A BEER
AT A BAWDY
HOUSE

A BEER AT A BAWDY HOUSE

David J. Walker

ST. MARTIN'S MINOTAUR ≈ NEW YORK

ISBN 0-312-25242-0

First Edition: January 2000

10 9 8 7 6 5 4 3 2 1

To Ellen, *ne plus ultra*

Chi-ca-go (*shi-kaw-go*) n., a city in northeast Illinois, on the shore of Lake Michigan; the name is said to be derived from the Native American *chicah goo*, literally "stink root" or, perhaps more elegantly, "wild onion."

ACKNOWLEDGMENTS

This is a work of fiction. The organizations and characters are imaginary or are used fictitiously, and are not intended to represent actual organizations or persons. I am grateful to them, though, for showing up.

I am also grateful to lots of actual persons, including: Dick Morrisroe, for stuff about bishops; Kirk Hudson, for stuff about real estate; Bill Hutul and Inspector Bob Jolley, for stuff about North Bay, Ontario, and police procedures there; Mike Mudrey of the Wisconsin Geological Survey, and David Long, for stuff about rocks and pipes; Kelley Ragland, my editor, who does just that with creative insight; and Jane Jordan Browne, my agent, who never stops working . . . or believing.

A BEER AT A BAWDY HOUSE

ONE

Peter Keegan was already on edge, of course, and anxious to get inside. But even so, he should have noticed that it wasn't only the garage door opener that wasn't working.

He punched the button half a dozen times, then gave up and pulled around to the front of the house. He'd have to park on the street, which he hadn't done since the night he moved in, two years ago. The next morning he'd found the window smashed and his new sophisticated sound system, an unexpected gift from his students when he'd left teaching, torn out of the dashboard. He'd never replaced it. He'd sold his car, in fact, taking cabs mostly now, or borrowing one of the other guys' cars on occasion, like tonight.

Not quite midnight now, with the bright lights of Old Town—that stretch of North Wells Street with its odd mix of chic restaurants and dingy bars, upscale shops and pornographic bookstores—just a few short blocks away. But here, where he lived, the street was dark and deserted, and even the tall lights at each end of the block seemed strangely dim and distant. He stood beside the car, shivering, struggling with the buttons of his rain coat. The cold March wind came and went in fierce gusts, rising suddenly in high, mournful howls, and then—just as abruptly—falling silent. At least the rain had stopped. He looked both ways. There was no one in sight.

But that was only an illusion. He knew the man was there, not far away. He'd always been there, since the day the phone calls began. Now, though unseen, that presence was as palpable as the gnawing in his stomach that hadn't really gone away since the first call—more than a week ago now.

He locked the car and hurried up the walk to the large, aging house he called home these days, not even noticing until he was up the steps and putting his key in the lock that the light high above the front door was out. He froze. So that's why the block seemed so dark. He often arrived home in a cab and went in the front door, and that light was always on. He went back down the steps and looked up at the front of the three-story house. Darkness at every window. It was late, sure, and the other two guys who lived here were always off to their beds right after the ten o'clock news, but you'd have thought there'd be some light showing, somewhere.

He wanted to run back to the car and drive away. But where in God's name would he go? To the police? Claiming a strange, unseen man was following him, watching him? He'd look like a fool. And the phone calls? They'd been nothing beyond a whispered "Hello, Peter," and then silence until he hung up. Until last night. Last night the whispering caller had a message. Not explicit, but clear enough. A message he'd been dreading—yet secretly expecting—for years. So he couldn't go to the police about the phone calls, either.

The message, though, had finally driven him to take some action. He'd made arrangements to consult someone. It was the right thing to do, the only thing to do, even though the thought of it made him shudder. His appointment was tomorrow.

But what about right now?

The answer was that there was no one around right now besides him—him and his own exaggerated emotions. A blown fuse was probably why the lights were out. God knows, the plumbing and heating in this place were well past their useful life, and the electrical system must be, too. The other guys wouldn't even know the fuse was blown until they woke up in the morning to a cold, dark house. He should save them that problem.

The trouble was . . . he was scared. He didn't like admitting that, much less letting it dictate his actions. He wasn't *supposed* to be afraid. There was, ultimately, nothing in this world to fear. His whole life was based on that truth—or that was the theory, anyway.

He went back up the steps and unlocked the door. He recalled seeing a flashlight once, in one of the kitchen drawers, and the fuse box would be somewhere in the basement. If he couldn't find it, he'd have to wake one of the others. Waiting until morning wouldn't do. He pushed open the door and stepped inside, and as he did the wind gusted again, whistling and creating enough of a draft through the little entrance hall to slam the door shut behind him. He listened hard then, but no sound came from within the house.

Only the hint of light from outside glowed through the narrow glass panes along the sides of the door. He found the wall switch, and wasn't surprised that it was already in the up position. There was an open doorway in front of him, and beyond that . . . only pitch darkness. He knew, though, that a wide corridor led to the rear of the house, past offices and parlors, past the stairway to the second floor, all the way back to the kitchen. He also knew there'd be boxes and old clothing and clutter piled everywhere along the hallway. For weeks, people had been dropping off used items for the spring rummage and toy sale. He'd have to feel his way carefully in the dark.

Then, apparently because his eyes had adjusted to what little light there was, he saw the candle. A single candle in a metal holder, sitting on the little table beside him. A packet of matches, too. Now a new, stronger fear gripped him. He'd been through that front door a thousand times, and there'd never been a candle sitting on that table. The wind whistled again, shaking the door as though someone were trying to get in, and he shuddered as he picked up the matches. It took two tries to get the candle lit.

He went through the doorway, holding the candle high, and hadn't gone two steps farther when he saw her. Halfway down the hall, at the foot of the stairway. A woman. A pale, naked woman. He stood paralyzed, staring. No, not a woman. No head, no legs; only a torso, from neck to hips. A torso impaled on a metal pole.

Strange shadows danced along the hallway, the candlelight's waver amplified by the trembling of his hand. It was a moment before he could force himself to move forward, even though he knew now that he had seen the object before. Somebody's cast-off, donated for the sale. Not the sort of anatomically detailed mannequin you saw in store windows these days, but an antique dressmaker's dummy.

Still, it was unmistakably female and, as though to emphasize that fact, someone had crudely darkened the tips of its breasts, and drawn it a navel, too, probably with a felt-tip pen. Above that navel, fixed to the belly with masking tape, was a three-by-five-inch index card, folded in half. He set the candle carefully on the worn carpet of one of the stairs and, his hand shaking even more violently, removed the card. He knew there'd be a note, and he knew—whatever the words—what the message would be.

Unfolding the card, he held it toward the flickering candle. The message, probably printed with the same felt-tip pen as the markings on the mannequin, was brief:

Let's all tell everyone the fun things we did on our vacations, shall we?
You first, Bishop Keegan.

TWO

The midday sun burned high and bright in a cool, cloudless sky. Among the piled rocks and still leafless trees, two full-maned male lions roared challenges at each other across a narrow, but impassable, ravine. Maybe there was a female pacing back and forth nearby, Kirsten thought, beyond the reach of both of them. The two lions might even be brothers.

She'd heard that battles between animal siblings, however furious, were usually brief and mostly a matter of display, before one turned and went on to other pursuits. Human brothers, though, were different. Their struggles might last a lifetime and all too often were far more savage—even deadly—and it was never smart to get caught in the middle.

So what was she doing here?

Kirsten shook off those thoughts and watched a couple of harried-looking teachers shepherd a flock of schoolkids—maybe nine- or ten-year-olds—who punched and chased after one another, giggling and chattering. They were obviously headed for the hot dog stand. When one boy dared to stray away to stand and gawk at the huge, roaring cats, a teacher hollered at him. "Daniel! Get over here. You musn't get separated from the group."

The boy jumped. "Comin', Miz Jones!" he called, and ran to join his classmates.

Kirsten shook her head. She and Dugan had no children yet, but some day they would, and already she feared delivering one of hers into the hands of a school system that—like all systems—had a hard time dealing with curiosity and fascination.

Looking around, she selected a small, concrete picnic table sheltered from the brisk Lake Michigan breeze. She placed her paper cup of coffee in the center of the table, unzipped the bright red, hip-length jacket Dugan had given her for Christmas, and sat down. This was the first time she'd worn the jacket and it hadn't even struck her—not until ten minutes ago when she was walking through the iron gate that said Lincoln Park Zoo—that the label called it a *safari* jacket. It wasn't the best shade of red for her, but the concept of *shades* of red was a bit subtle for Dugan's shopping sense. He'd been too proud of his choice—and she loved him too much—for her even to consider exchanging the coat. Besides, it had lots of bulky, square pockets, which was handy because she hadn't wanted to carry a purse.

It was the third day of April, a Wednesday, the bishop's day off. Kirsten had never known any bishops before and, while she'd never had occasion to think about it, was vaguely surprised to hear they had days off.

"Oh yes," the soft-spoken man had said on the phone. "In fact, that's why I picked Wednesday, and . . ." He had paused, as though hesitant to go on. "And the zoo, you know? I often go there on Wednesdays, to walk and . . . well, I don't want anyone to see me with you. I wouldn't want anyone to think . . ." His voice dropped away again.

"It's up to you," Kirsten had said, not really anxious to have a priest, with all of his hang-ups, as a client. "I could arrange to bring along a chaperone, if it's scandal you're—"

"No, no. It's not that." There was another pause. "He

6

warned me, you see, not to tell anyone. He said they'd be there, watching me."

"Who said? Who warned you?"

"He didn't give any name. But I have this feeling that the one who had him call was . . . well, was my brother. He's with the—"

"I know who your brother . . . I know who he's with." She wondered if the bishop had detected the catch in her throat, her sudden shortness of breath. "What . . . what makes you think it's him?"

"I . . . well, it's a premonition, or instinct or something. Anyway, the caller warned me not to seek help. Otherwise, he said, they'd go public with everything and I'd be destroyed."

"Go public with everything? What's that mean?"

"He didn't say. But it could only be one thing. I don't know how my brother would have found out about it. But if it *is* my brother—and somehow I feel certain it is—and if he really knows, he'd do it. He has no scruples. He'd tell."

"What?" she asked. "Tell what?"

"Oh." There was a pause. "Well, about my . . . my being arrested."

"Arrested? A bishop? For what?"

"I'd rather not . . ." Again, a few seconds of silence. "Well, I suppose . . . It was up in Canada. I wasn't a bishop then, just an ordinary priest." His words came in a rush now, running together. "And the precise charge, I think, was frequenting a house of prostitution, but—"

"Wait . . . let's wait on all this until we meet, okay?"

So they'd made their appointment and now Kirsten sat in the sun and listened to the lions roar, her left hand wrapped around the fast-fading warmth of the coffee in her cup, her right hand wrapped around the Colt .380 in the pocket of her bright red safari jacket. The gun was a seven-round semiautomatic pistol, the Pocketlite model that weighed in at just under a pound.

1

Kirsten knew exactly who the bishop's brother was. Over the last twenty-five years Walter Keegan had killed—by official count, at least—two men, two teenage boys, and one pregnant woman. For each of the men he'd gotten a medal; for the two boys, and later the woman, he'd been investigated and exonerated. Two mayors had proclaimed him a hero, even if Kirsten's dad—an old-line Chicago homicide investigator—had given him other titles: *lying snake, bully*, and *back-shooter* among them. Walter Keegan's ruthless ambition and absolute lack of conscience made him a man to be feared, her dad had said—and her dad had been as brave as any cop she'd ever known.

By now, though, the lying snake had slithered a long way up the ladder. He was a deputy chief, and right now acting chief of detectives, Organized Crime Division, Chicago Police Department. If her dad had still been alive he'd have been sickened. Of course he'd had personal reasons for that. He had, as he would have put it, a *history* with Walter Keegan—one in which Keegan came out looking just fine and her dad came out full of regrets that dogged him to his grave.

Kirsten only learned all the facts later, then had to struggle with her own anger and resentment of Keegan for what he'd done to her father. Eventually, though, she'd left those feelings behind her—or thought she had—and the whole affair might have been forgotten. But that was an illusion. Now, in an instant, it all flooded back—not only her own anger and resentment, but her father's warnings, too . . . and even an unwelcome touch of her father's fear.

And the snake's brother was Bishop Peter Keegan.

Kirsten had never met the bishop in person, and didn't recall ever having seen his picture. He said he'd be dressed in street clothes. "My civvies," he called them. But she was certain she'd know him when she saw him, and there was no sign yet of even a remote possibility. Mostly young mothers pushing strollers, and more groups of school children with their teachers. The only man in sight who didn't look like a retiree was that tall, husky guy leaning against the shoulder-high iron picket fence off to the side of the lion house. He held a *Sun-Times* open in both hands and was carefully staring down at the pages, the same two pages he'd been staring at—between occasional furtive glances around—for maybe ten minutes now.

Kirsten smiled to herself, but still kept fingering the grip of the pistol in her pocket. Another thing her dad had said about Walter Keegan: he had no friends, but many allies; he had a hold over lots of people, many of them even farther off the edge than he was.

THREE

His Excellency Peter D. Keegan, one of seven auxiliary bishops for the Archdiocese of Chicago, wished the number 156 bus would pick up the pace a little. He'd stayed too long at the nursing home. That wouldn't ordinarily have made any difference on a Wednesday, but he didn't like being late as a matter of principle, and meeting this . . . this *investigator* was bothering him anyway. He shuddered. This whole thing was so bizarre.

He'd been visiting his mother three times a week for two years now, ever since he'd reluctantly placed her in the nursing home. His best friend, Bud Burgeson, the pastor of St. El-myra's, kept telling him he should skip Wednesdays. "Jeez, Peter, you oughta relax on your day off." Bud considered visiting a parent—especially one who seldom even knew anymore that there was someone else in the room—as a duty. Peter Keegan, though, didn't think of it that way. He enjoyed visiting his mom. He always brought her Holy Communion, and lots of people thought that was foolish, too. To put it in Bud's words, "Your ma doesn't know what Communion is anymore, Peter. She doesn't know Jesus is there in the bread. She doesn't even know *you're* there, for heaven's sake."

That was the truth. He always had to make sure she swallowed the host after he put it on her tongue. Once, she'd peeled the little wafer off the roof of her mouth with her index finger and given it back to him. "Glory be to God," she'd said, "that thing needs some salt." The theologian in him might argue with his bringing her Communion. But the pastor in him— and the son in him, too—had no hesitation. So what if his mom didn't know Jesus was there? Jesus knew his mom was there.

Today, though, he'd stayed longer than usual. Because today she'd broken through again, just briefly, which happened so rarely now. This was twice in one week, almost as though she were trying to tell him something—which he knew it was foolish to imagine.

He'd been reading Luke's gospel to her from her old Bible and she'd been staring out the window, mumbling incoherently from time to time. He'd gotten to the crucifixion of Jesus when suddenly she spoke up. "Peter," she said, and there was a flash of intelligence in her eyes, "is that you?"

"Yes, it is." He could hardly get the words out. "It's me, Mom."

"Would you read that again? What Jesus said to the good thief on the cross."

So he read again, his voice trembling. " 'Amen, I say, this day thou shalt be with me in paradise.' "

"Ah," she said. "So that thief, Peter, the criminal . . . did he get turned around right there at the end and make it into heaven?"

He knew exactly what she was thinking about. He said, "Yes, Mom. That's what Jesus said."

"So maybe Walter can, too," she said. "Are you prayin' for Walter? Are you?"

"Yes, Mom, I am. Every day." Which was true. At least he was trying to—even now, when he had more reason than ever to fear his brother, even hate him.

"Ah, you're a good boy, Peter," she said. "But you be careful.

Walter's a mean one, y'know, and he'll be comin' to visit." She shook her head slowly. "Remember that Christmas Eve he came . . ." Her voice drifted away.

"Mom? That's twice in a week you said Walter's coming, and—"

"Look at that." She'd turned her head away, and was looking out the window, out onto the yard with its fresh spring grass and the tiny green leaves on the trees. "Look at that snow," she said. "My gramma's comin' on Christmas."

He'd spent a fruitless half hour trying to get her back.

And now he was on the bus and running late. He knew what Christmas Eve his mom was talking about. Walter had joined the army and he was home from Fort Leonard Wood, in Missouri. He'd always been an angry boy, sullen and mean—but now he was all that and more. Now he was no longer afraid of their father, who'd kept Walter in line up till then with his fists and a leather strap. That Christmas Eve everything changed. That was the last time their father ever hit Walter. It was also the first time Walter ever hit their father—but not the last. After that, there was some sort of incident every time Walter came home. A few years later, when the booze finally took the old man away for good, Walter was still in the army. He could have come home for the funeral, but he didn't.

Peter had come home, though, home from the seminary. And he'd taken care of everything. He always did the right thing. And always in the background there was Walter—criticizing him, envious of him, ridiculing him. Always. Now he was convinced, for reasons he couldn't explain, that Walter was behind the phone calls. And his mother's sudden talking about Walter, out of nowhere, seemed to be a sign that he was right.

So here he was, *Bishop* Peter Keegan, riding the number 156 bus in black loafers and a light blue windbreaker. He took the business card out of his pocket and read it again: *WILD ONION, LTD., Confidential Inquiries—Personal Security Services.* He'd scrawled the name of the woman he spoke to on the back of the card. *Kirsten*. A young person's name. He shouldn't have blurted out so much on the phone. He wondered if she were Irish. And he wondered whether any other bishop since the days of Saint Peter himself had ever hired a private investigator.

He didn't consider himself much of a bishop, anyway. He'd never wanted to be one in the first place, had no interest in playing ecclesiastical politics with the guys who did. But here he was, just the same. And now this talk of his being given his own diocese somewhere. . . . Funny, he'd become about as successful as you could possibly get in the priesthood. And he kept wondering what all that was worth.

The bus lurched to a stop and he almost forgot to get off.

Successful, maybe. But still the same old Peter Keegan—and still frightened to death of his big brother Walter.

Dugan wasn't even aware that his back was aching until he saw the bishop. That's when he suddenly realized he hadn't moved a muscle—except to glance up from his *Sun-Times* every so often—for probably fifteen minutes. His plan was to hang around looking nonchalant and disinterested, and keep his eyes open. Kirsten would spot him, of course. Probably already had, and was probably angry. He hadn't told her he'd be there. But what could she do about it?

God, she looked great in that jacket.

He folded the newspaper, surprised to notice he'd been holding it open to a two-page spread on organic gardening, and lifted his rear end off the fence behind him. Arms outstretched, he rolled his head around on his shoulders, easing the kinks in his upper back muscles—and eyeing everyone in the vicinity. There weren't many people. That school group over by the food stand, a few women with toddlers, and now a couple of tall, husky kids in baseball caps and wraparound sunglasses, weaving idly around on skateboards. And the bishop, of course.

Because that man walking toward Kirsten had to be the

bishop. Black shoes, black socks, black pants, green sport shirt that even Dugan knew was a terrible match for the light blue windbreaker. Medium height, maybe a tad overweight. He had a pleasant, friendly face with curly gray hair backing away from his forehead toward the top of his skull. He was decidedly unremarkable. And if his posture and gait seemed too tight, too rigid somehow? If his body seemed stretched taut by some hidden tension that might set him to flight at the snap of a twig? Well . . . maybe that was in Dugan's imagination.

That the bishop and Kirsten acknowledged each other at a distance of maybe twenty yards was reality, though, and not his imagination. He saw them both nod, nearly imperceptibly, to each other, and then the bishop turned and walked straight toward where Kirsten sat.

Dugan leaned forward then, staring past the bishop in disbelief. He sure didn't want to cause a scene. But he moved forward now, despite his uncertainty. Maybe he was overreacting. Maybe that big bozo in the baggy pants, gathering speed on his skateboard, careening across the square, wasn't going to blind-side the bishop after all. Wouldn't send him sprawling, smashing into the concrete picnic table where Kirsten sat.

But by then Dugan was running. Sprinting, in fact, and waving his *Sun-Times* wildly in the air. "Miss Jones!" His voice boomed across the concrete. "Miss Jones!" Heads turned, especially in the group by the food stand. He kept running, timing his speed, judging the angle of impact. "Miss Jones! It's Daniel!" he shouted. "He fell into the lion's—"

And then, at full speed, he collided with the big kid on the skateboard.

FOUR

T he big kid wasn't a kid at all, of course, but a man. Dugan
had seen that, just before he dipped his shoulder and
rammed into the midsection of the onrushing attacker. After that Dugan was out for a few seconds, or at least so dis-
oriented that he might as well have been out.

When he had his wits back the lions were roaring at each
other again, and he was on the ground, with lots of moms and
teachers gathered around him. There were schoolkids, too,
whooping and high-fiving and arguing about who'd seen
what—and two of them showing off skateboards they'd just
fallen heir to. But there were no men dressed up in baseball
caps and ragged, baggy pants.

And there was no pretty woman in a great-looking red safari
jacket, and no man dressed up like a middle-aged priest on his
day off.

Dugan gave the two little boys twenty bucks each for the
skateboards, and carried them with him out of the zoo. He
wasn't worried about Kirsten. No way she'd been grabbed by
the two goons. Not without a fight that would have quieted
the lions and made those kids forget all about Dugan's colli-
sion. No sense looking for her now, so he left the zoo and
looked for a cab.

"Nothing like a quiet walk in the park, huh?" Kirsten said. They were in her car, pulling onto the ramp for Lake Shore Drive, southbound. She was trying to put the bishop at ease, even though her own pulse hadn't slowed down yet. "That's why the sign says 'no skateboards.' Because kids can be so careless."

The bishop sat in the passenger seat. His seat belt was on and he was fiddling with the buckle. "I suppose you wouldn't have rushed me away from there so fast if you really thought what almost happened was accidental."

"You're right." She smiled. "And I suppose you wouldn't have been so cooperative if *you'd* thought it was."

"I didn't think anything. You grabbed my arm and I just ran. I don't even know if anyone was hurt."

"The guy on the skateboard sure wasn't. Not badly anyway. He and his buddy were almost out the zoo gate, and still running, last I saw."

"But what about the man who got hit?"

"Oh, he'll be all right. He was back on his feet, too, by the time we were turning the corner by the primate house." She switched lanes. She'd drive right on past the Loop, along the lakefront, maybe as far as McCormick Place, then turn around and head back north. The car was as good a place as any to talk. "Besides," she added, "it's his own fault. He should have been at his office."

"I'm afraid I don't follow you."

"That was my husband. He's a lawyer. Wednesday's not *his* day off, so he had no business interfering with—" She glanced across at the bishop, and saw him looking back at her—and smiling. "Are you laughing at me?" she asked.

"You might say so," he said. "Or at least at your pretense of anger. I think you're happy your husband showed up, not angry. You're not as happy as I am, of course, since I'm the one who'd have gotten the broken bones."

16

"You're only half right. The fact is that I really *am* angry, because it bothers me that Dugan would sneak around to help me, as though I weren't able . . ." She let it go. "But I'm also very thankful he was there."

"Funny, isn't it?" His smile had disappeared. "Funny how we can have two conflicting feelings at exactly the same time." There was a long silence, but she waited him out, and finally he said, "I kept an eye out, as you suggested, for anyone following me. But I have to admit there were times when I forgot to pay much attention. They . . . I wonder if they could tell I was headed toward you in particular."

"Hard to say."

There was another period of silence. She wasn't about to steer the conversation anywhere. After all, he wanted to hire *her*, not the other way around.

"They want to frighten me, let me know how powerless I am." He paused. "Maybe I should just . . . Maybe it's God's will."

"Uh-huh." She drove on past McCormick Place and decided to go all the way out to the end of South Shore Drive before turning around.

"But that can't be true," he said. "This whole thing is . . ." He rested his palms on the dashboard in front of him and sighed. "Maybe I should just tell you what's been going on."

"Uh-huh."

So he talked and she listened.

And when he suddenly claimed that was all, and said he wanted to go home, she didn't press him. She gave him some instructions, then dropped him a few blocks from where he lived. Driving away, she tried to sort out her own disturbing mix of feelings: anger, apprehension, even an old sadness renewed. But through it all a sort of amusement. The bishop— as bright and sensitive and insightful as he was—clearly had no idea how obvious it was that he'd omitted the most important part of what there was to tell.

FIVE

For starters," Dugan said, "there's one part of the story that's especially hard to believe." He crouched on his haunches and peered into the refrigerator. Kirsten had picked him up at his office and on the ride home told him what Bishop Keegan had said. Not everything, though. He could always tell when she was holding things back. Now she'd asked for his opinion. Actually, disbelief was his second thought. His first was that he wanted a beer. "Yes, sir. Hard to believe," he repeated.

"You mean that a decorated Chicago police officer, a man who's worked his way up to a command position in the department, would be involved in criminal—"

"Not so much that part," he said. "There is, as we lawyers like to say, convincing precedent for that." He popped open a Berghoff for himself and handed her a bottle of her own latest drink of choice, wondering again why spring water should cost as much as beer. "What's hard to believe is that a respected Chicago priest, a man who's worked his way up to being a bishop, would admit he knows a guy like Larry Candle."

"Hey," Kirsten said, "Larry's *your* partner, after all. Which wasn't my idea, if you remember."

"He's my *associate*, an employee, not a partner." He sat down and faced her across the kitchen table. "And it turns out he's a pretty good lawyer, too. It's just that Larry's reputation's never been the greatest, y'know?"

"So I've heard," she said. "Anyway, the bishop says he got one of my business cards from Larry Candle. I didn't ask how he knew Larry, because I didn't want to get sidetracked. The poor man had a hard enough time telling his story as it was."

"So Bishop Keegan thinks the problem is his own older brother, whom he never got along—"

"Half brother. Same father, different mothers. No other brothers or sisters for either of them. The father's dead. Walter's mother's dead. And the bishop's mother's a saint from the old sod who's in and out of reality . . . mostly out."

"She had just the one kid, though, huh? Not very saintly-sounding for an Irish mother of her generation."

"We didn't get into that, either." Kirsten was paging through their stack of take-out menus. "How about Thai food?" she asked.

"How about going out for a corned beef sandwich?"

"Sorry," she said. She was already tapping out numbers on the phone.

She put in a pretty large order, he thought, considering she'd only recently developed a taste for Thai and she knew that he'd hardly eat any at all. Meanwhile, he looked through his wallet and found one of her Wild Onion, Ltd., cards. When she set down the phone, he said, "So the bishop got one of these cards from Larry Candle. Amazing." He paused. "I suppose what he wants from Wild Onion is what the card advertises: personal security services, and a confidential inquiry into why he's being threatened by his own brother."

"He *thinks* it's his brother," she said, "but he's got no proof. What I think— Anyway, I dropped him off near where he lives, in a rectory at a parish on the west edge of Old Town. I told him I'd call later with my decision on whether I'll take the case."

"Call later?" Hesitating wasn't her usual style.

"Yes. There's . . . well . . . a special circumstance here." She took a long drink of bottled water. "The problem is Walter Keegan."

"Oh?" Dugan was surprised at the strange new tone in her voice. "I remember hearing about some sort of dispute your *dad* had with Keegan, but—"

"The dispute part didn't turn up much on TV or in the papers, and I never explained it to you. The thing is, it affects how I feel about Keegan, and about whether I should take the bishop's case."

"It was a shooting incident, right? On the West Side?"

"The *South* Side. I suppose I should tell you just what happened." She paused and slowly rotated the bottle on the table in front of her, as though studying the label. "My dad was in Area One, assigned to what they called homicide back then. He'd dropped his partner off that morning at Twenty-sixth and California to testify at a trial and was on his way to pick up two other state's witnesses to take to court. He was bored, and was scanning through the different bands on the police radio when a call came through: domestic disturbance, shots fired. Not his responsibility, but it was right around the corner from him and he responded. He was the first on the scene, followed right away by Walter Keegan and his partner. Keegan was younger than my dad, and was working a tactical unit. Plainclothes and aggressive as hell, like all those tac guys.

"The scene was one of those huge old mansions on King Drive near Thirty-ninth Street. Some of them are being rehabbed now, but back then this place was a hell hole, cut up into maybe eight or ten tiny apartments. My dad and Keegan ended up inside, in a first-floor rear apartment. A skinny little fifteen-year-old boy had just shot his father. The boy's mother was there and she said the victim was high on something and had stripped the boy's brother—her other son—down to his shorts and wouldn't stop whipping him, with an extension cord. The brother was a tall, husky guy, about seventeen. Built like a pro linebacker, but he had Down's syndrome, and an IQ of maybe fifty or sixty."

"The other kid—the shooter—was he still there?"

"They were *all* there—the mother backed up into a corner, the big slow kid lying on a sofa in his underpants with raw, bloody welts all over his legs and back, the father sitting on the floor holding his belly and moaning . . . and then this terrified fifteen-year-old, crying and holding a cheap little twenty-two caliber down beside his leg. Police units were pouring in from all over, and my dad sent Keegan's partner out to tell them they had a hostage situation, and then started talking the kid down. He tried to get Keegan out, too, but he wouldn't go."

"It wasn't exactly a hostage situation," Dugan said.

"No, but he wanted to keep them from charging in and getting more people shot. The real problem, though, was Keegan. He wouldn't shut up, kept yelling and cursing at the kid, so my dad's trying to calm Keegan down as well as the kid. He told me he knew he had the kid just about ready to give up the gun, when Keegan starts waving his own revolver—a three-fifty-seven Magnum. The kid got scared and jumped, and his gun hand—still down by his leg—jerked up a little and . . . and Walter Keegan shot him. Point blank. Blew a big hole in the center of his chest.

"The mother started yelling then, and the boy with Down's syndrome jumped up and just went crazy, hollering and throwing himself around. Then he took one step toward Keegan, and Keegan shot him, too. Caught him in the shoulder but the boy kept coming. My dad was pulling on Keegan, trying to get him to back away, but Keegan put two more bullets into the poor guy and put him down."

"My God!"

"It was senseless, vicious. Neither boy had to die. By then the woman was completely hysterical and screaming. Two sons shot to death in front of her eyes. Keegan just ignored her. He pushed my dad aside and turned and headed for the door, yelling to the cops to come on in, that it was all over. Except, it wasn't over. Not yet. The woman grabbed the twenty-two off the floor and fired two shots. One went wild and the other hit Keegan's right arm and his gun went flying. He spun around to face her. He had a backup weapon, but it was on his right hip and he was struggling to get at it with his left hand, while she kept yelling, 'Murderer! Murderer!' She raised the twenty-two again, screamed 'Murderer!' one more time, and . . . and then . . ."

"And what? What, for God's sake?" Dugan said, but was afraid he knew what was coming.

"And then . . . then my dad shot her."

"Jesus. Did she . . ."

"She died on the spot. Next thing my dad remembers is a dozen cops are swarming all over him, pumping his hand, yelling congratulations for saving a fellow officer's life. Later, during the shooting investigation, my dad tried to tell them Keegan had killed the two boys without sufficient cause, but nobody'd listen to him. After all, one of the kids was armed, and the other was a huge guy, out of control."

"Keegan convinced them he'd had no other choice?"

"Right. And they tried to tell my dad he was a hero, but he wouldn't accept the award they wanted to give him. He'd been on the job thirty years, and he was one of the best. But he'd never killed anyone, and after that the bottom just fell out of everything for him. A lot of his fellow cops turned on him when he told the truth about Keegan. He kept doing his job, dragging himself down to area headquarters every day, but there was no life in him anymore. Six months later he was diagnosed with pancreatic cancer, and six months after that . . . he was dead." She stopped and stared down at the table. "You see what happened, don't you?"

"Yeah, I see."

"Walter Keegan murdered those kids," she said, "and he as

good as murdered my dad, too." She looked across at him, her eyes bright with tears. "That twenty-two the woman had, you know, it was . . . it was empty when he shot her."

Dugan opened his mouth, then closed it.

"Anyway," she said, "I told the bishop I'd call him."

"I know you don't like to back off from anything."

"No."

"But maybe . . . maybe this time you'd be carrying too much baggage."

She stood up and drank the last of her water. "We always think we can get rid of the past, don't we?" She stared at the plastic bottle in her hand. "Sunday's *Trib* had this article about landfills," she said, "and how some things are buried and don't decompose, but just rise and pop right up through the ground, years later." She dropped the empty water bottle into the blue recycling bag by the back door. "Anyway, I told him I'd call. I want you to listen in on the extension in the hall."

He walked from the kitchen to the entrance hall at their front door, crossing the wide-open, high-ceilinged living area. He was sure she'd take the case, but not sure why she wanted him listening in. By the time he picked up the phone, she'd gotten through and a male voice was saying, "I'll see if the bishop is available."

There was a brief pause, and then a pleasant voice said, "This is Bishop Keegan."

Kirsten identified herself and got right to the point. "That matter we discussed this afternoon? We don't really know who's behind—"

"Wait," the bishop interrupted. "Considering what happened today, I'm . . . well, I'm afraid, actually. I'm not even sure I know what it is that I think you can do."

"I understand," Kirsten said, "and I was about to say that you're up against someone—whoever it is—who plays in the big leagues. Sometimes one has to accept one's limitations." Kirsten's voice had a sad, defeated tone that Dugan had never heard before. "I hate to say it," she continued, "but . . . I've decided not to take the case."

"Well, that's strange." The bishop sounded as surprised as Dugan was. "I was told that you—"

"I know, but. . . . Anyway, I could recommend another agency, if you like. Someone larger?"

"No. I guess . . ." He paused. "I believe you're right. I hate to give in, but sometimes it's best for everyone."

"Well," Kirsten said, "thanks for thinking of Wild Onion, Limited. And . . . good luck, Bishop."

"Yes. Thank you, too. Good-bye." And he hung up.

On his way back to the kitchen, Dugan thought he should be happy that Kirsten had made a wise choice for once. Instead, he felt vaguely depressed. He wanted another beer. And a sandwich or something. None of that damn Thai food she'd ordered, though, or . . .

That's when it came to him.

In the kitchen, Kirsten handed him another Berghoff. "Sit down," she said, "and let me—"

"Wait. I have a question." He opened the beer and stared at her. "This Bishop Peter Keegan," he said, "does he happen to like . . . Thai food?"

SIX

Peter Keegan hurried along the passageway that led directly from the second floor of the rectory into the darkened church. From the sacristy behind the altar, where the priests vested for mass, a stairway went down two flights to the janitor's room and the boiler. But he was going just one flight down, feeling his way through pitch darkness, to ground level. He'd never used this way out of the church before, and he suddenly pictured himself like some second-century bishop—Polycarp or someone—creeping down into the catacombs to avoid the emperor's soldiers.

That afternoon, Kirsten and he had agreed that if someone was following him around, they'd probably be watching the front of the rectory. On the other hand, maybe it was a phone tap that had picked up today's meeting at the zoo. If so, their conversation about him giving up and Wild Onion not taking his case might throw them off—at least for a while.

One flight down, he slid his hands along the wall until he found the door that opened onto a small parking area and the alley behind the church. As promised, there was a car waiting in the alley, a dark-colored four-door sedan. This Kirsten seemed quite competent, and very down to earth, somehow. She had a sense of humor, too. The sign she'd promised was on paper taped to the inside of the rear door window, just behind the driver. The words were printed large: *WILD ONION CAB COMPANY.*

He got into the backseat and even before he had the door closed the car began moving forward. "Thank you," the bishop said. "I was—"

"Just tear that damn sign off the window and get down on the floor till I tell ya." The driver's voice was harsh and impatient, like an angry father to a slow child. "Hurry up, for chrissake!"

He complied, folding his legs and jamming himself into too small a space. Kirsten had said the man she'd send for him was absolutely trustworthy, but warned him to brace himself for what she called "a pretty abrasive personality." Even so, he was taken by surprise. He couldn't remember when, if ever, anyone had spoken to him in quite that tone of voice.

The car turned out of the alley and they headed east at first, but within ten minutes he'd lost all sense of which direction they were going, or what street they were on. By then his feet were asleep and there were pains shooting through both legs, from his calves to his buttocks.

"My legs are cramping," he finally said. "Can I sit up now?"

"Stay down!" It was more a bark than a human command. "I told you I'd say when to sit up."

He didn't argue.

Another five or ten minutes went by before the car stopped. "We're here," the man said. "I'll sit here till they buzz you in. Tell Kirsten I gotta get back to watchin' her other friend again, so I won't be here to take you home."

The bishop struggled out of the backseat. He tried to stand as he closed the door, but his legs buckled at the knees and he had to lean against the side of the car. The front passenger window slid down then and the driver, a huge man with a drooping mustache and a thousand creases in his face, leaned across toward him. "You okay?" The man didn't sound really concerned, just in a hurry.

"Yes," he answered, pushing himself away from the car. "And thanks. I really—"

"What the fuck, I'm gettin' paid." The window started to glide up.

"Wait," the bishop said, and the window opened again. "Did Kirsten . . . uh . . . tell you I was a bishop?"

The big man stared as though surprised at the question, then pointed a huge finger right at the bishop's face. "That stuff don't mean shit to me, pal. I was a beat cop for thirty years. I knew your brother. He's a deputy chief now, and you're a bishop. Till I learn different, I'm guessin' you lied and kicked and pimped your way up the line, same as him and all the other so-called big shots." He paused and, as the window was closing again, added, "I wouldn't have said that, y'know, but you asked."

The car just sat there and Peter Keegan finally turned away, reminding himself that at least there was something to be said for honesty.

SEVEN

Kirsten was in the kitchen, worrying about whether she'd made the right decision about the bishop and sorting out the packages of Thai food, when Dugan called out from up front. "They just pulled up. I'll go down and meet him at the door."

She set plates around on the kitchen table. There was corned beef in the refrigerator for Dugan, but she decided not to put it out. How could a person live in Chicago and not learn to like Asian food? It seemed . . . well . . . un-American, somehow. Maybe he'd eat some beef satay and some pad thai. She'd steer him away from that chicken and curry combo the menu called original hot number one.

She could hear Bishop Keegan's voice from the front of the apartment, and then Dugan laughing as they came through to the back. ". . . and he takes a little getting used to, that's for sure," Dugan was saying, as the two of them came into the kitchen.

The bishop was wearing black pants and the same blue windbreaker he'd worn earlier that day, but a white dress shirt now. He smiled when she said hello, but he looked tired, and seemed at a loss as to what to say.

"You said you like Thai food, so sit down and join us," she said. "You don't look so good, if you want my honest opinion."

"See, Bishop?" Dugan said. "All you get around here is honesty, whether you like it or not." She caught the slight wink Dugan gave her as he took the bishop's jacket. "The bishop here just got an unexpurgated dose of Cuffs Radovich," he explained. "That's enough to wear anyone out."

"Sorry, Bishop," she said. "Maybe I should have given you a stronger warning." Actually, she'd discovered that warning people about Cuffs was of little use.

"That's all right," the bishop said. "That food smells great. I haven't eaten since breakfast." He sat down in the chair Dugan held for him, and she noticed he seemed to take for granted that people would attend to him. "Mr. Radovich said to tell you he's gone back to watch some other person. Is he always so . . . gruff?"

"Yes," Dugan said, as he poked around in the white boxes of food set out on the table. "Gruff. And obscene, generally. Also opinionated, arrogant, permanently angry, and about as racially and ethnically . . . ah . . . *insensitive* as a person could be. Fact is, Cuffs doesn't like authority figures, or any other group of people in the world, and very few individuals, either."

"But he's tough," Kirsten said, "and dependable."

"Yes, there's that." Dugan winked at her again, more openly this time. "And even if he'd never say so, Kirsten's one of the people he likes."

"That's right," she said. She was dishing rice and noodles onto their plates. "Alarming, when you think about it."

"Glass of white wine, Bishop?" Dugan asked.

"Thank you."

Kirsten watched Dugan pour the bishop's wine and then, without comment, dig the package of sliced corned beef out of where she'd hidden it in the refrigerator and make himself a sandwich. They all ate for a while in silence, as though sharing an unspoken agreement to enjoy the meal before getting down to business. The bishop seemed to relax a bit, and truly to savor the Thai dishes.

When they were finished, she and Dugan cleared off the table. "More wine, Bishop?" she asked. "Or coffee, maybe? It's not decaf, though."

"Thanks," he answered. "I'll have coffee, please. I don't usually—"

"Fine," Dugan said. "It's right over there on the counter. Mugs are in the cabinet right above."

The bishop seemed slightly startled and Kirsten smiled inwardly. Cuffs Radovich would have said: *Get up off your ass and get your own coffee,* or something more graphic. But Dugan's meaning was equally plain, and the bishop got his own coffee— and poured mugs for Dugan and Kirsten as well.

"Now then, Bishop," Kirsten said, "let's get down to business. First, I wanted you to meet Dugan. He's already . . . well, *butted in.* So I asked him to assist me with your case."

"You did?" Dugan asked.

"Sure. Just now." She turned back to the bishop. "We have to decide—"

"Wait," Dugan interrupted. "If I'm helping, I want to ask the bishop one preliminary question."

"What is it?" the bishop asked.

"How in the world does a bishop know a lawyer like Larry Candle? I mean, he's got a pretty bad reputation. Lots of people think he's nothing but an ambulance chaser, a pugnacious little loudmouth, and—"

"And your partner," Kirsten put in, not able to resist. "Or . . . associate, I mean."

"I know a little about Larry's reputation," the bishop said. "But I've also known him personally for years. Ever since I was a priest in Rogers Park and he and his bride-to-be came in to make wedding arrangements."

"You mean Larry's a Catholic?" Dugan asked.

30

"No. But his wife—ex-wife, now—was born and raised Catholic. She insisted on getting married in the Church, and on Larry learning all about the faith so their children could be raised Catholic. He wouldn't go to the usual classes, but he came and talked to me, twice a week for a couple of months. I didn't approve of him, either, at first."

"Not surprising," Kirsten said.

"But we got to know each other. And . . . we get together regularly, about once a month. We talk." The bishop drank some coffee. "He's not what you'd call a religious person. But he always asks me to pray for him. He says I'm his ticket to heaven."

"So," Kirsten said, "he told you about me, and Wild Onion, Limited?"

"Right. He said you helped him once when he was in trouble. He's a little unpolished, maybe, but very bright. And he certainly seems to trust you. Anyway, I asked him for a referral."

"A referral?" Kirsten asked. "Did you explain what the problem was?"

"Only a bare outline, and I didn't say it was for me. I said it was for someone I knew, someone who couldn't go to the police. It wasn't until a few days later that he gave me your card and . . ." He shook his head. "Gosh, could you get me a glass of water? That chicken and curry dish was very hot."

EIGHT

Kirsten got up and got the bishop some water. She was about to suggest they adjourn to the living room, but changed her mind. She sat down while he drained his glass in one long drink. She hadn't pressed him that afternoon for the important facts he'd skipped. Now he seemed more relaxed, maybe ready to open up a little, and she was afraid even moving to another room might break the mood and make him clam up again. Dugan poured coffee for everyone, put the glass carafe on the table, and sat down.

It was as though that were a signal, and what followed was dead silence that lasted probably five seconds, but seemed interminable.

"So . . . um, Bishop," Kirsten finally said, "I've already told Dugan about how someone's been following you, calling you."

The bishop nodded in agreement. "They're trying to scare me into doing something, and I don't even know what it is."

"Right. I told Dugan that, too." She leaned forward across the table toward him. "But now," she said, "now, why don't you tell us the hard part. Then that'll be over with, and we can try to decide what to do."

"The hard part?" the bishop asked, obviously trying to sound as though he didn't know what she meant. But that was just a stall. Even Dugan could tell that, she was sure, although she hadn't mentioned the arrest, so she had a better idea than he did what the *hard part* was. "I'm afraid . . ." The bishop shook his head, as though he couldn't convince himself to go on. "Well, *that* much is true, anyway. I *am* afraid, truly afraid." He stared down at the table.

"Who wouldn't be afraid, if they got threatening phone calls?" Dugan asked, but Kirsten knew the bishop was referring to something else.

"No. I mean I'm afraid to talk about it, now, to the two of you. I shouldn't be, since I already blurted the gist of it out on the phone, God knows why."

"God might know, but I know, too. I know just why you blurted it out," Kirsten said, holding the palm of her hand out toward Dugan to keep him quiet even though he hadn't said anything. "Because it's crucial and you were afraid you might hide it, and that was the best way to make sure you got it said." She paused. "So?"

"I . . . the entire incident is very difficult to talk about." The bishop spoke slowly, deliberately, as though hoping someone would intervene to stop him. "I mean, it's not as bad as it must sound, but . . ." His voice trailed off, but when neither Kirsten nor Dugan said anything, he continued. "It was nine years ago. There were three of us—my friend Father Burgeson, his twin brother Kenny, and I—on a fishing trip in Canada, near North Bay, Ontario. We flew to Toronto, and from there it's another flight, due north, of about a hundred-fifty . . . no, I think it's probably two hundred and—"

"We can look at a map later, if it's important," Kirsten said. "Meanwhile . . ."

"Yes, sorry," he said. "Well, it was a package deal—four days, three nights in one of those rustic fishing cabins, but I'd made arrangements to stay an extra three days. It was August, and I was to start teaching in the seminary in the fall. That was a new assigment for me and I planned a sort of retreat, three days alone in the back country. So, when the other two left, I drove them—we had this beat-up rental car—to the airport at North Bay." He paused. "They said I was crazy to stay on alone, and they were right. I sure wasn't ready for three days and nights of total solitude."

"What happened?" Kirsten asked.

"Actually, nothing. That was the problem. I'd sort of romanticized it. I thought I'd read, meditate, walk in the woods. But it was cold and rained all day the first day. The next day was the same and by afternoon I couldn't stand it and I drove into North Bay."

"Great idea," Dugan put in. "I bet there's *lots* of excitement there."

Kirsten wanted to punch Dugan, but the bishop didn't seem to mind his sarcasm. "Not much to do," he said. "Pretty remote, and kind of a rough and tumble place; at least it seemed that way to me. I later learned that their economy was slumping and there was a lot of alcoholism, and . . ." The bishop drank some coffee, then looked up at Kirsten. "Anyway, that's where I got arrested."

"What?" Dugan said. "Bishops don't get—"

"Dugan," Kirsten said, "I love you. But please shut up."

"I wasn't a bishop then. But I *was* a priest, and I got arrested. It was outside of town, actually, maybe a mile or two, along a little river called Yellow Bird Creek. There was this bar in the middle of nowhere called the Yellow Bird Falls Saloon. Sort of run-down. The guys and I had gone by it a couple times on our way in out of town. There'd always be a few cars there. It was . . . the sign said: 'Topless.' " The bishop stared down into his coffee mug. "No, that's not quite true. One sign said 'topless, bottomless.' The other sign said: 'Totally nude dancing.' I'd bought some groceries and I ate supper at a cafe in town. I was headed back to the cabin, and I—"

"You went inside," Kirsten said, "and got arrested." She couldn't believe it was she who'd interrupted this time, and not

Dugan. But she knew why. She didn't want to hear this bishop—no, this very nice, very embarrassed man, bishop or not—explain how he'd snuck into this creepy, sleazeball dive and got busted with some naked dancer squirming around on his lap, or . . . or whatever. She just didn't want to hear it. Now *she* was the embarrassed one, dammit. "How long did the cops keep you in cus—"

"Kirsten," Dugan said, "why don't you let him tell the whole story. Okay?"

"Sorry. Just trying to make it easier on the bishop." That was a lie. "But you're right. Go ahead, Bishop."

"Well, first I drove on. Then I turned around and drove back. I must have driven back and forth in front of the place six times, arguing with myself. Telling myself I'd just look around. That it couldn't hurt. That my life was too cut off from reality, too prudish. Telling myself lots of things, when really I was just experiencing what they used to call in the seminary 'prurient interest.' What finally tipped the scales, though, was fear."

"Fear?" That was Dugan, and Kirsten didn't mind.

"Yes. I realized I was *afraid* to go into that place. A very sensible fear, of course. But I decided it would be an act of courage to go in, have one beer, and then leave. So I parked the car and went inside. Very frightened. And . . . very foolish."

"In hindsight, at least," Kirsten said. She found herself, surprisingly, sort of proud of the bishop.

"It was dark inside, and smoky, with music blaring very loudly. It was only about seven in the evening, but it was a Friday and it was pretty crowded for such a small place. A bartender, a couple of waitresses, and maybe ten or fifteen customers, all men. There was a woman dancing, up behind the bar. She was topless, but she had something on . . . below her waist, you know. Not much, but something. I sat at a small table by myself and one of the waitresses came over. She had no top on either. I was really embarrassed, but I ordered a beer.

35

I remember being surprised at how expensive it was. This was a long time ago, and it was ten dollars or something. The waitress brought back the beer and I paid her and then . . . then she leaned over and asked me something. At first I didn't understand, and then I suddenly realized she was asking if I wanted . . . well . . . a sexual thing I'd rather not repeat now, unless—"

"That's fine," Kirsten said.

"I must have been blushing, and my voice was probably shaking, too—just like it is now. Funny thing, I remember my exact words. 'No, thank you,' I said. 'Maybe some other time.' I was very nervous. Anyway, she didn't make fun of me or anything. She was quite courteous, and left me alone to finish my beer." The bishop drank the last of his coffee and reached out for the carafe.

"That's it?" Dugan asked, and Kirsten thought his disappointment was a bit too obvious.

"As far as anything I *did*, that was it. I drank my beer in a hurry. I didn't belong in there. Not only because of the women, you know, but the other men, too. They . . . there was a lot of loud talking. All of them looked like laborers or something. Mostly big men. A few, I'm sure, were Indians. Everyone—even the bartender—was kind of mean-looking, like ready to fight. And that's exactly what happened. A brawl broke out, all at once, right by the front door. It was scary. I jumped up and ran down a hallway to the back where a sign said 'Exit,' but when I got there the door was locked. I was trapped. There was a little bathroom that smelled like a sewer, and I locked myself in. The fight just kept going on and on. People were screaming and cursing. The whole building was shaking. It was really bad. Not like on TV or something."

"Nothing in real life is like TV," Dugan said.

"So the police came then?" Kirsten asked.

"Yes. I finally heard sirens pulling up outside. I was so thankful. I figured they'd just send me on my way, but they didn't. I got the impression they were looking for an excuse to shut the place down, and they arrested every single person there. I told them I was a U.S. citizen and that didn't seem to impress anyone." He paused. "So, to make a long story short, they charged me, and I guess everyone else, with frequenting a house of prostitution, or something equivalent to that. They said I'd have to stay in jail until Monday, but they finally said I could make one phone call. They suggested a lawyer, or a family member or friend. I had no idea who to call. All I could think of were people I didn't want learning about . . . about where I'd been. Certainly not the cardinal or anyone at the archdiocese, and none of my friends, either."

"What about a lawyer?" Kirsten asked.

"Back then I only knew two lawyers and one of them was Bud's twin brother, Kenny Burgeson. But then Bud would probably find out and . . . besides, I didn't think Kenny'd be much help. He's at a big downtown firm and I think all he does is trust work for religious and nonprofit organizations. I decided I'd skip the call and see if they'd let me go in the morning."

"Not such a bad idea," Kirsten said.

"But then . . . then I got more worried. I changed my mind and made a call." He paused. "I took their advice and called the only—"

"Don't say it," Dugan said. "I think I can guess."

"Me, too," Kirsten said. "You called the only *other* lawyer you knew."

"That's right." The bishop seemed genuinely surprised. "How did you guess?"

NINE

Peter Keegan thought he might actually be able to sleep. He'd told Kirsten what Mr. Radovich said about not taking him home, so they'd gotten him a cab. But he'd barely fallen into bed when the sound ripped through his room. He sat bolt upright, breathless. Just the phone, that's all. Eleven o'clock. It might be the nursing home. It wouldn't be, though. It would be the same man, the same message. But it might be the nursing home.

At the third ring he picked up.

It rang again. The call wasn't on his private line. He hung up, grabbed the other phone.

"Hello?" A woman's voice. "Hello?" she repeated. "Is someone there?"

He recovered his breath. "This is Bishop Keegan."

"Oh . . . I . . ." There were some clicking sounds. Maybe she was calling long distance, or from a pay phone. "Are you still there?" she said.

"Yes. Are you sure you have the right number? What number are you—"

"No. I mean . . . yes. I mean, I think so." She paused. "I think I can help you." More clicking—or static, maybe—on the line. "If you're the right Peter Keegan."

"Help me?"

"It's about when I . . . you know, about when you got arrested, in Canada." A deep breath then. Smoking maybe. "Do you know what place it was? I mean, like, what color bird?"

He waited, frightened, not knowing if he should say anything.

"Well? What color bird?" More aggressive. "I musta called ten times since noon and it's never you. Now it is, but I gotta know you're the right Peter Keegan."

"I . . . I'm sure that I am. Yellow. Yellow Bird Falls."

"Good. I figured you hadda be from Chicago, 'cause the man was from there." Another deep breath. "I can help. I don't want a lotta money. I just—"

"What man? Who are you?"

"I know you're in big trouble, 'cause Bobby tole me this man came all that way, askin' about me, about what I told the coppers. Sayin' he's gonna give me money, and Bobby, too. But Bobby told me there was something funny, and he didn't trust him and he wasn't gonna tell him where I was, and . . . and . . ." She stopped and he didn't know what to say. "Anyway," she finally said, "you want help, or not?"

"Yes, but—"

"I need some money. I mean, not a lot. I'm not a bad person, whatever you think."

"I don't think any—"

"But if you want my help, then you have to promise. Okay?"

"What kind of help?"

"No. First you have to promise. I didn't know back then you was a priest or I wouldn't've . . . Anyway, now I found out. And that's good. Priests don't break promises, right?"

"Well, they . . . yes, that's right."

"So promise not to tell no one about me, okay? Promise?"

"Yes. Yes, I promise. But—"

"Not no one. Swear to God?"

"I . . . yes, I swear." God forgive him. "But who are—"

"Not on the phone. We gotta meet. I . . . I'll call back to-morrow, during the day. Tell you where I'll be, and when."

"I'm never here during the day." He gave her his chancery office number. "That's a direct line, just to me. If I don't pick up, leave a message on—"

"No messages. I'll call. I gotta go." She hung up.

TEN

J eez, Kirsten, gimme a break, huh?" Larry Candle peered up at her, looking like a dwarf from behind the huge desk in his tiny office, down the corridor from the library in Dugan's suite. He was a short, pudgy man, with a round head full of curly, jet-black hair, permed and probably dyed. "What is it? Eight o'clock? Jeez, I haven't even finished my morning java."

"*Java?*"

"You know, coffee."

"I know what it means. I just never heard anyone . . . Anyway, don't change the subject." Larry Candle had that hurt expression he slipped into whenever someone suggested he was trying to get away with something. No wonder his reputation was so bad. He managed to *look* guilty, whether he was or not. Was it his nature? Or did he practice? She repeated her opening question. "What happened in North Bay?"

"Jeez, you expect me to remember some case I mighta had something to do with nine years ago?"

"Not just some case, Larry. A phone call from your friend, a priest. A cry for help in the middle of the night. Not something you'd forget."

"Oh, I got it!" She didn't believe Larry's look of sudden insight. "You mean *that* case. Father Keegan."

"*Bishop* Keegan now. Yes, *that* case. The one I didn't say was nine years ago, but you did. *That* case."

"Sorry." Larry's full-moon face adopted an apologetic smile. "Can't talk about it. Lawyer-client privilege, you know."

"You wouldn't even *be* a lawyer today if I hadn't saved you when those disciplinary people tried to pull your ticket, dammit."

"Right. But all you did was prove the truth." The look on her face must have scared him, because he held up his hand. "That is, not that I'm not thankful for—"

"Now it's the bishop who's my client, Larry, and I will personally put your attorney registration card through Dugan's paper shredder, and your round little body along with it, if you don't tell me what happened, how you got him out of jail and put such a quick lid on the whole affair."

"You know how it is," he said, his ever-pliable features turning smug now. "Situations like that take finesse, just the right touch of—"

"Try again, Larry. What did you do?"

"Okay, okay. Thing is, I knew Father Keegan. Man's a saint or somethin'. The charges hadda be phony. But hell, I didn't have a clue what to do about it. So I did the only thing I could think of."

"Which was?"

"Which was call his brother, Walter. He was this tough-guy cop and I figured maybe he'd throw some weight around, give me a hand. I got him on the phone and after about three sentences he told me to shut up. 'I'll take care of it, you shyster.' That's what he said. I mean the guy didn't even *know* me, I don't think. Anyway he told me he'd handle it, I should do nothing, and if I ever coughed up a word about it, or about my call to him, even to Father Keegan, he'd cut my nuts— I mean he threatened me, anyway. So that was it. Pure and simple.

Father Keegan never knew what happened. All he knew was those Canadians cut him loose with no explanation. He couldn't thank me enough next time he saw me. Said I must be a genius."

"And did you tell him you didn't do anything at all?"

"Not exactly. I mean, I didn't actually lie. I just said I didn't want to talk about it. I told him I didn't want a fee, just don't forget me when he's praying people into heaven. He never brought it up again." Larry leaned back in his chair. "So what's up now?"

"I can't tell you."

"Fine. I can handle that." Larry winked. "It was me sent him to you, y'know?"

"I know."

"He told me it was for a friend, but I knew better. I could tell it was him was in trouble, so I wanted him to have one of the best, y'know?"

"Thanks a lot."

"Think nothin' of it." Larry gave an embarrassed smile, then said, "I . . . uh . . . should tell you, though, I did ask another investigator to look into it first."

"Oh? Before you recommended the *best*?"

"Well, before I knew whether the bishop was just imagining things. I mean, he told me this *friend* of his *thought* someone was following him. So, there was this guy said he needed work." Larry rummaged around in his desk drawer and came up with a business card and handed it to her. "Clayton Warfield. I asked him to check into it."

"And?"

"And he called back a couple days later and quit. Wouldn't say why. Sounded kinda scared to me. Then I gave Father . . . I mean Bishop Keegan your name. I never even told him about Warfield."

"Sounded scared?"

"I don't know, just his voice or something. Anyway . . ."

Larry dug a pen out of the mess on his desk and twirled it in his fingers, and she wondered what was coming. "Anyway, I was just gonna say, guys like Father Keegan—priests, and I guess bishops, too—most of 'em don't have much money, y'know? I mean for stuff like your fees. So . . . whatever he can't pay, I'll pay for him." He spread out his hands, palms up, then added, "Of course, just now I'm a little flat. But I'll pay, I mean it."

"I know. I know." He meant it, all right. That was the trouble with Larry—just when he had you convinced that you were right to be furious at him, he'd show signs of a real human heart beating inside that pudgy body.

ELEVEN

I t had taken him a long time to fall asleep after the woman called, and then he slept late the next morning, all the way till eight o'clock. Now it was after ten and Peter Keegan was still in church, on his knees in the front pew, trying to pray. He'd said the weekly nine o'clock mass for the children of the parish school, and now he had the silent, empty church to himself. He always took his turn saying the kids' mass, although he could have gotten out of it, being a bishop and only "in residence" at the parish. But one of the other two priests was very old and in poor health, and the other one—the pastor—was badly overworked.

He pulled his mind back to his prayers by saying one for the pastor. Who wasn't overworked these days? Parishes that used to have five priests were lucky now to have two. Most places had just one. There simply weren't enough priests, and the proposed solutions were too controversial. In his mind he knew the world wouldn't end—nor the Church, either—if they let married men be priests. And ordaining women priests? Deep down, he couldn't buy the arguments against it. But he never expressed such thoughts out loud, not even to friends. The pope had spoken and Peter Keegan was, after all, a loyal son of Rome. He'd signed that seven- or eight-page solemn oath of orthodoxy before he could be ordained a bishop. Besides, he'd never been one to rock any boats. Sometimes he wondered if he wasn't too—

Uh-oh, his mind was wandering again. Anyway, he knew the Lord would provide workers for the vineyard, in his own good time. The Lord knew best. He truly believed that. Even when we mortals weren't able to make sense of things. For example, only God knew why his mother should have to keep on living, when all her life she prayed she'd die before becoming a burden. And only God knew why his brother kept on hating him, after decades of virtually no contact. He wondered whether it was really Larry Candle who'd told Walter what happened at North Bay—as Kirsten and Dugan suspected— and why Walter waited until now to act on what he knew.

Because it had to be Walter who was behind the phone calls, Walter's thugs who almost ran him down at the zoo. Kirsten agreed, the intent must be to frighten him, show him how vulnerable he was. There wasn't much sense in reporting the incident to the police. Just a couple of unknown kids goofing around. Besides, Walter would find out if he made a report, and their plan was to keep Walter ignorant of how he was reacting, or even whether he was reacting at all. For his part, he was to do nothing except wait for the next call, and meanwhile make sure he was always with other people whenever he left the rectory. That wouldn't be so hard, since—

A sudden, soft noise startled him. Caught him a million miles away again, far from where his body was kneeling. He started to ask the Lord for forgiveness—then froze. That noise—what had it been? It had come from the rear of the church. Not a stifled cough. Not a door closing. More like a quiet thud—but ominous, somehow.

He forced himself to stand up and turn around. Compared to most other pseudo-gothic churches around the city, this one wasn't large. But when the floodlights in its high, vaulted ceiling were turned off—like now—it stayed surprisingly dark even during the day, with narrow stained-glass windows that seemed to shut out more light than they let in.

As he peered through the gloom, something—another sound? some slight movement?—drew his attention to the choir loft. But there was nothing to be seen up there now. Besides, the first sound surely hadn't come from high up. It had seemed close to the floor, down there by the double wooden doors that led to the vestibule.

He stood motionless, straining to hear. There was nothing.

Then new light suddenly filled the cracks around the double doors. Someone had opened the outside door. Coming in, or going out? The two thin-lined rectangles of light disappeared again, as the outside door closed. Still no sound. No one came into the church.

He wanted more than anything to run away, to race back to the sacristy and then through that fire-proof, burglar-proof door that guarded the passageway into the rectory. But he didn't run. He sidled out of the pew, automatically going down on one knee—genuflecting toward the tabernacle on the side altar and the flickering red flame of its candle. He turned and walked slowly down the wide center aisle toward the rear of the church.

Maybe it had been some harmless, common sound—some unnoticed old woman dropping her purse as she rose stiffly from the back pew and went out into the vestibule. Or maybe his instinct was accurate. Maybe a real menace lay behind the dread that still had the blood churning wildly through his body. He had to know.

As he walked he kept his gaze fixed on that set of double doors, wondering if someone was out there in the vestibule, waiting for him.

He was nearly to the doors and, because he wasn't looking, it caught him by surprise. Something picked up out of the corner of his eye. A shape unidentified, almost unnoticed. He'd already passed it by when he stopped, then backpedaled a step.

There it was, lying on the polished wood of the pew to his right, the one just beneath the front railing of the choir loft, fifteen feet above.

It was nothing but an ordinary pigeon, fat and mottled-gray, one among a million others in the city—cruising the canyons between tall buildings, flapping into noisy landings, waddling in circles like drunks around downtown plazas and neighborhood parks. This particular pigeon, though, lay on its side where it had fallen, in the shadows of the dimly lighted church. Its wings were bound to its body with yellow twine that was wrapped around and around and even held its feet tied together, too.

This particular pigeon lay very still, very silent.

TWELVE

Kirsten took the Dan Ryan south to Eighty-seventh Street and then headed west. The signs weren't easy to read in the morning fog and the rain, but she couldn't miss May Street. There was a huge brick church on the corner—St. Kilian's. She made a left turn there and drove south. Once she got past the church, houses lined both sides of the street.

She was a northsider herself, but as a cop she'd spent some time here in the Twenty-second District, and had gotten to know the area well. She also knew, mostly from Dugan and his relatives, that back maybe thirty-five years ago most of these modest, solid homes had been filled with O'Briens, Sullivans, Maloneys, and the like. Now the neighborhood was 99 percent African-American, middle-class and well-maintained. Signs of age and economic distress were showing, though, especially in the apartment buildings that anchored the corners of many blocks.

It was 10:30 when she pulled to the curb and stared across the street at Clayton Warfield's home. She'd called right after talking to Larry and, when Warfield wouldn't talk to her, she'd left her name and told him to check her out. "Call Larry Candle," she'd suggested, just before Warfield hung up on her. That was over two hours ago.

Now, using her cell phone, she called back to Dugan's office. "Larry's out," Mollie said. "But he said to tell you he talked to your friend, and he doesn't think it did much good."

She tapped out Warfield's number again, and this time an automated voice informed her that the phone was "temporarily disconnected." That was quick, although it didn't seem surprising, now that she saw the house.

It was a single-story, 1950s brick house with a small, well-kept front yard. There wasn't much to distinguish it from the other homes on the block, except that at Clayton Warfield's every shade at every window was pulled down tight, and the space where the front door used to be was covered with a sheet of plywood, with the words A-ABLE BOARD-UP in bold block letters. The house looked as disconnected as the phone.

She spent some time cruising Warfield's block and the surrounding streets, finally parking around the corner from his house. It was mid-morning, yet dark enough so the street lights were on. Pulling the hood of her jacket up over her head against the soft, steady rain, she walked up the alley. The waist-high chain-link fence around Warfield's backyard looked brand new, as did the swing set, and the sandbox with a plastic cover that looked like the shell of a green turtle. A rusting Ford Escort sat on a concrete square that once must have been the floor of a garage that was no longer there. The shades were down here, too, but light showed behind them at two windows to the left of the back door, in what she assumed was Warfield's kitchen. She opened the gate and walked along a narrow sidewalk to the back porch. The rain beaded up on the freshly painted wood, and the paint can still sat on the flat porch railing.

She went up the steps. Not too loud and aggressive, she told herself, but not too tentative, either. Then she knocked on the door.

Almost immediately, the lights inside went out and a floodlight high above her head went on. She waited. Finally, one edge of the curtain over the window in the door was pulled aside. She smiled and held up one of her business cards, shielding it from the rain and tilting it so it could be read by the man looking out at her. The curtain dropped back over the window, and she heard muffled voices through the door. Then the lights went on again inside, and the door swung open.

"Okay," the man said. "I s'pose you should come in outta the rain." He wore khaki pants and a dark blue pullover shirt that showed off a slim, muscular build. His complexion was light brown, except around his left eye, where the swollen tissue was yellow and purple and black. What little could be seen of the white of the eye wasn't white at all, but a cloudy red.

"Thank you." She stepped into the kitchen. Across the room, and just beyond a doorway leading into the darkened interior of the house, an attractive, dark-skinned woman in a long beige robe stood in the half-light, with an infant, maybe three months old, cradled in her arms. "I'm sorry," Kirsten said. "I don't mean to intrude. I called and—"

"I'm Clayton Warfield," the man said, walking past Kirsten until he stood between her and the woman with the baby. "What do you want?"

"You talked to Larry Candle, right?" she asked.

"I did. Now what—"

"You might ask her to rest her coat, Clayton." The woman with the baby had a soft, soothing voice. "And maybe to sit down." The woman nodded at Kirsten. "As for me," she said, "I have to go feed the baby." She stepped backward, and disappeared into the darkness.

"Your wife and baby?" Kirsten asked.

Warfield nodded. "Katrina," he said, "and Clayton Junior." When he took her jacket and draped it over the back of a kitchen chair, she noticed for the first time the splint on the little finger of his left hand.

"They're lovely," she said, "both of them."

"Thank you." His tone was neutral, and he didn't smile back at her. "What is it you want from me?"

51

"I don't know, really. I'm . . . looking into something for a Bishop Peter Keegan, and Larry Candle told me you—"

"Anybody know you're here? Anybody see you?"

"No one knows, and no one followed me. There's no one watching your house, either. I checked . . . and I'm good at things like that."

"I don't know." He glanced at the doorway where his wife had been standing, then sighed and shook his head, as though concluding a discussion with himself. "C'mon in here," he said, and turned to his right. She followed him into a room the size of a small bedroom. There was a washer and dryer on one side, under the windows, and a row of tall cardboard U-Haul cartons against the opposite wall. Odds and ends of furniture filled much of the rest of the room.

"Oh," she said, "you're moving?"

"We just moved *in* a month ago. Haven't even finished unpacking yet."

"I know what you mean," she said. "It took my husband and me—"

"There's three bedrooms, and we—Treena and me—we decided we'd make this one into a combination laundry and playroom for the little guy. Treena quit her job, you know, so she could stay home and . . . and . . ." He stood for a moment and looked around, as though he didn't recognize what he was seeing. "I don't know if I should be talking to you I . . . anyway, we ain't moving. I don't know what we're gonna do."

"I guess I don't understand," she said, which was an understatement.

"Look here, this washer and dryer—brand new. Me and Treena picked 'em out together at Circuit City. And I put up that fence out back with my own hands, and painted the porch and . . . and I didn't even know I could do that kinda stuff. Anyway, we knew we'd have the house note, and big credit card bills, but we figured . . . we stand together we can make it. But then, like I told Mr. Candle . . ." Warfield lifted the lid on top of the washer and stared down into it, then let it fall with a bang. "I went to see Larry Candle and told him things had got slow and I needed work . . . bad."

"Do you mind if I sit down?" Kirsten asked, and then sat on an uncomfortable wooden rocking chair, more to make sure the conversation kept flowing than because she was tired. "Are you . . . um . . . licensed by the state as a private detective?"

"Oh yeah, I got the license. I got a degree and I worked security for a while. Then I went on my own. What I do is take pictures of accident scenes for lawyers, interview witnesses, stuff like that. Mostly in black neighborhoods, y'know? Anyway, I went to see Larry and he said he had just started with a new law firm and so he didn't have anything for me just then. I pressed him—I wish I wouldn't have—and finally he said there *was* this one guy needed something, but not the kind of work I usually did."

"This one guy . . . that was Bishop Keegan?"

"Yeah." Warfield shook his head. "Larry told me there was this guy, this bishop, had an idea some weirdo was following him around—stalking him, like—and I could just watch and see if I saw someone. He said it might not be anything, but if I *did* see someone, and the dude didn't see me, I should follow him. Larry said be careful, just find out where he lived or worked or whatever. That was it. Seemed pretty simple."

"Did you talk to the bishop about it?"

"Uh-uh. He didn't even know. Larry said he'd pay me himself just to watch for a couple days, see whether this bishop was imagining things. He gave me five hundred dollars and told me where the bishop lived."

"Five hundred dollars," Kirsten said. "That's a lot of money for a couple of days."

"I know. Anyway, the next day was Saturday and I was watching outside the bishop's house and someone came and picked him up and drove him to this other church, and—honest to God—there *was* someone following him, a man, in a black Buick. So I followed, too, in my car. And when we got to the other church there was a big crowd and some sort of ceremony and the bishop was a part of it. The man who was following him went right into the church, and I followed him and . . . and somehow I lost track of him. Dude musta gone right out by another door and drove away."

"You see his face?"

"No, not really. Not that I could recognize him again. White guy, maybe six-one, husky, dark-colored clothes."

"And you never saw him again?"

"Oh yeah, I did. The next day I went back to watch the bishop again, and it was Sunday and he had a service right there at the church where he lives, and I saw the Buick again, parked around the corner, with a man sitting in it."

"The same man?"

"I figured it was, but I guess I don't know for sure. Anyway, I sat in my car and when the service was over the bishop came out and a cab picked him up and the Buick followed the cab and I followed, too."

"Where did the bishop go?"

"I don't know. I was following the Buick and lost track of the cab. Then all the sudden the guy starts going faster and making sudden turns and at first I kept up and then I realized he must be trying to shake me off."

"And then?"

"And then he was gone and I realized I was in over my head. I drove home and called Larry and told him I was gonna pay the money back, because he was right in the first place. It wasn't the kind of job for me." Warfield paused, then held up his left hand, the one with the splint, and stared at it. "But it was too late."

"I don't understand," Kirsten said, although she was certain she *did* understand. "What do you mean?"

"That same night we were watching TV. Me, Treena, and the baby. And wham! The whole front door just, like, flew in.

They busted the door in, tore it off the hinges. There was three of 'em, I think. They were in plainclothes, you know, white guys. They never said so, but I swear they acted like cops." Warfield was pacing around between the cartons and the laundry appliances. "I mean, it all happened so fast, with Treena screaming and the baby wailing. I jumped up, but one of 'em hit me with something, a sap or something, smack in my eye. Another dude had a gun and told Treena and me to turn and face the wall. One of 'em ran back toward the bedrooms and the bathroom and I could hear him throwing stuff around. Then he came back and said there was nobody else in the house but he found something."

"Found something?"

"Yeah. One of them reached around and held a little fat plastic bag in front of my face. Said he found it in our toilet tank, and I said that was a lie and I was calling the real police. I started to turn around and then . . . Treena was beside me holding the baby and the one with the gun held it right by my little baby's face. And then he said, 'You make that call, Clayton boy. You just do that. And then say good-bye to the little pickaninny here. Drug houses like this,' he said, 'lotta shootin' goes on sometimes. You know what I mean?' That's what he said. So I just stood there." Warfield was breathing hard now, leaning over the top of the dryer, both hands flat on the smooth white surface—and tears were running down his cheeks. "I just stood there and stared at the wall."

"Was . . . was there anything else?" Kirsten could scarcely speak above a whisper. "Did they say anything else?"

"Just . . . just the man said I should stop messing in stuff that got nothing to do with me. He didn't say what stuff, but I knew. And then he said he knew me and Treena wouldn't say nothing to nobody, because he knew I didn't want anybody to get hurt, especially not a new mama, or a helpless little baby. Then he said, real calm and slow, 'Give me your hand.' So I held out my hand, behind my back. But he said no, the left hand was good enough, this time. And I didn't know what he meant. But he took my left hand and pulled it behind my back, and then he bent my little finger backward until . . . until it broke. Just like that. Not like he was mad, or anything. He just did it. Then he said none of us wanted anything else to get broken, did we."

Warfield didn't move, just kept staring down at the top of the dryer, silent for what seemed a long time, and Kirsten herself felt physically unable to speak.

Finally he turned to face her. "And then they were gone," he said. "I wasn't even gonna talk to you. But Treena said I ought to. So I did. And now you should go away, and never come back here."

"I won't," Kirsten said. She stood up. "And . . . thank you, Mr. Warfield." She turned and was surprised to see Warfield's wife standing in the door to the kitchen. "Thank you, too, Mrs. Warfield."

"It's best this way," the woman said. "And it wasn't just me decided Clayton should tell you. We decided together. Mr. Candle told Clayton we could trust you. We don't want something bad to happen to us, or our baby. But we thought we should at least tell *some*one, maybe keep someone else from being hurt."

Kirsten got her jacket and turned toward the back door. Her legs felt weak, as though she'd been running a long distance.

"One more thing," Warfield said. "You remind Larry I'm paying his money back, like I told him. I mean, we spent it right away, but when we have it I'll pay it back. I didn't earn it. Didn't even get the license number of the Buick."

"No way," Kirsten said. "You earned that five hundred and then some. I'll work it out with Larry. I'm sure he won't want it back. Period. Forget it." She pulled the hood up over her head and started out the door, then turned back. "And by the way, I *know* that lawyer who runs the new firm Larry works for. You call Larry. They'll have *lots* of work for you."

She pulled the door closed behind her as she left, then dug her billfold out of her purse and slid two folded fifty-dollar bills under the paint can on the railing. She was nearly running by the time she got to her car. By then, too, she was already over her anger with Larry for getting Clayton Warfield into something that could have destroyed him. Larry was only trying to help.

But that didn't mean he should get his five hundred dollars back.

THIRTEEN

You couldn't con Mollie. She'd been the firm's secretary forever, even before his dad died and Dugan stepped in, and had been as important a part of the operation as Fred Schustein and Peter Rienzo, the two lawyers who'd worked for his dad. Mollie had more savvy about the in-office side of handling plaintiffs' personal injury claims than most lawyers ever would. But that wasn't exactly neurosurgery; anyone interested enough could learn it. The special thing about Mollie was, you couldn't fool her.

Of course, that never stopped him from trying, and he figured she enjoyed the game, too, even if her no-nonsense demeanor never showed it.

"Ten-thirty meeting, Tort Law Committee, at the Chicago Bar Association," he told her. "Lucky it's just around the corner. Gotta keep up with the changing law." He dropped a dictation tape on her desk. "You can sign most of these letters for me. The rest I'll look at tomorrow morning."

"Better hurry," Mollie said, and looked at her watch. "Oh . . . and don't be surprised if the CBA isn't there when you get there. They moved their headquarters, you know, six or seven years ago." She picked up the tiny cassette tape and waved it at him. "You're getting mixed up in some of that stuff with

Kirsten again," she said. "I can tell. Not in till noon yesterday, leaving early today. I mean, it's a darn good thing you've got Larry Candle in the office, someone who's able to handle—"

"Wait!" Dugan stared at her. "Mollie, did you hear what you just *said?*"

"Of course I did," she said, but he could tell she was trying to hide her own amazement. He turned and went out the door, leaving her to wonder if she were losing her mind.

When he'd first suggested it, Mollie told him a dozen times that bringing Larry into the office was something "no one in their right mind would even consider." Dugan hadn't been sure it was a good idea, either. But his long-standing need for another lawyer became even more compelling some months ago, during another time he'd gotten "mixed up in some of that stuff with Kirsten," as Mollie put it, and was out of the office so much.

The problem was that he hadn't needed just some competent lawyer. He'd needed a competent lawyer who wouldn't go ballistic if he or she happened to discover that some of Dugan's clients with accident injuries were sent to him by police officers, and that the police officers got paid for their referrals. The group of referring cops was something he inherited along with the law firm when his dad died. The cases they sent him were never phonied-up accidents, but his paying for the referrals was still considered unethical.

As time went by some of his cops got reassigned to desk jobs, or retired—like Cuffs Radovich—or died, and Dugan never recruited any replacements. Personally, he didn't think his way of paying to get clients was any worse than wining and dining corporate hotshots like the big-name firms did, or dropping cash for those pseudo-slick ads on cable TV like some of his personal injury competitors. But the people who wrote the rules, and the Attorney Registration and Disciplinary Commission that enforced them, thought otherwise. So, if he ever got caught . . .

Larry Candle had seemed a logical, if unexpected, choice for Dugan's new associate. Even before he'd been temporarily suspended on charges of stealing from a client—charges later dropped—Larry had had a questionable reputation. It was a reputation worse than his actual habits, but one Dugan suspected Larry enjoyed, maybe even helped promote. That was something Dugan could understand, since he, too, enjoyed thinking of himself, even portraying himself, as something of a maverick.

When Dugan stepped into the empty elevator outside his office, he was happy that Mollie was changing her mind on the Larry Candle issue. But by the time he got down to the building lobby, he wasn't so sure. Except for Fred and Peter, who handled workers' compensation cases, he'd been the only attorney in the office since he took over. Naturally, he considered himself irreplaceable. To think that his own role could be assumed so easily by anyone at all, not to mention Larry Candle, was a bit sobering.

He decided to walk the two miles from downtown to Renfroe Laboratories, near Chicago Avenue and Halsted. He'd dropped the skateboards off there yesterday, and ordered an expedited examination. Today there was a light, steady rain, but he had an umbrella and the walk might help him clear his brain.

The night before, they'd sent the bishop home a little after ten o'clock. Dugan had gone down to the street with him and hailed a taxi—a real taxi this time, not Cuffs Radovich. The bishop was to call Kirsten's office from a pay phone the next time he saw someone suspicious, or got an ominous call. All three of them agreed it was *when*, not *if*, but Dugan was less certain than the bishop and Kirsten that it was Walter, in fact, who was behind the stalking.

And *stalking* was the correct term, even if the bishop hadn't used it. There were the calls on his private line for which only a few close friends, and his mother's nursing home, had the number. There was the elusive man in dark clothing—the bishop wasn't sure it was always the same man—so often staring at him from the edges of crowds at affairs like confirmations, fund-raisers, funerals. And, what Dugan guessed to be worst of all, there was the feeling the bishop described as a "constant sensation of being observed," wherever he was, all the time.

Kirsten had explained to the bishop that once he became aware he was under surveillance it wasn't unusual that his feeling of being exposed would persist, even at times when it was unlikely—or impossible—that someone could actually be watching. There is a comfortable, if not always accurate, sense of security that one's privacy offers. When that bubble of privacy is broken, one feels vulnerable. It takes time to create a new bubble, Kirsten had said, and even longer to regain the sense that one is safe inside its fragile walls.

So the bishop was to report any new contact.

All Dugan had to do was follow up on the skateboards—check possible fingerprints, see if they'd been reported stolen, and the like—a task which would prove fruitless and was probably designed by Kirsten to keep him out of her hair while she conducted her investigation in her own way, about which she was irritatingly uncommunicative.

"I'll call if there's anything else for you to do," Kirsten had said. "Meanwhile, you should be at your office. They can't possibly get by without you."

Uh-huh.

FOURTEEN

It wasn't quite noon when Kirsten got back downtown, parked, and went to her office in the old jewelry district on the east edge of the Loop, at Wabash and Washington. The headquarters of Wild Onion, Ltd., was a tiny, two-room suite on the tenth floor, tucked between Mark Well Diamond Company, Inc., and Brumstein & Brumstein Wholesale Jewelry, Inc. Both corporate neighbors were owned by Mark Brumstein, who was the husband of one of her first clients and gave her a break on the rent.

Kirsten went through her little reception room and into her office. She checked her voice mail and then called Mark Brumstein's receptionist, Grace, who took her calls during office hours. There were none so far that morning. She sat at her desk, throwing away mail and wondering whether Acting Chief of Detectives Walter Keegan had the slightest idea who she was. If he'd intercepted a call from the bishop to her office, he surely knew plenty about her by now. Otherwise, who could say?

Kirsten's father had spent his entire adult life as a cop, and she'd spent a few years with the department herself, long enough for her to sense the early symptoms of chronic cynicism, something cops develop as a sort of vaccination against a far worse disease—despair. Not wanting a lifetime of either condition, she quit the department and joined up with a large security firm. There, she'd had one brief moment of fame—or notoriety, anyway. That had to do with the so-called Magnificent Mile Bomb Scare, a big deal in the media for three or four days that had left one perpetrator blown into several dozen pieces, while his co-conspirators went unidentified and unapprehended. Several upscale stores along North Michigan Avenue missed a day of cash flow, but otherwise remained intact. Kirsten got lots of credit, or blame, depending on who was dishing it out. She also got promoted within the big firm to a management position she hated. But even that worked out for the best, because it convinced her to walk away from that job, too, and start her own agency.

With the resources at his disposal, Walter Keegan could have found out most of that in fifteen minutes . . . if he was interested. But was he? It would be nice to know for sure.

She had no real proof that it was Walter who was behind the bishop's problems, although the signs pointed that way. One way to find out for sure was to walk up and ask him. That would be fast, cheap, and—if the signs were right—not very safe. She needed something more indirect, maybe a way to rattle Walter's cage a bit, to see how he responded. It would take more time and expense, but seemed worth it.

Larry's suspicion that the bishop couldn't pay her fees was reasonable, but may have been inaccurate. During their drive after fleeing the zoo, the bishop had told her—with a naivete she was learning was typical of him—that he had "plenty of money, so don't worry about that." His mother, although by no means wealthy, had been left some money and a piece of land in northern Wisconsin by her own widowed sister, who'd died childless. She put the land in a trust, planning to donate it for use as an orphanage or a camp for children some day, but had never gotten to it. The money she'd given outright to the bishop. He had no use for it and simply set it aside for his mother's care.

"But it's more money than she'll need, even if she lives ten more years," he'd said, and dealing with the threats, while keeping his reputation intact, was clearly more important to him than expense. Kirsten didn't blame him, although she didn't know how much "plenty of money" added up to. She doubted he had much of a handle on what a job like this might cost, and noted his flinch when she stated her per diem. But he'd left a check with her before Dugan took him down to the cab the night before.

Larry Candle had given two reasons why he sent the bishop to her after Warfield quit. First, she was one of the best. Second, she was honest and wouldn't shake the man down for his last penny "and then walk away from the poor guy," Larry said, "like a lot of your asshole com—oops, sorry, greedy competitors would."

She knew Larry was stroking her, but actually he was right on both—

The phone rang.

She let Grace answer it and picked up when the call came through to her. It was the bishop. His voice had a nervous, strained sound to it, but he described in detail what had happened when he was praying after mass.

It turned out the pigeon wasn't dead after all. "I untied its wings," he said, "and saved the yellow twine, just like Dugan saved those skateboards." He told her how he gave it some water and the bird still wouldn't fly away, and how he'd taken it to the principal of the parish school. She was a nun, and rather disagreeable, but liked him ever since a few weeks ago when he and Bud Burgeson, and Bud's brother, Kenny, had helped sort out donations to the annual rummage and toy sale. The principal sent him to Miss Hardaway's classroom. "Turns out Miss Hardaway's famous for helping injured animals," he explained. "Even keeps a huge bird cage in her room." Her third graders promised him they'd help Miss Hardaway take care of the pigeon and pray for it, and send it to the bird hospital if it didn't get better overnight. "I . . . I'm not reading something into it that's not there, am I?" he asked.

"No way," Kirsten said. "It couldn't be more obvious. Yellow bird falls."

She told him to save the yellow twine in a plastic bag for her. That was only to encourage him, really, since she expected the twine would be about as much help as the skateboards—which she expected to be of no help at all.

"Anything else happen?" she asked

"I . . . no, nothing." She had the impression he was hiding something—again.

She hung up, wondering whether she'd have been so willing to handle that poor bird. Don't pigeons carry some strange disease? She decided Bishop Keegan was turning out to be a complex and rather surprising man, all things considered. More important for now, though, she was getting an idea for an interesting, and rather inexpensive, cage-rattling technique.

What with waiting for traffic signals and not being in a hurry to begin with, it took Dugan forty minutes to walk the two miles to Renfroe Laboratories. If the name was nondescript, the building was even less than that. A brick, three-story structure, it might have been built in the thirties as a small factory or warehouse. The first floor windows had been filled in with cement blocks maybe forty years ago, and the metal sheeting over the only door was rusting around the bottom corners.

When he pulled on the handle the door didn't budge, so he pressed the button in the shoulder-high intercom to his right and the response came back at once. "May I help you?" A female voice, firm and pleasant.

"I'm here about the skateboards."

There was a buzz from the lock and he pulled open the door

and stepped into a harshly lit vestibule, about eight feet square, with a very high ceiling. The door closed behind him and when the lock clicked into place he turned back and saw that there was no handle at all on the inside. The walls were a flat gray, and paint and plaster both were flaking off. High up and to his left, what looked like a convex mirror built into the corner sent him back a distorted image of himself, but the image being sent to whoever was watching the security monitor was apparently clear enough, because there was another buzz from the lock of the steel-clad door in front of him.

He went through and walked nearly to the end of a fifteen-foot corridor to the only other door, on the right. That door was glass, and opened into a waiting room that was bright and cheerful, and somehow reminded Dugan of childhood visits to his orthodontist, except for the convex mirror high up in one corner of this room, too, something his orthodontist hadn't needed.

A briskly efficient middle-age woman led Dugan beyond the waiting room and through a jumble of six-foot-tall office cubicles to an elevator. He rode alone up to the top floor of the building—the third floor. Leroy Renfroe met him and took him back to a spacious, comfortable office with a wall of windows that faced the west, to tell him what the Renfroe technicians had found on the skateboards.

"Only one significant thing, I'm afraid," Renfroe said, opening a thin manila folder that lay on the desk between them. "Otherwise, just some prints too smudged to provide any match, but almost certainly those of a child, or children. Which is consistent with your narrative."

"Right," Dugan said. He'd described the incident at the zoo to Renfroe, without identifying the bishop. "But what about the significant thing?"

"After the carbon dusting we moved on to the Super Glue technique, which, as you probably know, doesn't actually use

Super Glue itself, but cyano acrylate, which is a chemical compound contained in Su—"

"And the significant thing?" Dugan knew Renfroe charged by the hour, and figured they could return to the lecture later, if necessary.

"Sorry." Renfroe consulted his notes. "One via—let's say usable—thumbprint, up under the rear set of wheels of skateboard number two. That's the only significant thing so far. First we verified that the print wasn't yours, and then—"

"You've got comparison prints of mine?"

Renfroe's only answer to that was one of those kind, condescending smiles which made Dugan think again of his orthodontist. "So we continued to run comparisons," he continued. "Those boards aren't new, obviously, and whoever it was probably bought them or stole them for the occasion, and apparently tried to wipe their own prints off. We found bits of fabric, which turned out to be cotton, like from an old T-shirt."

"What about the one print. No match?"

"Oh, we finally got a match. A real surprise, too, but not a guy likely to be involved in some street mugging. Name's Keegan, and he's—"

"I know who he is," Dugan said. "Walter Keegan, deputy chief of detectives or something. And—"

"What are you talking about?" Renfroe, clearly confused, looked down at his file again. "Not *Walter* Keegan. *Peter* Keegan. Says here he's a Catholic priest."

FIFTEEN

Kirsten knew the perfect place to call from.

She walked a few blocks from her office to the Richard J. Daley Center, a thirty-story glass-and-oxidized-iron rectangle housing the downtown branch of the Circuit Court of Cook County. She went past the Picasso sculpture in the plaza, to an entrance on the east end of the lobby where metal detectors guard the elevators up to the courtrooms. She skipped those, and rode the escalator down.

The Daley Center was connected at its lower level to a subterranean "pedway" through which the nonclaustrophobic could wander under the northeast quadrant of the Loop, and beyond. On a rainy morning you could ride a subway or a Metra commuter train downtown, file your property tax appeal at the County Building, drop in on your alderman at city hall—assuming your alderman ever showed up there—then dash along to meet your lawyer at her office and walk with her to Domestic Relations Court for a fight over who gets your kids. After that, you might unwind with lunch at one of twenty different possibilities from Arby's to the Walnut Room at Marshall Field's, follow up with some rehabilitative shopping, and then hop a train back home—all without going out in the rain.

Kirsten knew the layout of the entire pedway, knew it very well because she thought she ought to. But she didn't like being down there. Rational or not, she always found herself wondering how many million pounds of concrete and steel were piled up over those tunnels at any given spot—say, for example, the spot where she was when she was wondering.

Stepping off into the open area at the foot of the moving staircase, she joined the midday throng she knew she'd find beneath the courthouse. The blind vendor at the newstand was making change and bantering with his regulars as always. There were a few people just hanging out, of course, but most rushed along, headed for lunch at the cafeteria to her left, or on toward one of the various tunnels leading away in different directions. It was an underground pedestrian crossroads, brightly lit and—to Kirsten, anyway—gloomy at the same time, but a great spot for urban people-watching.

And the perfect place for making a phone call she didn't want traced back to her.

"Acting Chief Keegan here," the man answered, after she'd bluffed and bullied her way through two telephonic road blocks.

"Mornin', sugar." That's all she said, trying to sound southern, or mountain or something.

"This the FBI or not?" Keegan asked. There was silence, and she didn't fill it in. "What the hell?" he finally said. "Who is this?"

"Why, it's your travel consultant, sugar. A big hit this season is Yellow Bird Falls. I recommend you watch for it."

"What're you talk—"

" 'Bye now." She hung up and hurried around the corner, down one of the tunnels, and up a wide stairway.

She stepped out onto the plaza at Clark and Washington. It was an easy corner to catch a cab, especially with the rain gone and the sun coming out, and catch a cab is what she did.

"Archdiocese of Chicago chancery office." A woman's voice, smooth and mellow. "May I help you?" A sexy voice, in fact.

"Is Bishop Keegan in?"

"Yes, but he's awfully busy right now. Could someone else—"

"No. It's a personal matter, and very important."

"Well . . . please hold," she said, so Dugan held.

Leroy Renfroe had insisted he tour the whole lab, which Dugan had to admit was impressive. They'd had lunch in the employee dining room, and now Dugan sat on the corner of a battered oak conference table in a room with no chairs, surrounded by floor-to-ceiling shelves, widely spaced and lined with things brought into Leroy Renfroe's lab for analysis, bulky items that were wrapped in black plastic. All very orderly. Kirsten claimed she'd seen more than one police crime lab that looked like a teenager's room compared to Renfroe's.

While he waited, he tried to identify the plastic-wrapped items by shape and size. He'd picked out a hockey stick for sure, plus a possible truck tire rim, when a different woman's voice finally came on the line. "This is Mrs. Gage," she said, "Bishop Keegan is unavailable just now, and he has appointments all afternoon."

"But this is very important."

"I'm sure it is." Businesslike, sympathetic, not rude at all. "You may leave your name and—"

He hung up and tried to call Kirsten. Her cell phone was off, and at her office Grace answered and said Kirsten was "out for the rest of the day." He called their home number and there were no messages. Finally, he considered calling his own office and handling the inevitable crisis or two over the phone, but decided the hell with that. Let Larry Candle live up to his emerging reputation.

Kirsten would have wanted him to check with her first, but

she'd dragged him into this mess—well, in a sense, anyway—
and he'd be damned if he'd confine his role to running errands.
Of course, he wasn't certain what he'd say to the bishop when
he got there, other than ask him about about the fingerprint.

SIXTEEN

Kirsten paid off the cab three blocks from home and walked the rest of the way. Parked down the block, in a tow zone, was the car Cuffs Radovich had left for her. It was a Ford Taurus he'd rented, using some credit card she certainly didn't want to ask about. She changed clothes and packed the Taurus with what she needed, including a lunch of radish sandwiches on a whole wheat bread—a personal favorite—and diet Coke. By two-thirty, after a stop at a Japanese gift shop near Clark and Diversey, she was driving south on the Dan Ryan Expressway.

Just past Sixty-third Street, where Interstates 90 and 94 split up, she took the I-90 exit. That put her eastbound on the Chicago Skyway, skimming high over the tops of the lookalike bungalows and abandoned mills and warehouses crowded into the city's little-known southeast corner. As it crossed the border, the skyway came down to earth just below the southern shore of Lake Michigan and poured itself into the Indiana toll road. Then, somewhere past Gary, the two interstates crisscrossed again and Kirsten switched back to I-94, still headed east.

She had no trouble remembering that Michigan City was in Indiana and that the Warren Dunes were fifteen or twenty miles farther along, in Michigan. But she could never keep all those other places straight: Long Beach, Grand Beach, Beverly Shores, Union Pier, and a bunch of other little towns that dotted the southeastern curve of Lake Michigan. Of course the condo developers were swarming all along the shoreline now, but for maybe a century those towns had been sleepy summer havens for who knows how many thousands of Chicago families, mostly southsiders.

Among those people were some big-timers in business and industry, not to mention law and politics. Most of the summer people, though, were more ordinary. They were middle-class, with a high percentage who were carried on some public payroll—either the city itself, or Cook County, or the Forest Preserve District, or the Sanitary District, or whatever—foremen and supervisors from various municipal departments and offices, plus teachers, firemen, and cops.

Quite a few cops, in fact. Chicago police officers were required to reside within the city limits, and this rule seemed pretty strictly enforced. But many of them had second homes, and Kirsten would have put the percentage of upper-echelon cops who did at very close to one hundred.

The bishop had told them that Catholic Charities, with an annual budget of over a hundred million dollars, operated out of a building on the Near North Side, but he spent most of his time at the chancery office—archdiocesan headquarters—in a high-rise on East Huron. That was about half as far as his earlier walk that day, and Dugan could use the exercise. Besides, it had turned into a sunny, warm day and he enjoyed being outdoors and able to enjoy it. He took his time and it was past three o'clock when he got there.

He was greeted by the same sexy voice that had answered the phone when he called—and a young woman who fit the voice perfectly. He identified himself as "Captain Nemo, to see Bishop Keegan," and she invited him to wait. He sat down and picked up a tabloid-style Catholic newspaper called *The New World*, but he couldn't take his eyes off the receptionist. It surprised him, for some reason, that visitors to this official church headquarters were greeted by such a vivacious, attractive woman. Every so often she'd casually tuck a wisp of straw-blond hair behind her ear, and he decided she resembled one of those trendy, young Manhattan types from some primetime network sitcom.

He was still peeking over the top of *The New World* when a priest in a white Roman collar stepped into the waiting room. His black shoes shone like a marine's, and French cuffs edged out from the crisply pressed sleeves of his black suit. It took Dugan an extra second to recognize the man.

But it was definitely the bishop, and he seemed relieved that it was Dugan who was waiting for him. "Oh," he said, "Captain Nemo. Please come in."

Dugan followed him down a hallway and into a large, wood-paneled office that might have been the lair of some high-powered partner in a Loop law firm—except it was larger and less cluttered than most lawyers' offices, and the books that filled nearly an entire wall of shelves mostly had something religious in their titles.

"Nice office," Dugan said. He sat in a comfortable chair facing the desk.

"Thank you." The bishop removed his suit coat and draped it very carefully over the back of a straight chair that sat by the windows. "I inherited it when I took over Catholic Charities." He sat down behind his desk. He looked tired, confused even, and then seemed to get a sudden thought. "Oh," he said, "I know why you're here."

"You do?"

"Well, I think so, anyway." The bishop reached down and pulled open one of his desk drawers. "Kirsten must have sent you to pick this up."

"Pick something up?" Even the bishop saw him as just an errand boy.

"This." The bishop pulled a tangle of yellow twine out of an envelope. "You know. From the pigeon?"

"I don't know what you're talking about. What pigeon?"

The bishop told him what had happened.

Dugan stuffed the string back in the envelope and put it in his jacket pocket. "We'll have that checked," he said. "Now, what I really—"

"Wait." The bishop suddenly stood up. He turned and looked out the window, then turned back. "There's something else. Something I didn't tell Kirsten. I promised I wouldn't tell anyone. I . . ." He sat back down. "My God, I just don't know."

Dugan waited. He'd let the bishop wrestle it out.

"As I said, I didn't tell Kirsten because I promised not to, but . . ." He leaned over and picked up a message pad from his desktop. "Last night I received a phone call from a woman. She said she could help me."

"Help you?"

"Yes. She knows about . . . about Yellow Bird Falls. She's apparently from up there. Said someone came there from Chicago and was asking a person named Bobby about her."

"Asking about her? Why?"

"She wouldn't explain on the phone. She seemed very afraid, but she promised to call me today. And she did, about a half hour ago. She wants to meet me. Alone." He shook his head, as though he couldn't believe what he was saying. "I said I would."

"Are you crazy? She might be—"

"She said tonight. But I said no, that I was tied up and it would have to be tomorrow night. I . . . what I really wanted was more time to decide whether I'd break my promise and tell Kirsten."

"Good for you." This bishop was tougher than people might think. "Where are you supposed to meet?"

15

"It's . . . a motel." He read from the message pad. "The Moonglow, on Lincoln Avenue, near Devon. Room one-one-nine. I was scared, but . . . what if she could really help put an end to all this? So I promised—"

A rasping buzz tore through the air and nearly knocked Dugan out of his chair. "Jesus Christ! What the hell . . . oh, sorry, Bishop."

"No, you're right. I should have that intercom adjusted." He half-turned and reached for a phone on the wide window ledge behind him. "This is Bishop Kee—Oh, of course, Your Eminence. Except I'm with someone and I . . ." There was a long pause, while the bishop sat down and his face sagged into a frown. "Uh, certainly, Your Eminence. I'm very pleased." But he sure didn't look that way to Dugan. "Yes," he said. "Right away." He put the phone down and stared at it, not saying anything.

"More bad news?" Dugan asked.

"What?" The bishop jumped a little and turned his way. "Oh. No, I guess not." He managed a smile that looked more resigned than happy to Dugan. "Please," he said, getting to his feet, "tell Kirsten . . . what I said. I'll call her later tonight, or tomorrow morning. Right now, though, the cardinal—Oh, Mrs. Gage."

Dugan turned. The place seemed to be full of pretty women. The one at the bishop's door was brown-haired, in her mid-forties, and fresh from either Bermuda or some local tanning salon. "Excuse me, Bishop," she said, "but I understand His Eminence wants to see you right away." She was tall and athletic-looking.

"Yes," the bishop said, plucking his jacket from the chair, "I just spoke with him. I wonder, Mrs. Gage, would you be so kind as . . ." His voice trailed off as he slipped his arms into the jacket. Dugan stood, too, but by then the bishop was out the door and seemed already to have forgotten he was there.

Mrs. Gage was shaking her head as she watched the bishop

leave, then looked at Dugan and shrugged her shoulders. "Bishop Keegan is very . . . *busy*," she said, obviously searching for the right word. "I'm sorry. Would you come this way, please?" She led him toward the reception area.

On the way, Dugan heard a smattering of applause from somewhere far behind them. Mrs. Gage obviously heard it, too, because she paused and turned her head, and there was disappointment in her eyes—or maybe sadness, or worry. Strange. He decided not to wait, not that anyone asked him to. They'd have to talk to the bishop later that night. In fact, Kirsten might be happy he hadn't mentioned the fingerprint. She'd want time to think about it. More important, what about the woman who called? Who the hell was she? What did she want? How did she—

"Bye-bye." It was the receptionist. He looked up and nodded to her. Once again slipping her hair behind her ear with one hand, she gave a little finger wave with the other. "You take care now," she said, and flashed him a smile to die for.

By the elevators he punched the down button, then had a new idea. He turned and walked back to check the sign by the door of the chancery office. They closed at five, a little over an hour away. He'd try calling Kirsten again. Then he could get coffee at the restaurant down in the lobby and wait . . . and try to dream up some really dynamite introductory line.

SEVENTEEN

The bishop had an idea. It might prove to be a mistake, but he had to do *something*. Dugan had left while he was talking with the cardinal, and that woman on the phone . . . he'd have to talk to Kirsten about her tomorrow morning. Meanwhile, he didn't want to go home, and he'd already turned down an invitation to go out to dinner with some of the chancery office staff. He had no desire to celebrate the "good news" he'd just gotten.

Now more than ever, he had to take positive action, and he knew what it had to be. So he called Bud Burgeson. He swore Bud to secrecy and told him what the cardinal had said.

"I know you hate the whole idea," Bud said, and he was grateful for the compassion in Bud's voice, "and I sure wish I could invite you over and commiserate. But I have a parish school board meeting tonight and, as pastor of this place, I can't avoid it. They're voting on whether or not I should renew the principal's contract for next year. It's like: 'Which half of the faculty do you wanna have walk out?' It'll be past midnight before the fur stops flying."

"I know you're busy," the bishop said. "The reason I called . . . could I borrow your car for the evening? I just want to drive somewhere and think about things, and—"

"Absolutely," Bud said. "Right now I'm headed for a pre-meeting meeting—God, what a mess this is—but I'll give the keys to the kid who answers the door. Keep it overnight, and I'll pick it up tomorrow sometime."

He'd decided against trying to call Kirsten or Dugan. They might want to talk him out of what he was going to do. He left the office and caught a cab on Michigan Avenue.

During the ride to Bud's parish he tried to put aside his worries and concentrate on thanking God for his blessings. For friends like Bud Burgeson, for example. *Use my car? Absolutely.* No questions, no hesitation. Bud was the one person he'd told, eventually, about his arrest in Canada. He'd listened, not been judgmental at all, and never again brought the matter up.

Friends like that were what he needed, with his life rushing forward, seemingly out of his control for the last couple of years. Most people probably thought things were working out perfectly for him, but it was just the opposite.

He'd enjoyed all his assignments as a priest, but where he'd really found a home was at the seminary. Teaching was hard work, but he was good at it and the students had liked him. The faculty did, too, and every so often someone suggested he might be the next rector of the place. His answer was always the same: "Just let me keep teaching till they get tired of me. Then I'll go to some small parish. That's enough for me."

Actually, being rector of the seminary might have been okay, except that so many previous rectors had gone on to be bishops. And that was the last thing he'd wanted.

"They can talk all they want about 'shepherding the flock,' " he recalled telling Bud at a restaurant a few years ago. It was a Wednesday evening, and they'd been waiting for Bud's twin brother, Kenny, a bachelor who often joined their little group of priests for dinner and cards. "But being a bishop looks mostly like office work to me. Drudgery."

"That's the name of the game," Bud had said, draining the last of one martini and signaling the waitress for another. His friend only drank on his day off, but he made the most of it. "Just like being pastor of a parish."

"Only worse," he said. "The ones who stay in Chicago as auxiliary bishops get assigned a vicariate and face problems in fifty parishes instead of one. A few even have other jobs, too, like head of Catholic Cemeteries or something." He waited while the waitress set the new martini in front of Bud. "Then confirmation ceremonies on weekends, and fund-raising dinners, and a million meetings."

"Some guys love that stuff," Bud said. "Plus they might get their own diocese."

"Yeah, and manage hundreds of employees spread out all over in churches and schools, social service agencies, whatever. Plus public relations duties, financial decisions, and God only knows what—"

"Hey, slow down, will ya?" Bud laughed and lifted his glass. "They ever ask you . . . you just say no. It's not like they can't get anyone for the job." He sipped, sipped again, then smacked his lips. "Shoot, I'll name ya twenty priests who'd give up their left nut to be bishop. Especially since they're not supposed to be gettin' much use out of that particular item, anyway."

Bud's remarks had made sense at the time, but then suddenly everything changed. First they yanked him from the seminary to be head of Catholic Charities, and in no time he was an auxiliary bishop. It seemed like overnight. He hadn't been able to "just say no."

"You got yourself an angel," Bud insisted, "someone with ecclesiastical clout."

Maybe that was true. But if he'd have known, he'd have told his angel to go foster someone else's career. God's ways were strange, but why in the world—

"Hey you! Priest!" It was the cab driver. "I say we here. Okay?"

"Oh . . . yes. Sorry." He paid the driver and rang the bell at Bud's rectory.

A teenage boy answered the door and gave him the keys to Bud's car. "It's parked right out in front, Father," he said. "That dark blue Chevy, right beside the fire hydrant. I put it there. I mean . . . not the hydrant, but the car. Father Burgeson told me to get it out of his garage and park it in front and the only place was by the hydrant and I hope Father's not gonna be mad at me 'cause—"

"Thank you, son." He still had the change from the cab driver in his hand, so he gave it all to the boy. "Father Burgeson doesn't get mad easily. Besides, he won't even know. I'll take care of it."

He went out to the curb and pulled the parking ticket from the windshield of Bud's car. He could pay it by mail.

His mind was whirling so fast he'd forgotten he might be caught in the heart of rush hour. But it wasn't bad at all. He picked up the Dan Ryan Expressway just past the Loop, kept going south, and then almost missed the turnoff for the skyway. He kept hearing his mother's words: *Walter's a mean one, y'know, and he'll be comin' to visit.*

She was right. Walter was a very difficult, very angry man. He disliked Walter. The two of them spoke to each other only once or twice a year, usually on the phone, and always on his own initiative. It never had a satisfactory outcome, but he couldn't just give up. He didn't want his dislike of his brother to solidify into hatred.

He knew, from Kirsten's call that morning, that she'd talked to Larry Candle, who told her that all he'd done back then was call Walter. It was Walter who'd gotten the charges dropped in Canada. So Walter must know everything—even what he himself hadn't yet told Kirsten and Dugan. In the face of a lifetime of hostility, he had no earthly reason to think Walter would be sympathetic to him now. But the man was still his brother and, with God's help, anything was possible—even miracles. Maybe, even if they'd never be reconciled, the two of them could somehow resolve this particular problem if they met face-to-face. Like it or not, he had to try.

That's why he'd called the police department. Whoever answered in Walter's office was very nice when the bishop identified himself, and apparently thought Walter would be disappointed he wasn't there to get the call. "That's a shame, Bishop," the man had said, "but your brother's off till Monday. He left early—you just missed him—for his place in Michigan."

He paid the first toll at the Indiana toll road and went only a few more miles before he realized how hungry he was, so he took the next exit. But then, as he drove along trying to decide which of several restaurants to choose, the hunger in his belly transformed itself into waves of nausea. He kept right on going and returned to the tollway. There was no way he could have kept solid food down.

That's how scared he was of meeting his own big brother, face-to-face.

EIGHTEEN

K irsten's watch said 4:30 when she left I-94 at the Union
Pier exit and headed north, but she recalled it would be
5:30, local time. Within about ten minutes she could see
the lake again, but it took another half hour to locate Walter
Keegan's place in that labyrinth of curving blacktop and gravel
roads. She might never have found it at all without the hand-
drawn map that lay open on the seat beside her. She'd eventually have found someone able to provide directions, but Cuffs
got the map in just a few hours, along with the information
that Keegan was starting a three-day weekend when he got off
duty that day, and seldom left headquarters before 6:00 P.M.
Kirsten differed with Cuffs on just about every political and
social stance conceivable, and didn't much like depending on
him. The problem was, he was so darn . . . well, *dependable*.

She drove around for a while longer and saw one elderly
couple strolling the roadway, one woman jogger, and not another soul. There were cars parked at only a few of the cottages.
Half a mile away from Keegan's, she parked, slipped her loose-
fitting jeans off over her running shoes, grabbed her sun hat
and beach bag, and headed back down the road on foot.

The rain that had passed through Chicago that morning had
moved on toward the northeast. Here, the temperature hovered

just under seventy and it was the end of a perfect spring day, almost no breeze, a bright sun sinking quickly over the lake to the west. In her broad-brimmed straw hat, sunglasses, shorts, and a light blue, man-tailored cover-up that came nearly to her knees, she might have been on her way home from the beach after a start on redefining those tan lines Dugan loved to trace.

Not a soul in the world would have considered her plan anything but foolhardy. So she'd told nobody—and especially not Dugan. The warning delivered by the heavies who Clayton Warfield swore "acted like cops" had Walter Keegan's return address all over it. She knew damn well that he'd think the bishop sent Warfield, and that he expected the message to be passed along to anyone else who might think about following in Warfield's footprints. Now she had to let Keegan know he was up against a more formidable opponent.

She'd give him a sign he couldn't misinterpret. Rattle his cage? Hell, she'd step right inside the damn cage, show him she couldn't be intimidated.

And, no fool herself, she knew *she* needed convincing, too.

Keegan's place was maybe a quarter-mile inland from the lake, close to the road just where it curved sharply, but up on a little bluff. There was a packed stone driveway that went straight when the road curved, then rose steeply and leveled off maybe three feet higher than her head. She walked ten paces past, then turned around—as though casually, but making sure there were no cars or people in sight—and walked back and up the driveway.

According to Cuffs, Keegan used his cottage year-round, just about every time he had two days off in a row. But right now he was on duty and wouldn't get there until well after dark, and the odds were against anyone staying at his place when he wasn't there. Divorced and childless, he was known to be something of a womanizer, but a man with no close relationships.

The drive leveled off and widened into a parking area in

front of a one-car garage built into the lower level of the home, which had the look of a cottage built originally for summer use only. The walls of the lower level were built of large rounded stones held together with concrete or mortar. Above that, the wood siding of the living area was painted white. The windows—and there were lots of them—were multipaned casement windows, with drapes drawn tightly shut. There were floodlights high up at either end of the front of the house, but no other security system that she could spot.

To the left of the overhead garage door, and up a few concrete steps, was a door made of thick wooden planks, painted white. She went up and rang the doorbell. She waited, rang again, waited, rang a third time, and waited some more. When there was still no answer, she went back down the steps and around to the side of the garage. She pushed her way through a thick growth of unkempt shrubbery that ran along the side of the house, trying to ignore the prickly branches that scraped and scratched at her legs, to peer through a small, four-paned window set into the stonework. The glass was dirty and covered with old gray spiderwebs, inside and out, but she could see that there was no car in the garage. Stepping backward through the bushes, she went to the rear of the house.

The sun had barely gone down, and she'd rather have done this after it was actually dark. She considered just getting the layout now, then coming back later. But she wanted to be long gone by the time Keegan showed up and she didn't want to wait until after the weekend. The house wasn't really isolated— not more than fifty feet from its neighbors on either side—but its location on a bend in the road, and the surrounding trees and brush, made it unlikely anyone could see her. She also realized that after dark, if the security lights were operating, she'd be as visible as she was now—and far more obvious.

More compelling than all that logical stuff, though, was the fact that she was here right now. She didn't want to leave and then have to talk herself into coming back again, especially now that she felt how hard her pulse was pounding, and how cold her fingers were as she pulled thin latex gloves over them.

She slid the beach bag off her shoulder and crouched down before the lock on Walter Keegan's back door. She had to leave her surprise somewhere inside the house. It would be so much more effective that way.

NINETEEN

The restaurant's glass wall faced out onto the lobby, and from where Dugan sat, nursing his coffee and pretending to read the *Sun-Times,* he could see everyone who came down on the elevators and left the building by the main exit. By 5:15 there'd been lots of people who seemed headed for home, but the one he was waiting for hadn't appeared yet. In fact, to his surprise, the first person he'd recognized going out was the bishop, and that wasn't long after he himself had left. He thought of catching up with him and resuming their conversation, but he'd made up his mind to speak to that woman, and that's what he was going to do—bad idea or not.

At ten minutes to six there she was, striding briskly along, as though she had somewhere to be and no time to lose. He chased after her. "Excuse me," he called, and several heads turned, but not hers. He went through the revolving door and finally pulled even with her out on the sidewalk. "Excuse me," he repeated.

She barely glanced at him and kept on walking, headed east on Huron toward the lake.

Maybe he'd misjudged her, but he wasn't about to give up. "Dammit all, Mrs. Gage, the bishop needs help."

Not quite the dynamite opening line he'd been searching

for, but it stopped her in her tracks. She turned and stared at him. "I'm sorry," she said, "but my mind was somewhere else. I didn't recognize you right away."

"May I walk with you, and talk a bit?"

"Well, I suppose so, but only because . . ." She started walking again at the same rapid pace, gracefully, like a natural athlete. He'd have described her as either attractive or curvaceous, depending on who was listening. "The bishop asked about you," she said, "after he'd spoken with the cardinal. He was disappointed to learn you were gone."

"Well, I—"

"You're the man who called earlier today, and then hung up." She seemed certain, so he didn't respond. "You should have said your name," she went on. "The bishop mentioned yesterday you were helping him with something important and he wanted to be interrupted for any call from you . . . or from your partner."

"Partner?"

"Yes. A woman's name. Kirsten."

"Oh, yes. We're not really partners, though. She's my . . . she lists me as her employee."

"I see," Mrs. Gage said, although Dugan wasn't at all sure that she did. They'd reached the end of Huron Street, and she headed north along the west side of Lake Shore Drive, continuing her long strides. "So I know that Bishop Keegan trusts the two of you."

"Really? And are there people, then, that he doesn't trust?"

"He . . . what I mean is he's been, oh, distracted lately. Worried, or . . . concerned."

"Frightened?"

"I suppose that's the right word, although I didn't like to say it." She shook her head. "I don't know whether others have noticed it, but I have."

"I have the feeling you're much more observant than most people." Her face flushed a bit under the tan. Maybe the flattery embarrassed her, or maybe there was some guilt about how closely she *did* observe things. "Like," he added with a smile, "you must have noticed I can hardly keep up with you and talk at the same time."

She slowed down. "I'm not really in a hurry," she said. "Fast walking's just one way I exercise. It's gotten to be a habit."

"So . . . what do you think the bishop is afraid of?" Dugan asked.

"I'm not certain, but—" She shook her head. "I wonder if I should even be talking to you."

"I thought we'd crossed that bridge already. You know the bishop trusts Kirsten and me, you know he's afraid of something, and you know we're trying to help him. So, what's the problem with talking to me?"

"Well . . ."

"That's right," he said. "No problem at all."

They came to Chicago Avenue and crossed the street. Lake Shore Park, a playground the size of a city block, stretched out to their left. "Let's go sit down," Dugan said.

She followed him into the park, past a field where young men were playing sixteen-inch softball, to a bench down the left field line. The setting sun had dropped below the high-rises to the west of the park, striping the grass with lengthening shadows. A cool, humid breeze off the lake carried the chatter of the ballplayers and the mixed odors of water and grass and dust—and even a faint, oily smell from the damp cinders of the running track that went around the perimeter of the playground.

"Isn't it lovely?" Mrs. Gage said. "Sometimes I forget how much I enjoy living in Chicago."

Dugan had often felt that way himself, and was about to say so, but something about her tone made him wonder whether she really meant what she said, or was just trying to change the subject. "You don't have to answer anything you don't want to," he said, "but you may know something that will help. You do *want* to help, don't you?" Getting a commitment.

"Of course, but—"

"Good." He paused. He'd made up his mind he'd be more than Kirsten's errand boy, but he had no clear idea what to ask, now that he had his witness. A secretary might know a lot, or almost nothing, about her boss's affairs. "So . . . uh . . . how long have you known the bishop?"

"I started working with him maybe six months ago."

"And has he been afraid that whole time?"

She seemed surprised by this question. "Really, I should think he'd be the best one—"

"We've talked to the bishop already, and will again. Now, though, I'm asking for *your* perception. A secretary might see things that others don't."

She stared at him, apparently mystified. "You're mistaken, I—"

"Please. It's important." Or he hoped it was, since it was the question that had popped into his mind. "Try to remember when you first noticed he was afraid of something."

"Okay, I'll try." She smiled, as though she'd decided to humor him. "But it's difficult to say, because I've never thought he was at ease in the job. Not that he confides in me, you understand, but sometimes, especially when he's tired, he does blurt things out. How he's feeling, and—" She stopped. "Don't misunderstand. I don't mean that there's anything personal or . . . do you know what I'm trying to say?"

"I think . . ." Dugan began, then decided to shut up and let her work her way through it.

"Well," she finally said, "what I mean is that I like the bishop. He's a kind, gentle man. But he wishes he were still teaching. Being a bishop, and especially running a big operation like Catholic Charities—which no bishop should have to do in the first place, with all his other responsibilities—is simply not for him." She was on a roll now, and Dugan let her go. "What I mean is, he can do the work but he doesn't enjoy it.

There's what he calls the endless paper pushing, the personnel problems, and then having to be nice to all those big-money contributors, no matter how egotistical and arrogant some of them are." There was a touch of venom in her voice with that last phrase. She paused and took a long, deep breath. "There. The bishop never complains explicitly, but that's the fact of it. I can tell."

Dugan let a few seconds pass, then asked, "But when did you first notice that he was afraid?"

"What? Oh, I guess I didn't answer your question." She frowned. "What I'm getting at is that all along I could tell he was dissatisfied. But recently he's been acting differently. Nervous, or jumpy. I thought it was just stress. But gradually I've come to believe he's frightened of something, or of . . ." Her voice trailed off.

"Or of some *person?*"

"Well . . ."

"Who?"

"I . . ." She turned her head and stared at the softball players as though the game were suddenly interesting. "I should think he'd be the best one to answer that question."

"Mrs. Gage, have you forgotten that bridge we've crossed several times already?" He paused. "I need to find out now what *you've* noticed." He was pressing her pretty hard, but all she could do was brush him off—and by now anyone who really didn't want to talk to him would have done just that. She hadn't.

"Well," she said, "to begin with, there's his brother, that . . . policeman. I think Bishop Keegan is afraid of his own brother. I can see it in his eyes."

"Uh-huh. And who else?"

"Who else?" she repeated, looking surprised.

"Yes. You said, 'to begin with, there's his brother.' So, who else?"

"Well, I mean . . . that was just a manner of speaking. I don't know that there *is* anyone else." She looked around her, then stood up. "That breeze is really getting quite cold, isn't it? And maybe I've been talking too much. I should be going."

Dugan stood up, too. It was getting dark and the ball game was breaking up. "Thank you, Mrs. Gage," he said, "and feel free to repeat our whole conversation to the bishop if you like. It'll be fine with him, I'm sure." He couldn't tell whether this reassured her or not, but the conversation was definitely over. "Now," he said, "can I pay for a cab to take you home?"

"Oh, no. I live just over there." She waved vaguely toward the west.

"But I've kept you late," Dugan said. "Are you sure it isn't far?"

"It's not far at all." She was walking already and he stayed with her. "I usually walk a roundabout way, just for the exercise. We have a condominium, in Water Tower Place."

"You do?" He was amazed. Those condos were among the priciest in town.

She turned, not breaking stride. "I know what you're thinking. You're surprised to find me at work there at the chancery office. But we have no children and my husband works long hours and travels a great deal. I need to do something with my life besides shop and sip cocktails all afternoon."

"Good for you," he said. It sounded as though she'd given this explanation before, frequently. "I suppose the Church is as good—"

"Actually, working for the Church is very fulfilling." She stopped walking. "Even a church so foolish it keeps Peter Keegan in the wrong job for him." She turned and walked away.

Dugan watched her go. She carried herself with the air of a model, or an actress, and—He suddenly realized he'd forgotten to ask her about the applause at the chancery office. Too late now, but he *had* learned one interesting thing to report to Kirsten. Mrs. Gage had an idea about someone the bishop might be afraid of, besides his brother—and she didn't want to talk about it. He wondered if the person was one of those "big-money contributors" she said the bishop had to be nice to, "no matter how egotistical and arrogant some of them are."

Or was that just her own personal hang-up?

TWENTY

It was only 5:45 when Charles Banning got home from his office, and he went straight to the kitchen. He poured himself half a glass of ginger ale, dropped in one ice cube, then went into the library and topped off the glass with Old Grand-Dad.

Supper would have to wait, dammit. He'd been putting on weight, anyway. For a boxer who'd have made the goddamn Olympic team twenty years ago if the coaches hadn't fucked him over, he'd let himself slide pretty far. He'd start working out again, though, as soon as he got this latest goddamn deal done.

He sat at the little desk by the window and looked at his glass. Half-empty already. Christ, he needed something better than alcohol.

The assholes had called him again that morning . . . at his office. He paid plenty to be certain his lines were kept clean, but it still pissed him off that they ignored his orders. He should have hired someone to take a closer look at them right at the start. But Christ, if he'd been in a position to do everything perfectly he wouldn't have been interested in their proposal in the first place. Now it was too late.

He'd sunk far too much into this project. To begin with,

he'd underestimated the costs—their fault, not his—then had to start spending money he didn't have. Leveraging was the name of the game in real estate, of course, and that was his bread and butter. The trouble was he'd already been spread way too thin by then, had been pledging one after another of his properties against loans, having to fudge on the debt some of them were already carrying. If this deal failed there'd be a domino effect, one fucking property lost after another, until he was wiped out. He'd be broke, humiliated—and goddamned lucky to stay out of jail.

He'd spent his whole life bootstrapping himself from nothing to where he was. Now each day brought him closer to real trouble with his lenders and the phonied-up financial statements he'd given. He'd hit a brick wall on the deal, been flexible enough to hire help, and then started facing threats and demands from the asshole for a bigger cut almost immediately. Last night was the final goddamn straw, and he'd put in a call to Miami. He knew the drill; the price was high—and you paid, or else—but he'd remove every obstacle and get this fucking deal done, whatever it took.

"Yes, I will," saying the words out loud, making himself believe, "whatever it takes."

He finished his drink, then stood up and stared out the window. Thursday night. He didn't want to go back out, but he would. There was something that had to be done . . . tonight; a task he had to take care of himself. He breathed deeply, slowly. From his apartment he could see the cars driving along Lake Shore Drive and, past that, Lake Michigan. Watching the unending movement of the water always calmed him, gave him confidence.

He'd have to be careful. He'd change into some old clothes, maybe grab a bite at Burger King or somewhere to kill some time, make sure no one saw him, and then get on with it.

Christ, he'd have to be fucking goddamn careful.

TWENTY-ONE

Kirsten's technique was improving, but it still took her fifteen minutes to work her way through the lock on Walter Keegan's back door. Once inside, and even though this wasn't a search mission, common sense demanded another fifteen minutes for a look around. Maybe she'd find something tying this guy for sure to the stalking of his brother or—if not—then maybe a bag of cocaine, or a cache of guns stolen from police evidence storage, or some eight-by-ten glossies of Acting Chief Keegan getting it on with . . .

But no such luck.

There was a low-ceilinged upper floor with three small bedrooms and a tiny bathroom, all with bare-mattressed beds and empty dressers. The main floor—with a small kitchen, another bathroom, a bedroom, and a living-dining area—looked well-lived-in, but clean and fairly neat. The only clutter was reading material: newspapers, lots of hunting and gun magazines, a couple of old Tom Clancy paperbacks, and one recent issue of *Playboy*. There was the sort of casual clothing, male only, you'd expect at a weekend place. Fresh towels and bedding were stacked in a linen closet, and a good supply of cleaning materials and equipment was stored near the back door. There were windows everywhere, and the drapes and curtains, none of them new, looked recently cleaned. All that, plus the absence of old grease on the kitchen walls and countertops, convinced Kirsten that there must be a woman who came in to clean. Maybe she did some shopping, too, because the refrigerator was nicely stocked, although with no fresh foods.

Her fifteen minutes were up.

She went down a short stairway from the living area to a small, square landing that served as an entrance hall at the front door. From there, another half flight of stairs led to a dark basement. She flipped the wall switch beside her and went down into a single large room, bright now with fluorescent lights. The floor was carpeted, and the rough stone walls were painted white, as was the wood-raftered ceiling. There were no windows, but a room air conditioner sat high up in the wall that faced the front of the house, and an exhaust fan in the back wall. There were a full set of free weights, a bench, and a treadmill, nothing extravagant. No high-tech bells and whistles, no whirlpool, no sauna or steam room. Just a place for serious workouts.

And fixed to the wall near the exhaust fan was a serious-looking gray metal box, with two vertical rows of round electrical fuses inside, each fuse carefully labeled as to which part of the house it served. Lined up along the bottom of the box were four spare fuses. But there was no spare in sight for the main fuse—a three-inch-long cylinder about a half inch in diameter—that controlled the whole box. She hadn't thought of bringing a fuse puller, but she managed to extract the main fuse, plunging the basement into darkness.

She took the fuse with her back upstairs and into the kitchen, where she'd left her beach bag on the counter by the sink. From the bag she took the decorative, white-feathered bird she'd bought at the Japanese gift store. There'd been several styles, and she'd chosen the one that looked like a dove at rest, with wings folded. Probably only a fourth the size of Bishop Keegan's pigeon, of course, but it certainly looked like a real bird, and Walter would get the idea—assuming it was really he who was the bishop's nemesis. The bird's feet were flexible wire, so it could be attached to something. "Makes nice Clistmas awnoment," the clerk had said.

But Kirsten had a better idea.

With little time to shop, she'd settled for yellow knitting yarn, which she now wrapped around the bird, as though pinning its wings to its body, then knotted the yarn and cut it, leaving a strand about a foot long. Next, she bent the wire feet around the cylindrical fuse, grasping it like a branch. Finally, on a sudden burst of inspiration, she added a few thick smears of ketchup from the refrigerator.

Perfect. A small dead bird, bloodied and bound up with yellow twine.

Outside, twilight was fading fast, but even at high noon Keegan's windowless basement would have been very dark. She found a flashlight in one of the drawers, grabbed a pair of scissors from another, then hurried back downstairs to the fuse box. It was a deep, old-fashioned box, with plenty of room to lay the bird beside the spare fuses. But instead, wanting a bit more drama, she hung the strand of yellow yarn over the thin metal door and closed the bird inside the box with the yarn hanging outside, caught by the tightly fitting door.

Then a test run. She pulled opened the fuse box again, and the tied-up bird dropped to the floor with a soft, satisfying *plop*.

She reset her little surprise, but this time she cut off the yarn hanging outside the door so close that it wouldn't be seen if you weren't looking for it. Hopefully, Walter Keegan would be next to open that fuse box. But whoever it was would have to be using a flashlight, just as she was, and the effect was bound to be just as eerie.

She crouched down with the light to wipe the traces of ketchup from the floor . . . and then something suddenly went wrong. For no reason that she could explain, she was unexpectedly swept up in an overwhelming urge to run, to get out of there. Of course she'd been a little edgy ever since she entered the house. But that sort of tension was helpful, and she'd been very much in control. Until now. Even as she rose to a standing position she felt a second wave wash over her. Fear. Cold, bone-deep fear.

She'd heard nothing, seen nothing. Was it intuition, or what? Imagination? Forcing herself to act calmly, deliberately, she went upstairs. Beyond the kitchen windows it was quite dark now. She put the scissors and the flashlight back in their drawers, picked up her sun hat and beach bag, and pulled the back door open.

There was a man standing there in the shadows, not three feet from the door, facing her. A slim, sharp-faced man, with jet-black hair and a dark complexion. The side of his left forefinger was pressed to his lips, in a quieting gesture. In his right hand was a semiautomatic pistol, with a long silencer fixed to the barrel.

TWENTY-TWO

With Mrs. Gage gone Dugan sat alone on the park bench down the left field line, past third base, and watched the players walk by, lugging bats and equipment bags. Most had baseball shoes tied together by the laces and hanging over their shoulders. Men in their twenties, boisterous and brimful of testosterone, joking and complaining about the "babes" and the "chicks," arguing about which bar to head for. They seemed so . . . well . . . *carefree.*

Meanwhile, it was only 6:30 and he should get back to the office. Evenings were when he could really get the paperwork done on his cases. And weekends, too. Otherwise, he was on the phone all day, negotiating with insurance adjusters, settling cases, making a living. Actually, quite a good living. Except, no time to play softball anymore. Or basketball. Or beach volleyball. Or . . .

Ah, well. He'd catch a cab to the office. In a few minutes.

The ballplayers were gone now, except for a couple of stragglers still hanging around over by the backstop, one of them smoking a cigarette and talking on a cell phone. They seemed a little older than the others. Maybe they had families or something and had to get home. Or maybe they'd been just spectators, since they didn't have gym bags or extra shoes dangling over their shoulders. The one without the phone, though, did have a softball bat in one hand, and was absentmindedly slapping the fat end of the bat into the palm of his other hand.

He noticed, suddenly, that the man with the bat was looking right at him. Dugan automatically turned away, like civilized people do when they catch each other staring at each other. He stood up and stretched and made a show of looking off into the outfield. But when he looked back the man was still gazing at him, and still slapping the bat into his palm.

He found being stared at by a man wielding a baseball bat a little unnerving. Even if the man was smiling, like this one was. Or sort of smiling, anyway, as far as Dugan could tell. It was getting pretty dark now, and hard to see, even though the lights on the tall poles around the perimeter of the park were going on. And where had the man with the cell phone disappeared to?

Lake Shore Park took up most of an entire city block, and there was a five-foot, wrought-iron fence around the whole thing, with open gateways every fifty yards or so. The nearest opening was about equal with third base, closer to Dugan than to the man with the bat. So Dugan started that way, in a hurry.

Unfortunately, that's exactly where the man with the phone had gone. Dugan turned and then, not quite sure how it was happening, managed to let himself be hemmed in, herded like one sheep by two dogs until he was backing up toward the wrought-iron fence, ten feet east of the open gate.

Both men looked a bit thick around the waist, but tough and hard-bodied. With their well-worn jackets and work pants, they might be dock workers or pipe fitters. Except they weren't ordinary laborers. Their eyes gave them away. Tired, hostile, cynical eyes that had seen way too much hurt—and knew they hadn't seen the end of it. It was their eyes that pressed his back against the fence, while the men themselves stopped five feet away.

"You guys have done this before," he said.

The man with the cell phone put it in his pocket. "Let's see some identification," he said, and Dugan had no doubt that the card and the star in the folder the man flipped open and closed were authentic. Chicago Police Department.

"I'm sorry," Dugan said, "but I didn't catch your name, or your star number."

"Let's see some identification," the man repeated.

Dugan showed them his attorney's photo ID that would let him skip the metal detector line in the courthouse. Not that he ever went to court anymore. He earned his money on the phone.

"This is expired," the cop said.

Dugan took the card back and looked at it. "So it is. But it's still me." He held it up beside his face and tried to match the grin on the photo.

"You got something more up-to-date, Counselor?" That was the one with the bat.

Wondering why policemen all seemed so fond of the word *counselor*, he pulled a thin card from his wallet. "Here's my latest attorney registration card."

"Fine," the man said.

"And here," Dugan said, handing them each three white cards. "Take a few of my business cards. You come across someone needs a good personal injury lawyer, give 'em my card. That's my specialty. That and civil rights-type cases. You know, illegal stop and seizure, false arrest, police brutality, that sort of—"

"Counselor, shut up." The cop with the bat was clearly tired of Dugan, and his partner was already walking away. "We got word a flasher's been exposing himself in the park here. Waits for a female jogger and shakes his wanger at her. We'd be remiss if we didn't check you out, sitting on the bench here."

Dugan looked around. "That's funny," he said. "I don't see a single jogger in the whole park."

" 'Course not. Perverts like that drive decent people away."

He smiled. "Thank you for your cooperation, Counselor."

The cop turned and tossed the bat high in the air and toward the infield. It hit the ground, flipped end over end a few times, then banged into the backstop behind home plate. Meanwhile, the other cop hurried to catch up with his partner, who'd almost reached the fieldhouse at the east end of the park, and who already had his cell phone up to his ear.

TWENTY-THREE

The slick-haired gunman reeked of some sort of musk-scented cologne—expensive smelling, but far too much of it. Maybe that explained it. Maybe she'd gotten a whiff of that odor through the exhaust fan grate near the fuse box, but not enough to register consciously. Even as the man moved her backward into the kitchen, the idea that her panic attack in the basement wasn't entirely unfounded made her feel better. On the other hand, if she'd been awake, been paying attention to what her senses were telling her . . .

The man stepped in and closed the kitchen door behind him. He wore a light-weight leather sport coat, a perfect shade of tan for his complexion, and moved gracefully, without a sound. "Who else is inside?" His whisper was mostly a hiss, but there was an accent, too. Hispanic.

"No one." She spoke louder than necessary, deliberately shifting her eyes from side to side. "There's no—"

"Silence," he whispered. He raised the gun toward her face. "You are lying."

"No," she said, but was happy to know that he thought so. She was still frightened, but this was a rational fear, not blind panic. "Jeez, I'm just here to . . . y'know . . . to clean the house." She set her beach bag casually on the counter beside her, and spread her arms. "See?" she said, flexing her fingers. "I still got my cleaning gloves on. An' I can tell ya . . . ain't nothin' here worth steal—"

"Shut up. There is no car, so he's not here." He spoke softly now, but no longer whispering. "You are his woman."

"Jeez, don't I *wish*." She started peeling off a glove, then thought better of it. "He's a big-time cop, you know? But hey, you got one thing right. Ain't nobody here." She tried again to look like she was lying.

He stared at her for a moment, then said, "You are trying to mislead me. I think there is no one," the man said. Then he gestured with the gun toward the steps that led down first to the landing by the front door, and from there on down to the basement. "But we will look."

"We?" She didn't want to go far from the kitchen, or from her beach bag, or from the Colt .380 automatic inside the bag. "Both of us?"

"Of course. That way, if there is a problem, you will die first. But," he added, still speaking very softly, "if you are truthful and good, you will live." He grinned.

"Oh, I'll be good," she promised, knowing it was he doing the lying now. She turned and walked to the stairway, very slowly, and started down. She had to stretch this out, think of something. At the landing by the front door, she stopped. "Um . . . it's pretty dark already right here and it'll be *really* dark down there, and—"

"Fool, turn on the light."

"Oh. Okay, but . . ." She flipped the switch and nothing happened.

"What . . . what is wrong?" For the first time, the hit man—and that's what he was, no doubt about it—sounded uncertain. A hopeful sign. Except he was on the landing now, right beside her, pressing the end of the silencer into her ribs, flipping the switch up and down with his other hand.

"The wiring's bad in this house," she said. Both her body

and her voice were trembling, but she forced herself to keep thinking. To have any chance at all, she had to be above him on the stairs. "It's old," she added.

"The wiring?"

"Oh yeah. Fuses blow all the time. But there's a flashlight in the kitchen." She brushed past him and started up the steps. "I'll go get—"

"Stop."

She stopped and turned around. She was three steps above the landing now, above where he stood with his gun raised and pointed straight toward her face. "We will go together," he said, "and more slow—"

They both heard the sound, and it froze them both for an instant. Then the sound again. A slight scraping noise, from the front door. A key in the lock? The man turned his head to the sound.

Now!

She brought her right leg up, and snapped it from the knee, toes arched back toward her as she'd been taught. The tip of her running shoe smashed into the butt of his gun, or maybe the bone of his wrist. Shock waves of pain roared up her leg, but she followed through and drove his gun hand upward as he fell back, thrown off-balance.

She definitely heard his gun go off, the report muffled by the silencer, might even have heard the bullet bury itself in the ceiling above her. But at the same time the heavy front door burst inward and smacked with a thud into the back of the gunman. Chaos then. Shouts, curses, noises like that of a body—or two bodies—slamming into walls or floors, as though someone might have tumbled down the half-flight of stairs to the basement.

But by then she was already up in the kitchen, feeling around in the dark on the countertop for her beach bag. She found it and was headed for the door when the shooting and the screaming started from the front of the house. At least one

106

muffled shot first, then one from a gun with no silencer. Then the screams. Not words, just unintelligible, animal sounds. Three more shots, rapid-fire. She pulled the door closed behind her. No more screaming. She stumbled across the backyard and into the trees.

She ran, losing track of which way she was going in the dark. A dog yapped, high-pitched and far away. Very few homes had lights on, and she veered away from them, staying in the wooded areas or cutting through dark backyards. The stabbing pain in her right foot—and her big toe especially—tortured her with every stride, and she lost her balance and fell at least twice, scraping her knees and bare legs. But she kept getting up and moving on. Running, but not as fast as she wanted to run, because she couldn't see, and she didn't want to keep falling, and her foot hurt so terribly.

She stopped finally, to catch her breath and get her bearings. She was in another backyard. This house, like most of the others, was dark and quiet, and she wanted to sink to the ground in the shelter of its walls. She'd just lie there until the pain in her foot went away and everything got better.

She made herself keep going, though, around to the front of the house. She was calmer now, not shaking. But when she came to the street she couldn't keep herself from running again—even though she didn't know which way she was going.

TWENTY-FOUR

Dugan had to walk all the way to Michigan Avenue before he could find an empty cab, and when he finally got to his office Larry Candle was the only person there.

His unspoken arrangement with his other lawyers, Fred Schustein and Peter Rienzo, was that they work their asses off seven or eight hours a day on the firm's workers compensation cases, and then go home. They made a decent buck and never worked weekends or evenings, never took files home. Fred and Peter were as old now as his dad had been when he dropped dead, and Dugan would turn away cases—unheard of in the legal profession—before he'd overwork them. Those two were like uncles to him.

Larry Candle, though, was a different story. Whether hiring him was a moment of weakness or a stroke of genius, the fact was that Larry worked pretty damn hard. That's why Dugan wasn't surprised to find him in the office.

"Hey," Larry said, looking up from his desk and breaking into a wide grin, "how ya doin', Doogie pal?" He'd given up telling Larry he hated being called that, because Larry always forgot.

"Fine, Larry. How's everything with you?"

"Couldn't be better. I made us a buncha money today. Been following your rule number one."

"That's great," Dugan said, "but right now I—"

"Okay. Rule one: settle every case you can without filing suit, but never sell a client short. And that's what I been doing. For instance, today I got fifty thousand on the Ben Hadjeem case."

Ben Hadjeem was an immigrant cab driver who'd fallen in a supermarket when he slipped on a piece of lettuce the size of an amoeba, and Dugan didn't even want to ask Larry how he got that much money to settle the case. "What about rule two, Larry?" he said.

"Negotiate like hell, but never actually lie to your opponent? That one?"

"Right. Rule two."

"Yeah. Well, I didn't actually *lie* about Hadjeem's employment and lost earnings. What I *told* 'em was—"

"Fine."

"Besides, I sent 'em all the records. If they don't wanna take time to go through things carefully, that's not—"

"Fine."

Rule three of Dugan's rules was never to take a case that had a stench of phoniness about it. That could land you in jail. Ben Hadjeem really had fallen down, and really did suffer a broken hip. His case was legitimate, all right, just pretty weak.

"Plus," Larry said, "I signed up three new clients. They just keep coming in."

"That's because we do a good job."

"Right," Larry said. "That must be it." If Larry had discovered that police officers were the source of some of the firm's new clients, he hadn't said anything about it. Not yet. "But . . . um . . . could we have a little chat?" Larry asked.

Uh-oh.

"Why don't we do it over a brew?" Dugan suggested, anxious for a little time to think.

They walked together to the tiny kitchen in the law firm's suite. Prior to Larry's arrival, Mollie had bought the beer for the office. It was always Budweiser or Old Style, whichever was cheaper at the time, and that had been fine with Dugan. But Larry took that job over in a hurry, and his tastes were more varied. More expensive, too, as Mollie pointed out.

Just now the refrigerator was loaded with Negra Modelo, and they each took a bottle and settled down in the conference room. Dugan was ready to defend his belief that paying police officers for cases was absolutely moral, just, honest, and humane. But since it was against the ethical code, and could drag Larry into trouble along with him, he was willing to cease the practice immediately. End of discussion.

He took a swig of the beer and nodded to Larry across the conference table. "So," he said, "chat away. I'm ready."

Larry swiveled his round head this way and that, and finally just stared down at the bottle on the table in front of him. "Good beer, huh?"

"Uh-huh."

Larry picked up the bottle of Negra Modelo. "Don't ya wonder," he said, "why the first word here ends in 'a' and the second word ends in 'o'? I mean, I took Spanish in high school, and—"

"No, I don't wonder about that. What I wonder is what you want to talk about."

"Yeah. Well, I don't wanna tell ya how to run your business, okay?"

"Okay."

"But it's just . . . well, the way you handle fees, y'know?"

"Fees?" Dugan was relieved. "Nothing unusual. I get one third of any settlement we get for a client. Any case we can't settle is referred out to litigation counsel to file suit. The fee to the client is still one third, but it's split between me and the other firm."

"I know all that. But some lawyers, y'know, charge *forty*

percent if suit has to be filed," Larry said, "so there's more to split."

"Right, but I've been doing just fine for years with a third."

"Anyway," Larry said, "the fee percentage wasn't the main thing I had in mind. It's more how you handle things when the cases settle. That is, I mean—"

"You mean I give away too much money."

"I wonder if you know how much it amounts to, that's all. Half the time you don't take your whole cut, for chrissake."

"First, you're exaggerating. Second, what's the difference to you? You get a straight salary, and as long as I make enough to pay you, what do you care?"

"I know, but some day we might be partners and—"

"Whoa! I never said anything about any damn partnership."

"Well, I . . ." Larry was blushing, a phenomenon Dugan hadn't thought could occur. "I was thinking, maybe, you know, way off in the future."

"Right, and way off in some distant galaxy." Dugan wanted that point clear. "No partners for me. And if once in a while I can get a client—like Lily Conway, for example—if I can get her what she wants out of a case by settling it and taking less for my fee, it saves me time and headaches. Good business."

"Yeah, but I settled Carlos Cruz and Mollie told me not to take out any fee at all. You call that good business?"

"Well, that's different. Carlos Cruz has three kids. He's out of work. And his wife's not well." Dugan stared down at the table. "I mean, Kirsten and I have pretty much everything we want and there's people out there who don't even have—" He caught himself and looked up at Larry. "What the hell am I defending myself to *you* for, goddamnit?"

Larry stood up. He kept his head down but Dugan had seen the grin on his face. "Jeez, I don't know, Doogie pal. I was just asking a simple question."

"Good-bye, Larry. Get outta here, will ya?"

Larry grabbed both empty bottles. He was still hiding that damn grin as he backed out of the conference room.

TWENTY-FIVE

The rented Ford Taurus was right where she'd left it, and Kirsten was so happy to see it she nearly yelled out loud. Her breath was coming in deep gasps now. How long had she been looking for the car? It seemed like an hour, but that was an illusion. Ten minutes, maybe . . . or twenty? Surely no longer than that. It must be nerves, more than simply exertion, that had her winded. She'd run aimlessly at first, and even on the road, with its dim, widely spaced streetlights, it hadn't been clear which way she was going. Finally, when she'd heard the soft lapping of Lake Michigan's waves against the beach, she'd regained her sense of direction and been able to find her way.

Her breath gradually slowed and, with one hand on the hood of the car, she stood on her left foot and gently rotated her right ankle and wiggled her toes. It hurt like crazy, but everything seemed to work fairly well. She dug the car keys out of the pocket of her shorts and went back and opened the trunk. Her jeans were in there. She'd put them back on over the shorts and stow the beach bag and the sun hat in—

The sun hat?

Where was it? Not on her head, not anymore. Had she taken it off when the gunman backed her into the kitchen? It was a floppy, broad-brimmed hat. Surely she wasn't wearing it when the man started her down the stairs. Was she? Or had she grabbed it from the kitchen counter along with the beach bag before she ran out the back door?

As hard as she tried, she couldn't remember what had happened to the hat. But she got her jeans on, with the cover-up tucked in like a shirt, and a navy blue sweatshirt over that. She stowed the beach bag with the gun in the trunk, got behind the wheel, and started the engine. It wouldn't do to be sitting alone in a car in the vicinity of Keegan's place when the police cars started arriving.

And where *were* the cops, anyway? By now there should have been sirens screaming and tires squealing. Someone must have heard the shots, and even if the few neighbors in the area had convinced themselves it was nothing, just noises in the distance, surely Keegan himself would have called it in. *Shots fired . . . police officer in trouble.* Calls like that ought to be bringing out the cavalry in force.

Then it dawned on her. Maybe Walter Keegan couldn't get to the phone. Maybe the struggle hadn't come out the way she assumed. A number of outcomes could have led to the police not being called. Maybe the hit man was dead and Keegan was injured and unable to call for help. Or they could both be wounded—or both dead. She cut the ignition and wrestled with whether she could just drive away, knowing that a man— possibly two men—might be lying in Keegan's cottage, bleeding to death. She had to call 911. Then suddenly another possibility arose, an idea that sent a cold shudder through her body. Maybe Walter Keegan was dead, and the sharp-faced hit man was alive and well. If so, he was coming after her—and he'd keep on coming.

She pulled the keys from the ignition, got out of the car, and stood there a minute, trying to think. The light from a tiny sliver of moon came and went with the passing of clouds. She noticed she still had the latex gloves on, and stripped them off, switching the keys from one hand to the other while she did. Then, as she stuffed the gloves into her hip pocket, something occurred to her. Four keys. Cuffs had left her four keys.

She tested them all. There were two ignition keys—which also fit the doors—and two trunk keys. She split the four into two sets, hid one set at the base of a tree beside the road, slid the ignition key from the other set into the ignition, and locked that set inside the car. Then, with the Colt .380 out of the trunk again and tucked into her waistband at her back, hidden by the sweatshirt, she headed toward Keegan's on foot. She wanted to know what had happened before she called 911. And even more than that, she wanted her sun hat. For all she knew, DNA testing, or some other sophisticated procedure, might be able to link it to her.

Streetlights were few and far between and there wasn't one close enough to illumine the cottage. Nor was there even a hint of a light on inside. Up on that little bluff among the trees, it looked as still and empty as most of the other homes in the area—waiting for the summer season.

But about thirty yards farther down the road, parked on the shoulder, was a car. She stared. There were two cars, in fact, one behind the other, both dark-colored sedans. One must be the hit man's, and the other was probably Keegan's, which explained why she hadn't heard either of them drive up. Keegan must have seen the first car and, if he'd noticed that none of the security lights were on at his place, might have been suspicious enough to approach the cottage on foot. He could have been standing by the front door, listening to the gunman and her inside on the landing. Timidity wasn't what had made Keegan notorious, and bursting through the door with gun in hand would have been just his style.

She stood on the road and looked up at the house for several long minutes. The drapes were still drawn and she'd swear no one was peeking through any of them. Favoring her sore foot, she started up the steep, dark driveway, pulling the latex gloves back on as she went. It was only after she got near the top that she could see the front entrance. The door was closed. Either it had been slammed shut during the struggle, or whoever survived had closed it. She went up the steps and tried it, very gently. It was locked. She turned away, stopped, then turned back and knocked loudly on the door. When there was no response, she made her way around the side of the house, past the garage window, to the back. The kitchen door, she knew, would also be locked.

Except it wasn't.

That is, even though the knob didn't turn, the last one to close the door—possibly she herself—hadn't shut it tightly enough and the spring latch hadn't caught. When she pushed, the door moved silently open. She waited, crouching low and off to one side, then leaned and peered in the doorway. The kitchen was empty. A little moonlight seeped in through the drawn curtains on the window over the sink, enough to see that the room was just as she'd left it. Even the sun hat was there on the counter, where she remembered now that she'd put it.

She stepped inside and closed the door behind her. Taking the floppy hat with her left hand, she used it to cover the Colt pistol she now held in her right hand. Then she just stood there, motionless, trying not even to breathe. Listening, hearing nothing. She moved cautiously across the kitchen and went through the doorway. The only sound was the slight creak of one floorboard as she stepped into the living area.

It was darker here than in the kitchen, with not as much moonlight making it through the heavier drapes, and she could scarcely make out even the shapes of the furniture. She waited again, motionless, and there was no sound. The place was the same, but somehow felt different than when she'd searched it such a short time ago. Gradually she realized the difference was a mixture of new odors: the gunman's musky cologne, burnt gunpowder, and something else . . . a sour sort of metallic smell. Maybe sweat, or fresh blood—or fear.

She waited some more, and was just ready to start moving again when she heard someone breathing. Slow, labored breaths, as though the very effort to stay alive were torture. Had the sound just begun, or had she not noticed it before? She couldn't place the direction it came from.

If someone was watching her, though, and wanted her dead, that would have happened already. She made her decision. "Hello," she called out in a high, trilling voice. "Is anybody home?"

Silence. No labored breathing now. No movement, no sound at all, as though the world were frozen.

Then a man's voice. "Help me." A whimper, too soft and strained to reveal any Hispanic accent. "I'm bleeding," he said. "Help me." The plea was coming up the stairway, possibly from the landing by the front door, or from all the way down in the basement.

She moved silently that way. Just short of the opening at the top of the stairs, she stopped and draped the sun hat on the barrel of the Colt. "I locked my keys in my car," she called, and eased the hat out beyond the edge of the wall about shoulder high. "May I use your phone?"

"Freeze! Don't move!" The harsh command and a sudden bright beam of white light shot up the dark stairwell together. "Or your fucking brains . . ."

His voice died away, or maybe she just didn't hear the rest, because she was already into the kitchen, headed for the back—

"Wait! Don't go!" A man's voice again, but louder. Not the same voice at all. "He really *is* hurt."

She stopped in her tracks. *What the hell's going on?*

"Please stay and help," the new voice begged. "He's . . . oh my God, he's unconscious again."

She turned around and went back into the living room. The bright beam from the flashlight bobbed as the person carrying it started up the stairs.

"Don't move," she yelled. "I have a gun, and I'll use it."

Then, when the light stopped moving, she added, "I want to know first if it's really you."

"It's me, and now I recognize your voice, too, Kirsten." The man was coming up the stairs again. "It's really me. Peter Keegan. The bishop."

TWENTY-SIX

His face was only a blur in the darkness, but his body seemed to sag and to shudder all at once. Kirsten wanted to take him in her arms and comfort him, but he was a bishop, after all, so she turned back toward the kitchen. "I'll call nine-one-one," she said, "and—" She stopped, suddenly hearing the sound of sirens whining in the distance.

"I called already," the bishop said. "I got here just before you did. The front door was open and I found Walter and . . . and I thought he was dead. But he came to, and told me the phone was in the kitchen. I must have closed the front door because while I was up here, making the call, someone knocked."

"That was me."

"I ran back to Walter. We waited, and then we heard someone come in the back door. Walter wanted to get them . . . you . . . to show yourself. When you poked your head out he started to shout, but then he just passed out on . . ." He turned. "My God, what about Walter? I have to—"

"Wait!" Kirsten grabbed his arm. The sirens were coming nearer. "We'll have to tell the police everything."

"Certainly." Then he seemed to realize what she was saying. "That is, you don't mean . . . not about *me*. This can't have anything to do with me. I—" He stared at her, eyes wide. "I mean, *you* didn't . . ."

"Shoot Walter? Of course not."

"No." He was shaking his head. "Anyway, I won't lie. I'll just tell them what I found, and nothing else."

"But what about *me*? I'll have to tell them you're my client, and—"

"No, please, don't open up this whole business about me. Especially not now."

"But they'll want to know what I'm doing here, unless . . . unless I'm *not* here." She realized she was still holding on to his arm, and she squeezed it. "Look," she said, "if I leave, are you sure—"

"I'll say I found Walter and called nine-one-one, and that's it."

The sirens were getting closer. No time to give it much thought. It was now or never. So she gave his arm a final pat . . . and ran.

She followed the route she'd taken before, through wooded lots and deserted backyards, with a better handle this time on which way she was going. Her right foot was killing her. Each time she landed on it, it screamed at her. And each time what it said was the same: *stupid, stupid, stupid.*

When she got out onto the road she forced herself to slow down to a walk and, as the muscles in her foot loosened up, the pain diminished. She felt less stupid, too. If the cops discovered her, she could tell them about locking her keys in the car and going for a phone, and finding the back door open. Then she could say she ran away because she thought someone in the house was going to shoot her. That made sense . . . sort of. Or, if she had to reveal that the bishop was her client, so be it. She wouldn't have to reveal the nature of his problem if he didn't want her to. Of course, there was the matter of the fake bloody bird in the fuse box. She couldn't just lie and say she knew nothing about it. What if the Japanese clerk read about it in the papers and somehow remembered she'd bought such a bird?

So, if the cops saw her, she'd just have to tell the truth.

Uh-huh. About how she'd picked the lock on the cottage and gone inside. Breaking and entering. And pulled the fuse and hidden the bird. Intimidation, or extortion or something? Or homicide? She was back to feeling stupid again, only worse.

She got to the Taurus and retrieved the keys by the tree and drove away. Out on the main road she met several police cars going the opposite direction. A moment later, she had to pull over and stop for a mobile trauma unit that came up behind her and then went past, lights flashing. Just one trauma unit, though.

The bishop hadn't said a word about the hit man, so probably he was dead. But she couldn't be certain. Maybe he was alive and Walter had died. She couldn't decide which of the two men she'd rather was still alive. Worse than that, she realized she had plenty of reason to wish that, whichever one was being rushed to the emergency room, he'd be too late for help by the time he got there. The fact is, she was hoping both men would die.

That's how she felt as she drove home alone through the dark. And she really didn't like feeling that way.

TWENTY-SEVEN

W hen he left the office after his chat with Larry, Dugan
was hungry and tired. He even dozed off in the cab, but
when the driver signaled to exit the Outer Drive at Ful-
lerton, he was awake enough to make a decision.

"Don't get off here," he said. "Keep going north."

"Whatever." The cab veered away from the exit lane, picked
up speed. "Where you wanna go?"

"Devon and Lincoln." Awake enough to make a decision,
not certain it was a good one.

Chicago's streets are laid out for the most part in a user-friendly
grid: north-south streets intersecting east-west streets with
waffle iron precision. But before the early planners had their
say, a dozen ancient Indian trails had already evolved into rut-
ted wagon roads, heading at all angles away from the ram-
shackle village by the lake, passing through onion-scented
marshland and out into the fresher air of the forests and the
plains.

Decades of bulldozers had scraped away many of those
roads, but others—worn too deeply into the land and people's
histories to wipe out—still survived as random lines across the
planners' careful gridwork. Most were called "avenues" now;

among them: Blue Island and Archer on the south side, Ridge, Milwaukee, and Lincoln on the north.

Devon's an avenue, too, but one laid out along the planners' rule, straight east-west, sixty-four blocks—a dead-on eight miles—north of the heart of the Loop. And where Lincoln angles across Devon, just west of the river and McCormick Boulevard, it creates a triangle known as Lincoln Village— which is not, of course, a village at all, but a shopping center.

The cab dropped him at Lincoln Village, and Dugan walked past the theater complex and turned onto Lincoln Avenue. The Moonglow Motel had been getting media attention in its old age. There were far worse places in the city, but that didn't mean the surrounding community, mostly homeowning families, had to tolerate the Moonglow without a fight. People didn't mind the sales reps or the budget-minded tourists, or even the furtive lovers who were usually checked in and gone again by 1:00 A.M. What the neighbors didn't like—and maybe exaggerated a little—were the prostitutes, the hustlers, the dope dealers. After thirty-five years on Lincoln Avenue, the neighbors wanted the Moonglow darkened for good.

He walked across the street and into the motel parking lot. Handling unscheduled interviews of mysterious women was not a job skill listed on his curriculum vitae, but he still hadn't gotten through to Kirsten, and the bishop had promised to meet this woman tomorrow, alone. If he went, Kirsten would certainly go with him. The whole idea was crazy.

They didn't know who the caller was—although Dugan already had his own suspicion—and the meeting might be some sort of setup. He sure wasn't going to let them go without him. But he wanted at least to see the woman first, possibly find out whether she was alone, maybe even talk to her. Which was equally crazy, of course.

Unit 119 was on the first floor, at the far end of the run-down, two-story building. He could tell the lights were on, even though the drapes were drawn across the window that opened onto the parking lot.

So he walked back and used a public phone at the Amoco station next door to the Moonglow. "Room one-nineteen," he said.

Four rings later, there was no answer. He walked around the block. It was ten o'clock and traffic was thinning out. He tried again. No answer.

Ah, well.

At a take-out place he picked out a pizza from the display case. A flat delivery box would look more authentic, so he asked for one, instead of the paper bag the clerk was sliding the pizza into, but she glared at him and said she'd have to talk to her supervisor.

He didn't need the attention. He paid for his pizza and left without a box.

About half the parking slots in the motel lot were vacant. The light was still on in 119, and through the door he heard a baseball game on TV. The White Sox, out on the West Coast. He knocked, ready to call "Pizza," when she asked who it was.

But there was no answer, so he knocked again, louder. There was still no response and, against his better judgment, he leaned his shoulder into the door. It swung open.

She was sprawled on her back across the bed, barefoot but wearing gray pants and a faded, blue-checked flannel shirt. Her mouth was open just a little. Her eyes were open, too, wide open—and she was never going to close them again.

He stood in the doorway, inhaling thirty-five years of stale cigarette smoke and hearing but not hearing the score of the Sox game. There was a half-empty bottle of Bud Lite on the bed stand, no glass. Two scuffed, brown penny loafers sat side-by-side against the wall, with a white sock stuffed into each one.

He didn't go inside.

It must have been about time for one of the movies to be over, because there were taxis waiting in front of the Lincoln Mall theaters. If the driver thought it was strange he brought a pizza with him in the cab, he kept it to himself. Near Belmont and Halsted, he paid the fare and joined the bustling swarms of night people.

There were fresh-faced yuppie couples, and aging men in tight T-shirts and too many earrings, and women with crew cuts holding hands and walking hip to hip, and kids with bright green hair smoking Camels and laughing too much. All of them prowling the streets, looking for something to take their minds off their own version of reality. A great night to be out, cool and clear, the air electric with hope and hustle.

He walked until he saw a chalk-faced scarecrow of undeterminable gender—maybe sixteen, maybe twenty-six years old—sitting alone on the curb by Dunkin' Donuts. The scarecrow peered up at him through wide, sunken eyes. "Lookin' for excitement?"

"Aren't we all," Dugan said, and handed down the pizza.

By the time he made it to the phone on the side wall of the doughnut shop, there were four of them at the curb, pulling the pizza apart. They might have been clones. He tapped out 911, said he thought he'd heard some shooting at a motel. "The Moonlight, or Moonbeam or something, up by Lincoln Mall."

"Sir, we need—" He hung up.

He wasn't sure he should have called at all. It certainly wouldn't help the barefoot woman who hadn't gotten to finish her Bud Lite. But that's what you did. You called 911. Maybe the sooner they got there, the fresher the evidence would be. He'd used his handkerchief on the edge—not the knob—of the door. He pulled it and it caught against the doorjamb and stayed closed, but he could tell the latch hadn't caught. Maybe the killer had used the same technique.

Maybe he'd smudged the killer's fingerprints.

He was nearly at the street entrance to the Belmont el station before he noticed how light-headed he felt, and how he was shaking. He leaned low over a trash barrel chained to one of the posts that held up the elevated tracks. People swirled past—some laughing and calling out to each other, others muttering softly to themselves. Finally he raised his head, breathing hard, embarrassed.

He looked around and remembered where he was. No one even noticed when you vomited in a barrel on Belmont Avenue under the el.

TWENTY-EIGHT

At eight o'clock Friday morning, waiting for Bud Burgeson to arrive and take him back to Chicago, Peter Keegan sat in the darkened hospital chapel and tried to pray—but couldn't. He was lacking sleep and overloaded with caffeine, and there were too many demons running around inside his head—whispering, congratulating, criticizing. He couldn't see them, but they were very real, and they were chipping away at his sanity.

One voice kept repeating how lucky he was that the police had treated him with deference, if not exactly kindness. He'd told them nothing about Kirsten being at the cottage. No one asked him that, and he was relieved at first. It didn't occur to him until he'd given his statement several times that Walter would probably say that the two of them heard a woman come into the cottage. But by the time he thought of that it was too late to change his story.

Besides, Walter hadn't been able to answer any questions so far. They bundled him onto a stretcher and the paramedics took him away. He'd gone right into surgery. Afterward, the doctor said Walter was a tough one, all right, but he'd lost a lot of blood. They weren't certain how long it would be before he regained consciousness. That's what the doctor *said*. The bishop was convinced that what he *meant* was that Walter might not regain consciousness at all.

One of his demons kept pestering him about what he'd say if Walter got well enough to tell the police what the bishop had omitted. Another voice said Walter might not even remember about Kirsten. As badly hurt as he'd seemed, it was amazing that he'd been able to think up a plan to draw Kirsten into view, or even shout as loud as he did when they saw the brim of her hat stick out, before he'd fainted again.

Then there was the demon of guilt. He could tell himself that he hadn't lied, but wasn't skipping a very important part of what happened the same as a lie? And, if that weren't enough, when they'd asked him about that toy bird, all tied up in yellow string, he'd said it had no meaning at all to him. That one was an out-and-out lie.

Another voice told him how much better off he'd be if he just told everything, brought it out in the open. The stalker, the threats, hiring Wild Onion, Ltd., his arrest in Canada. Everything. His career and his future in the Church would surely be ended. But wouldn't he be better off without this humiliating secret weighing him down; haunting him for the rest of his life?

The voices went on and on.

But the worst demon of all was quiet and constant, whispering beneath all the rest. Repeating, over and over, how much easier things would be if Walter never did regain consciousness. How much better it would be, the whisperer kept saying, if Walter—his own brother—would only die.

This demon was worse than the others, because this one was the most convincing of all.

TWENTY-NINE

To his amazement, Dugan was long asleep by the time Kirsten crawled into bed and, apart from a connubial nudge or two, it was breakfast before they actually communicated.

"You look a little . . . tired," Dugan said. He set a plate with two slices of dry toast—whole wheat—in front of her, along with coffee and orange juice.

"I look awful."

"Right," he said. "Horrible, in fact." Who was he to disagree? He scooped apricot preserves onto his own buttered toast. "At least, awful and horrible to the extent that a face like an angel and a body that—"

"Thank you." She picked up a piece of toast and stared at it. "You know what I'd really like?"

"Yes." He stood up and went to the refrigerator. "Breakfast."

"Thank you."

So he whipped up some scrambled eggs and fried some sausages and, while he did, she buttered her whole wheat toast and ate it, and they started telling each other what had been happening since they'd split up about twenty-four hours earlier.

There was a lot to tell, and he told it all—from the bishop's print on the skateboard, to his own head in the trash barrel.

He suspected, though, that she slid over some parts of her report, maybe because she didn't want him telling her to be more careful, which he still did now and then—but more out of habit these days than because he thought it would have any effect.

They'd finished eating and were washing the dishes when Kirsten suddenly said, "Another day away from the office?"

"Huh?" He turned and saw her looking at her watch. "Oh, yeah. It's a great life, isn't it? At least with a highly experienced lawyer like Larry Candle to step in." He wiped the counter and draped the dish cloth over the back of a chair to dry. "And if the ship goes down, with its captain absent from the wheel, we'll just have to depend on Wild Onion, Limited, for a living."

"Fine." She stood up and he watched as she seemed to be testing her right foot, rising up on her tiptoes and then back down on her heel. "On the other hand," she said, "you might come out ahead with Larry running the ship."

"Don't be silly." But he knew what she was getting at.

"Larry might start collecting fees from all your clients," she said. "And not be 'giving away the store,' as Mollie puts it."

"Uh-huh. And then we'd be on easy street and you wouldn't have to take cases where people shoot at peope and—"

"I wonder if the bishop's home," she said, changing the subject without skipping a beat. She picked up the phone and started punching out the number.

"Hold it," he said.

But she went ahead and got through to the rectory. The bishop wasn't there and she left a message.

"I thought you were worried his phone might be tapped and someone could trace the call back to you."

"I had Renfroe check that yesterday," she said. "No taps at the rectory or his office. Besides, you already identified yourself."

"I had no choice. When a couple of crooked cops—"

"I'm not criticizing. And those cops weren't necessarily crooked. They get an order from a superior to find out who somebody is, and they do it."

"They didn't look honest to me."

"Maybe they're undercover," she said. "Supposed to blend in with the bad guys."

"Yeah? Well then, those two are doin' a helluva job." He paused, kicking himself for the five hundredth time. "I still can't believe I didn't get their names."

"Might not even be helpful," she said, and he knew she was just being kind. "What's important," she went on, "is what to do now that Walter Keegan knows we're involved."

"We don't know for sure it's Keegan who's behind this. Hell, we don't even know if he's gonna survive."

"He's part of it, at least. I'm certain of that. Who else could send those two to check up on you?" She paused. "And he'll live, too. People like him, they don't die when you want . . . they don't die easily."

"If he *does* die, and if the stalking and threats stop, then we'll know."

"An easy thing to hope for, under the circumstances." She closed her eyes for a moment, then added, "That man needs a lot of support right now."

"You don't mean Walter."

"No. I mean the bishop. Right now he can't help wishing his own brother—half brother, anyway—would die. And I'd say he's beating himself up pretty bad about feeling that way."

"How do you know what the bishop is—" He stopped. He knew the answer. Kirsten could read the bishop's mind because, like him, she couldn't help wishing Walter would die. And like him, she didn't like feeling that way. "Yep, the bishop needs a lot of support," he said. "And don't we all?"

THIRTY

I can drop the rental car in Michigan City," Bud Burgeson said. "You think you're up to following me in my car that far? Then I'll drive the rest of the way home."

"Of course," the bishop said. "You needn't have come all this way, Bud. I'm fine. I could have driven home."

"Baloney. I suppose you called me because you're fine." He paused. "You look like hell. Anyway, you think I want you having a wreck? I mean, with *my* car?"

So the bishop followed Bud to drop off the rental car. Then Bud joined him and started the drive home to Chicago.

"Better fasten your seat belt," Bud said. "Be a shame if you survive a shootout one day, and go flying through my windshield the next."

He snapped the belt into place and they drove in silence for maybe five minutes, until Bud said, "The doctor says Walter's gonna pull through, huh?"

"Yes."

"Be in the hospital a while, though, huh?"

"Yes."

"And you'd rather not talk about it?"

"Yes. I mean no. That is . . ." He could feel it starting. First just his hands trembled, then his head, then his whole body

131

was shaking. Before he knew it he was sobbing, struggling to get some control, blowing his nose, then sobbing again. It went on and on, and he finally gave up fighting and just let the tears flow. Then, even after they subsided, he was scarcely able to talk. "I . . . I'm sorry. I couldn't help it."

"Yeah. Well, I'm no psychiatrist, but I'd say letting all that pent-up emotion pour out can't do you any harm." Bud turned and glanced at him. "Although I must say . . . you still look like hell."

That was Bud's brand of humor and the bishop had to smile, despite how embarrassed he was. He must look like a blubbering child but he did feel a little more relaxed. "The worst thing, you know, is . . ." He stopped, deciding to keep that to himself. Bud knew nothing of the stalking or the phone calls, much less his belief that Walter was behind them. "It doesn't matter."

"Of course it matters, but you don't have to say it," Bud said. "The worst thing is that a part of you was hoping that Walter wouldn't pull through."

"You know that?"

"Well, I suspected it, and *now* I know it. And guess what, I don't blame you. It's a natural reaction. That guy's a jerk, and he's been a problem for you, and your poor mother, too, for way too many years now. That there'd be some small part of you secretly wishing he'd be gone and done with? I can easily understand that."

"I appreciate your saying that." The bishop felt surprisingly relieved. "In fact, though, the part of me hoping Walter would die wasn't really so small."

"Small part, big part. What's the difference? I still don't blame you."

"I keep trying to make peace with him, but it's no use. I really envy you, being so close to Kenny."

"Yeah, well, it's different with twins, y'know, especially identical twins—and especially with no other siblings to interfere.

Kenny and I have our separate lives, but we're about as close as you can get. I mean, we argue a little now and then, but it's like arguing with yourself, trying to reach a conclusion."

"I was always surprised he didn't become a priest, too."

"Never had any interest in it. He always dreamed of being a lawyer, partly to make money to help my parents in their old age. Then they both up and died young and he's still at it. He says setting up endowments—or trusts or whatever—for charitable organizations is his calling. Now he's one of the top— Oh, by the way, didn't you ask him once about doing something with your mom's property? You two ever get together and—"

"Yes, about a year ago. He said with her mental status being so questionable, even then, it could complicate things and I'd be better off waiting until . . . until she—"

"Right. I got it." Bud reached out and turned on the car radio. "Now, why don't you get some sleep?"

"Wake up, Peter. We're almost there."

The bishop lifted his head. He couldn't believe it was past noon already, and they were just two blocks south of the rectory. "You mean I slept the whole—"

"Hold it!" Bud slammed the brakes hard and the bishop, still half-asleep, flew forward. The belt across his chest caught, and kept him from crashing into the dashboard. "See?" Bud said. "I *told* you that belt would come in handy."

A loud blast from the horn of a car behind them jolted the bishop. The car pulled around, its driver leaning on the horn the whole time, and kept on going.

"If I didn't have this darn Roman collar on," Bud said, "I'd give him the finger."

"Well, you have to admit you stopped a little suddenly."

"Yeah, I know. But look up there. You got company." Bud pointed ahead through the windshield. In the next block, parked in front of the rectory, was a white van with a satellite dish on top. "Channel Five," Bud said. "And look, farther down."

"This never occurred to me," the bishop said. A woman stood on the sidewalk in front of the church, facing two other people, one of whom pointed a minicam at her.

"You ready for your ten minutes of fame?" Bud asked.

"I suppose I have to face them sometime." The bishop thought for a moment. "But for now, turn at the corner and go down the alley behind the church. I have a key to a back door. I'll sneak in that way."

"If I was you I'd hide out tonight at my place," Bud said, already driving forward. "Tomorrow's Saturday. Maybe the press will lose interest in you by then."

"Thanks, but there's an affair I have to go to tonight. A cocktail party, with lots of big contributors to Catholic Charities. People I can't afford to ignore." He didn't mention that he also had an appointment with an anonymous woman at a motel.

"Nothing worse than a cocktail party," Bud said, turning into the alley. "I'd take even a parish school board meeting over that."

"Gosh, I'm sorry," the bishop said. "I forgot all about that. How'd your meeting go last night?"

"A disaster. The board voted to fire the principal. But I told them I wouldn't do it, 'cause she's only had the job one year and deserves more of a chance." Bud stopped the car behind the church. "So most of the board and half the faculty and parents started yelling that I was being dictatorial, arbitrary, paternalistic . . . and other things less complimentary. They're gonna go to the cardinal and—"

"Must have been awful." The bishop opened his door, feeling guilty about cutting Bud off, but too tired to keep listening.

"Yeah, well, maybe we should pray for an earthquake," Bud

said. "Then nobody'd care how dictatorial I am, and the press would forget about you and Walter." He reached across and patted the bishop on the shoulder. "And you wouldn't have to go to any god-awful cocktail party, either."

THIRTY-ONE

ocktail party? You *know* how much I hate that sort of thing." Dugan tilted back in his desk chair and looked up at Kirsten. He'd gone to his office for the afternoon, and gotten lost at once in phone calls and correspondence. "What time is it, anyway?"

"Just about six-thirty," Kirsten said. "And I'm here to be escorted to, as they say, an 'intimate gathering,' at what's probably a very nice condominium, up on Lake Shore Drive, north of Oak Street Beach."

"I'll have to go out and rent a tux or something. I mean, look at *you*."

"Like my outfit?" Kirsten smiled and did a little fashion model's twirl. She wore a hip-length jacket that hugged her body like a shirt and looked like silk, dark green and shimmering with sequins and tiny beads, over a black skirt that went straight down to her ankles and clung so close she wouldn't have been able to walk if it hadn't been slit up one side—way up, until the slit disappeared under the jacket. "I had just enough time, and credit cards," she said, waving a little hand-held purse at him, "to do a bit of shopping this afternoon."

"Sure. While I was busy settling a few cases, to maybe cover the cost." That was meant as a joke, since—apart from Christmas presents and the like—Kirsten paid for her clothes out of her own income. "And speaking of covering," he said, "are you wearing anything . . . um . . . *under* that jacket?"

"Well," she said, "yes. A *little* something."

"Uh-huh."

"Anyway, it's Friday night, and I'm told most of the men, and a few of the women, will be coming from their offices and therefore business attire is entirely appropriate. The party started at six-thirty and only goes on an hour or two. Then people scatter for dinner, I guess."

Dugan stood up and retrieved his suit coat from a hook behind the office door. He gave the coat a couple of shakes, but it still looked a little wrinkled. "I take it we're not merely stopping by for a good time with a bunch of congenial people."

"Right. It's a thank-you event for people who put together the financing for some infant nutrition centers the Catholic Church just started up on the West Side. We'll be a couple of new kids on the block, rather vaguely invited by somebody— the cardinal, maybe, since he won't be there—to meet this bishop who's in charge of Catholic Charities. Bishop Kagan, is it? Or Meegan or something? Maybe you've heard of him."

"Oh . . . you mean that guy whose brother was shot?"

"Half brother, actually. Who is, according to news reports, going to survive, but be laid up for a while."

Fifteen minutes later, they were in a cab, headed north.

"I guess you spoke to the bishop," Dugan said. "How's he doing?"

"A little shaky. He hadn't heard about that woman being beaten and strangled, and that hit him hardest of all. He's trying to dodge the press if possible, but didn't feel he could skip this party. So I want to be there, too. Partly because I want to see how he's doing; partly because of something Cuffs told me; and partly because you said the bishop's secretary thinks some of those big donors are people worth worrying about."

"I said that *seemed* like what she *almost* said."

"So we go with your hunch, trained observer that you are, and since those are the people who'll be at this cocktail party . . . well, where else would *we* want to be?"

"About a thousand other places," he said. "I'm thinking Walter—assuming he's involved in this—might have gotten my name from those two cops and passed it along to someone else before he was shot."

"Exactly. And maybe that someone else will be there tonight. That's one reason why I'm bringing you along. Maybe between us we'll see something sinister flicker in someone's eyes."

"Very dramatic," he said, "but not very likely." He paused. "What's the other?"

"The other what?"

"The other reason why you're bringing me along. You said one reason was—"

"Oh." She snuggled closer to his side. "Because I kinda like you," she whispered, and then kissed him lightly on his earlobe. The tip of her tongue barely brushed his skin, and a very nice shiver ran down his spine, or up—or both. "And if that's not enough," she added, still whispering, "there's something else, too."

"Oh?" he said, thinking they should skip the damn party and go straight home and get on with the shivering. "What's the something else?"

"Well . . ." She gently removed his hand from her thigh. "I'm carrying just this *teeeeny* little pocketbook and it's bursting its seams. So maybe, darling, you could help out." She took her lipstick, a nail file, a compact, and a thin wallet from her purse and dropped them all into his suit coat pocket.

"There can't be much left for you to carry," he said.

"Not much. Just our front door key, some tissue, and my Colt three-eighty."

The condominium covered one half of the top floor of an eighty-year-old building facing the lake. They stepped off the elevator into a small parlor with a huge mirror on the opposite wall that had them looking right back at themselves. To their left was the closed door to the other apartment on the floor, and to their right was an open door with the sounds of soft, stringed music and polite conversation floating out. Directly in front of them, against the wall with the mirror, were a tiny, fragile-looking table with a lamp and a tiny, fragile-looking chair beside the table.

Between them and the open door loomed a man neither tiny nor fragile-looking. He would have appeared uneasy and uncomfortable in any white shirt and tie, Dugan thought, even if the shirt hadn't been too small for him. It was Cuffs Radovich and his ensemble wasn't improved by his plaid sport coat, nor was the hostile scowl on his face improved by his unkempt, drooping mustache.

"I wouldn't have been worried about my wrinkled suit," Dugan said, "if you'd told me Cuffs was invited."

"Don't be silly," Kirsten said. "I just thought—" She stopped short when another man, this one in a gray business suit, appeared in the open doorway. "May we go in?" she asked, but obviously directing her question to Cuffs, not letting on she knew him.

"Show me some identification," Cuffs said. "And if you're with the press, turn around now . . . before you wish you would've."

Dugan held out his business card and Cuffs snatched it and shoved it into his pocket without looking at it, then waved them toward the open door with a guttural growl that reminded Dugan of his recent visit to Lincoln Park Zoo. By then, the man in the gray suit had disappeared back into the apartment.

They headed inside and down a short hallway, and Kirsten said, "As I started to explain, I thought the bishop could use a . . . a chaperone, and his wanting to keep the press at arm's length gives him a good excuse, in case anyone questions the need."

"You mean a bodyguard, and that much I understand," Dugan said. "But Cuffs Radovich? He'll offend everyone who shows up. They'll slam their checkbooks shut and *poof* . . . those nutrition centers vanish overnight."

"Oh, I don't know, he seemed pretty polite and restrained to me—I mean, at least for Cuffs."

"That's because you're used to his *usual* behavior." The hall opened onto a large, high-ceilinged living room, and Dugan gestured toward the throng milling around in front of them. "But these people? They step off the elevator and all they see is *surly* and *rude*. They have nothing to compare—"

"Speaking of these people," she said, "put on your game face and let's go introduce ourselves. Shall we start with the bartender?"

They picked up a couple of drinks, and were off on a bewildering round of handshakes, name exchanges, and small talk. Dugan concentrated hard, determined to remember as many names as possible. He was equally determined to suppress what Kirsten always called his "chauvinistic, *trophy* impulse," but couldn't help being pleased at the number of men who looked envious when they caught sight of her at his side.

They spent what seemed to him like an hour weaving their way among groups of chattering people and, drinks held high, sidling carefully between furniture and human torsos. From what he overheard, Dugan knew much of the talk concerned the shooting of the bishop's brother, and how the bishop was taking it. But each time he and Kirsten approached, the conversation shifted politely to the weather or the stock market—something more neutral, for strangers.

Finally, Kirsten nodded slightly toward the grand piano by the windows overlooking the lake, and Dugan followed her that way. Beside the piano an earnest young woman, a slim brunette with clear, pale skin and a black strapless gown, was playing a harp. They moved close to her, as though captivated by her rendition of "Greensleeves."

"No sinister flickers so far," Dugan said.

"That might be because you're too busy *strutting* to pay attention, Tarzan."

"I am *not* strutting," he said, "and you love it when I do, anyway." But he wasn't certain she did, so he decided to change the subject. "I guess the bishop didn't make it, huh?"

"He's here somewhere, or Cuffs wouldn't be here. It's probably a big apartment, you know, and we've only done one room so far."

"Damn, I was thinking we were about ready to hit the road. I'm hungry. Besides, it's just too . . . crowded, or something."

"There aren't really that many people for a room this size. Maybe twenty, twenty-five. It's something else." Kirsten looked around. "What do you think of the decor in here?"

"Actually, I hadn't really—"

"The furniture, for instance. It all looks expensive, and comfortable enough, I guess, but why so much? And all this artwork. It's overpowering. This place would feel crowded with no one in it."

Dugan studied the room. It must have been twice the size of their own living room, and it wasn't the people sitting and standing around that made it look so crowded. Kirsten was right. There were just way too many chairs, sofas, tables crammed into the space. And, besides the furniture, there were *things* everywhere. The place was cluttered with every conceivable type of artwork: paintings and photographs—large and small—all over the three walls that weren't windows to the lake; sculptures, vases, and general bric-a-brac on every available shelf and tabletop. "Some people," he said, "like to collect things."

"Look again, though, and tell me the one thing you *don't* see," she said. "Something not depicted in any piece of art or photograph in this room."

"Well . . ." The harpist gave up on "Greensleeves" without really finishing it and started in on Pachelbel's *Canon*, which Dugan had once loved, but had overdosed on about a decade ago. "Human beings," he finally said. "People. There *are* none. I mean, except for the live ones."

"One of which," Kirsten said, looking beyond his shoulder, "is headed our way right now."

Dugan turned. It was the man who'd appeared in the doorway momentarily when they first arrived. His gray suit looked tailor-made, and he exuded success and a sort of salesman's good cheer. And under that, something else, too—Dugan thought—like pent-up aggression, or maybe just stress. He was also taller than average and slightly overweight, things which Dugan hadn't noticed earlier, probably because he'd been overshadowed by Cuffs.

The man switched his wineglass to his left hand and reached out with a practiced smile to shake Dugan's hand. "Bishop Keegan told me a couple of newcomers would be here, wanting to meet him and maybe get a little involved with Catholic Charities. Figured it had to be you two. The bishop's in the library. Still quite fatigued from last night. Don't blame him. Awful thing to happen. You heard about it, right?"

"Yes," Dugan said, "we—"

"Well, come along with me and I'll introduce you to Bishop Keegan." The man paused, then laughed a bit, as though at his own foolishness. "Although I don't believe I introduced myself yet. I chaired the fund-raising committee for the nutrition centers, and I'm your host," he said, "Charles Banning. But please, just call me Charlie."

THIRTY-TWO

There must have been another dozen people in the library, and anyone who didn't already know could never have guessed the bishop wasn't meeting Dugan and her for the first time. That he could carry this off showed Kirsten a reservoir of strength that might easily be overlooked.

They sat down and, like everyone else, listened to a thin, bald man drone on about the DeBeers Company and the South African infrastructure . . . or something. She gave that about ten minutes and then stood up. "We really must be going now," she said. "We have another engagement, don't we, Dugan?"

"We sure do," he said, and she could tell how anxious he was to leave. "A dinner engagement," he added.

"Thank you for coming," the bishop said. "I hope to see you again before too—"

"Oh, don't worry, Bishop," Charles Banning said. "I've got Dugan's card. He won't get away."

"Sounds ominous," Kirsten said. Banning seemed odd, for some reason.

"Oh, he means he'll be asking you to pitch in." The bishop smiled. "Charlie's always on the lookout for volunteers."

They managed to ease away after a few more pleasantries. When they got to the little parlor by the elevator, Cuffs was still there. "Bring Bishop Keegan to our place when this is over," Kirsten said. "And please, be careful."

"I'm always careful."

"Of course you are. I just . . ." She paused, then decided to go ahead and ask something she'd been wondering about. "It seems unlikely, with all these people here, but what about the back entrance to this apartment? Couldn't someone sneak in? I mean, with the bishop inside and you out here and—"

"I took care of that, for chrissake." Cuffs glared at her, obviously offended. "Nobody's gonna get in or outta the back door of this place, not for quite a while. And they're gonna need a locksmith."

"Great," Dugan said. "I just hope there's not a fire or something."

"Yeah?" Cuffs shook his head, as though disappointed in Dugan. "If there is, I'll get my man out. The rest of them phony, big shot assholes'll have to take care of themselves. Fact is, the world would be better—"

"Okay, Okay." Kirsten raised her hands in surrender. "Sorry I brought it up." Cuffs blamed his disgust with just about every person and group in the world on bad experiences when he'd been a cop, but she figured it ran a lot deeper than that. "See you later," she said.

"Yeah, later," Cuffs said. "Long as you don't shoot yourself with the gun in that little purse of yours."

Coarse, rude, cynical—but also very good at what he did.

"Thai food again?" Dugan asked. Kirsten had changed into jeans and a sweatshirt when they got home, and now they were waiting in the kitchen for Cuffs to show up with the bishop. "Twice in one week?"

She wasn't surprised at his objection. "At least for the bishop and me," she said. "It's nine o'clock and he told me last time that eating this late is hard on his stomach, especially fatty foods. You can order pizza or ribs or whatever you—"

"You think that'll happen to me? I mean, when I get old will I have to watch what I eat when it's late?" He swirled the ice cubes around in his glass and drank some of the scotch he'd poured for himself. "For that matter," he added, "will nine o'clock be *late* when I get old?"

"I doubt that the bishop thinks of himself as old," she said. "Besides, I wouldn't worry about it. With your habits, darling, you probably won't live long enough to find out."

"There's that 'darling' stuff again. Did I ever mention that you only call me 'darling' when you're working on something and you want my help?"

"Yes, you have, but I don't know that it's true. Besides, did I say I wanted you to show up at the zoo? Or to interview the bishop or his secretary?"

"No, but you're glad I did, aren't you?" She pretended to be too preoccupied with putting water on for tea to answer. "And you *did* ask me along tonight." He paused. "There was something I wanted to ask you. Something about why we were going to the party . . . but I can't remember what it was."

"If you stop trying, maybe you'll think of it." But she hoped he didn't. It probably had to do with Cuffs and his keeping an eye on Walter Keegan's activities, and she wanted to keep that to herself for now.

"Anyway," he said, "you wanted me to help watch for sinister flickers."

"Notice anything?"

"Nope. What about you?"

"Nothing." She kept quiet about thinking Banning seemed odd. "Maybe Mrs. Gage has more insight than we do."

"And maybe I was just wrong about what she kept herself from saying."

"She did a great job tonight, though," Kirsten said. "I mean, there she is in the library with the bishop, listening to her husband bore everyone to tears explaining the *real* problems in South Africa, when Banning drags us up and introduces us."

"I was surprised a secretary was even invited to an affair like that," he said, "until I realized her husband's probably a big donor. Anyway, I thought she'd burst out with 'Oh, we've already *met*,' or something."

"But she picked up on the bishop's cue right away, and acted like she'd never heard of either of us." Kirsten paused. "I wonder whether she might prove helpful somewhere down—"

The buzzer interrupted her and she went to the intercom in the hall. It was Cuffs. He was sending the bishop up, but he'd stay outside and watch the street. They could reach him on his cell phone. When she returned to the kitchen, Dugan was coming in the door from their back stairway. "Where'd you go?" she asked.

"Just making sure Cuffs hasn't nailed our back door shut,"

They lived in a loft building, and the downstairs door that opened onto the alley was steel-plated. If either of its two deadbolt locks hadn't been thrown, their security system would have alerted them. "So, is there anyone in the alley?" she asked.

"Not a soul in sight," he said.

There was a knock on their front door and she went to answer it.

The bishop was standing there in his black suit and Roman collar, with a white plastic bag hanging from each hand. "The food," he explained, and held the bags up in front of him. "Mr. Radovich wouldn't let the delivery man come up. He paid him and said you could add the cost to his bill."

He obviously expected her to take the food, but she didn't. She led him back to the kitchen and, when he set the bags on the counter and turned to sit down, she said, "Would you mind setting the food out on the table? Oh, and there are plates in that cabinet, and the knives and forks are in the drawer by the toaster. I'll make the tea."

Dugan had been rummaging around in the refrigerator, probably looking for corned beef again, or something else with too much fat. He looked up, though, and glanced at her, and she knew he was enjoying himself. She never let *him* get away with sitting on his behind and waiting to be served, so why should the bishop be any different?

She and the bishop had tea with their pad thai and seafood ka prao, and Dugan added more ice and water to his scotch and made himself a couple of ham and cheddar cheese sandwiches. "Whole wheat bread," he said, slathering on the mayo, "very healthy."

"He doesn't mean *healthy*, bishop," Kirsten said. "He means *healthful*. And he knows it's not."

"Very tasty, though," Dugan said. He held out half a sandwich to the bishop. "Want some?"

"No, thank you. This is fine." The bishop drank some tea. "This ka prao is very hot, though. Would you get me . . ." He paused, then stood up, found a glass, and filled it with ice cubes and water. She decided they were making progress. On top of that, when he sat back down, he handed her a twenty-dollar bill.

"What's this for?"

"For the supper," he said, "and the one the other night, as well. And I just realized, you must be paying Mr. Radovich, too. So you should add that to what I'm paying you."

"I'll keep the twenty," she said, "even if it's more than your share. But, unless I warn you ahead of time, my expenses are included in the fee I quoted you. That's why it's so high, actually."

"It's not my business," Dugan said, "but I'd charge Cuffs's fee extra, as a penalty, to any client who insists on calling him 'Mr. Radovich,' as though he were an ordinary person or something."

The bishop smiled. "I'll try," he said. "Where does the name 'Cuffs' come from, anyway?"

"It goes back to his early days as a police officer," Kirsten said. "There are several versions of the story, but essentially he put handcuffs on a young man in his custody, put them on way too tight, and then forgot about the prisoner—or at least later he claimed he forgot—and then . . ."

"And then," Dugan chimed in, "the shackled prisoner got panicky, all alone there in the dark for so long. Just where he was being kept, or how cold—or hot—it was, depends on who you listen to. Eventually, though, most of the skin was scraped off his wrists. Pretty soon you got him hollering about brutality and complaining of pain shooting up his arms. And cops too busy with a multiple homicide to pay much attention to another whining punk. Next thing you know, blood poisoning. Finally, emergency surgery."

"He ended up with one arm pretty much useless," Kirsten said. "Of course, he was *not* a very nice young man, and he did finally give up some important information to the police."

"Only after which, of course, he finally got medical attention," Dugan said. "The thing is, his statements, although true, were found inadmissible as evidence because they were found to be coerced. And everything else the cops turned up based on what he'd told them was thrown out, too. 'Fruit of the poisoned tree,' the judge said, and he was right. So the bad guys walked . . . and Cuffs got his nickname."

The bishop stared at them. "And this is the man you . . . Is that story really true?"

"Maybe yes, maybe no," Kirsten said. "What's more important, though, is that Cuffs was careful never to deny it—except during the official investigation, of course. Some versions of the story are a little more graphic. I don't suppose you'd like—"

"No." The bishop looked pale and tired. "When you say some bad guys *walked,* do you mean—"

"We mean they didn't get found guilty of those particular crimes. Not to worry, though. They're probably all in jail by now, anyway—or dead." Kirsten poured herself more tea. "We could tell happy tales like that for hours, you know? But it's late, and we need to talk."

"Well, yes, I . . ." The bishop laid his fork carefully on his plate. His body sagged lower in his chair.

"You haven't eaten your twenty dollars' worth," Dugan said.

"I can't eat." He smiled a little, but it didn't last; as though the muscles around his mouth weren't up to the task. His eyes were watery, veined with red. "You know, I'm a man who's supposed to be able to pray and . . . Anyway, I'm not doing well at all. It's not only this business with Walter. It's . . . it's everything. I really don't know what I'm going to do about any of it."

Kirsten wasn't sure what he meant by "everything," and while she was searching for a response, Dugan spoke up. "Of course you don't know what to do," he said. "That's exactly why Kirsten had Cuffs bring you here. I'm sure she's got a plan."

Kirsten opened her mouth, but didn't say anything. She had plenty of questions, but she certainly did *not* have a plan.

". . . struggle to act normal at that damn party would wear anyone down," Dugan was saying, and he reached out and laid his hand on the bishop's arm. "Anyway, you're here now. And everything's gonna work out all right, goddamn—Oh, sorry."

"He's right," Kirsten said. "Now, I have some questions. First, have you ever ridden a skateboard?"

"What?" His eyes were wide with surprise.

"Or even touched one?"

"No, not that I can remember."

"So," she stared at him, "how did your fingerprint get on one of those skateboards Dugan retrieved at the zoo?"

"That's not possi—" He shrugged, as though this were just one of a thousand unexplainable things. "Well, if it *is* there, it's possible. But I can't imagine how."

"If you think of a way, let me know." She couldn't have caught him more off-guard, and she believed him. "Let's move on to something else. What do you have that someone else

149

wants, and wants very badly?"

"Nothing." He shook his head. "I'm sure there's nothing."

"Okay, maybe we'll come back to that," she said. Obviously, there *was* something. She just hoped it was something the bishop hadn't thought of yet, and not something he was hiding from them. "Or maybe we won't come back to it, because my next question might make all the rest moot. I'm wondering . . . why not just get rid of their hold over you?"

The bishop was silent for a moment, then said, "I'm not sure I understand."

Not quite untrue, Kirsten thought. He couldn't be absolutely certain what was in her mind. But he wasn't stupid. He had a pretty good idea. "Take away their leverage," she said. "What's going on here is blackmail, even if you don't know yet what the blackmailers want. So . . . go public right now. Tomorrow morning. Talk to the cardinal or something. Tell the world about your arrest, the whole thing. I mean, take your punches and then get on with your life. A year from now, who'll care? Who'll even remember?"

"I've thought of that, of course, and in some ways it makes good sense. But I just can't do it. Nude dancers? Arrested in a place of prostitution? And . . . anyway, the media would have a field day. They'd make it out to be much more serious than it really was. Worst of all, people who . . . who *believe* in me would feel that I've betrayed them. Especially . . ." his voice was shaking, "especially now."

"Why especially now?" she asked.

"It's . . . I've gotten a new assignment. I didn't ask for it, or expect it. But it's quite an honor, and it will bring my name to the attention of bishops all around the country. And, I guess, people in Rome, too. The cardinal just told me yesterday. I've been named to chair a new committee created by the National Conference of Catholic Bishops. A press release was going out today, to make the announcement."

"What kind of committee?" Kirsten asked.

"Bishops, theologians, psychologists, and experts from various disciplines to work on something the conference of bishops has struggled with for years, but can never quite agree on. I'm the chairman, and we're to try again to draw up a set of uniform standards and procedures for use all across the country."

"That *does* sound like quite an honor," Dugan said. "Also sounds sort of boring. You might as well become a lawyer."

"Uniform standards and procedures," Kirsten said. "Standards and procedures for what?"

"For dealing with charges made against priests," the bishop said. "Ways to act promptly and—insofar as possible—without the veil of secrecy."

"By charges against priests," Kirsten said, "I suppose you mean . . ."

"Yes," he said, "for the most part, charges of sexual misconduct."

THIRTY-THREE

The cocktail party was over and the last boring asshole had said good-bye. The caterers had to haul everything out through the lobby, because the lock on the door to the alley had somehow gotten hopelessly jammed. But they were gone now, too, and Charles Banning was alone. He sat by the window with a ginger ale and tried to think.

The party had been a success. And why not? Back when he was getting started, he and his wife had socialized constantly. Theater, the opera, the symphony. Always a party, sometimes before *and* after. Always business, networking, the usual bullshit. He was good at it, but hated it. Hated the people he had to pretend were so bright, so interesting. Hated the way the ones with real money smiled when they looked down on him.

He'd broken away from that. Men like him made it by working their balls off and having the guts to make tough decisions, not by sucking up to a bunch of pompous assholes and their anorexic wives.

Getting his own damn wife out of the picture had made it easier to skip the social crap. He still had to keep his name in circulation, of course, so he'd looked for an organization he could use, and Catholic Charities fit the bill. You had to drop a few bucks now and then to seed the pot, but mostly you hit up other people. Do it right, and you got a reputation for success, generosity, even a fucking social conscience.

The religion angle didn't bother him at all. He was good at pretending—learned it as a kid dealing with an endless string of foster parents. Some of them made him go to church. One couple, old enough to be his grandparents, even dragged him in one day and had him baptized. He was about eleven then, and that same night the old lady was drinking and tried to slide her hand up under his shorts. He burned the inside of her ear with her own cigarette and the agency came and took him away.

He looked at the clock. Past midnight now, but no way he'd be able to sleep.

From the news reports he couldn't tell what had happened at Walter Keegan's cottage. He had to assume the man from Miami had escaped unidentified. He was one of the best and if Keegan didn't die he'd be back and get the job done. But what had gone wrong? What was the bishop doing there, anyway? How bad was Keegan? If he didn't die, was there some way he could figure out who ordered the hit? He better die, the sonovabitch.

Christ, he wanted some bourbon in his ginger ale. He didn't move, though. If a man couldn't discipline his own desires, what chance did he have against the will of others?

He couldn't stop thinking about last night, and the errand he'd taken care of. He'd been smart enough to know it had to be his imagination, and tough enough not to let it stop him, but he'd had a feeling he couldn't shake off. It was like someone was watching him the whole time, witnessing the entire incident.

Fuck the ginger ale.

He stood up and walked across to the revolving bookcase that held his leather-bound set of the works of Jack London. As far as he knew, not one of the volumes had ever been opened. But he pulled out *The Call of the Wild* and *White Fang*, and removed a little metal box from behind them and took it back to the desk. His hands shook—too much fucking stress—as he tapped some of the white powder out of the box and stared down at it. It looked like a lot, but surprising how fast the shit disappeared.

He leaned his face low over the desk, lifted a hit from the tiny spoon, and sat upright again.

Christ, that fucker better die. He twisted and turned his head, stretching out the muscles of his neck, then leaned low again. Another hit. This shit was good, but it was the last batch for him. It was too goddamn expensive, for someone who didn't actually need it.

He waited awhile and felt the shit start to kick in. He stood up, then, and stepped closer to the window. Outside, past the Outer Drive and the beach, endless waves rippled across the surface of the lake in the moonlight. He watched.

They were much the same, the lake and he. Winds came and went, blowing from various directions. On the surface there was adjustment, a shifting this way and that, the illusion of being tossed about. But deep down the water ruled, untouched by passing commotion. These people who tried to stand in his way, they were nothing. Fucking puffs of wind. He was proving it. True power always lay deep and unseen—and it would not be denied.

THIRTY-FOUR

S o, a national committee to deal with charges of sexual misconduct against priests," Dugan said, when the silence
hanging in the air was finally too much for him. "Um . . .
suppose being arrested at a house of prostitution qualifies."
When that got no response, he tried again. "Maybe you could
say you were doing research, or—"

"Dugan!" Kirsten obviously didn't agree with his approach.

"Okay. Sorry." He stood up and took his and the bishop's
glasses—both of them empty—across to the counter beside the
sink and poured a couple of inches of scotch into each one. He
turned and held up the bottle. "Kirsten?"

"None for me, no."

"Me, either," the bishop said.

"You don't get a choice." Dugan held up the bottle. "I got
this for Christmas. It's a single malt scotch and they say it
settles the stomach, among other effects. They also say only a
rustic would add water to it, which is what I do. You want any
water in yours?"

"No, thanks. I probably won't drink it, anyway." The bishop
took the glass, though, and did sip a little of the scotch. "It's . . .
very good, I guess."

"It oughta be. You could fly round-trip to Glasgow for what

it cost." He sat down. "Now, let's try to keep our perspective here. Committee or not, I still think you should tell the world what happened."

"I agree," Kirsten said. "It's the only way to handle blackmail."

"I can't. You don't understand."

"Of course we understand," Dugan said. "The most important thing here is that you didn't *do* anything up in Canada. I mean, you told us the whole truth about what you did, right?" He watched the bishop's face as he said it, and began to have doubts immediately. "You told us everything that happened?"

"I told you the whole truth about what I *did*, yes. But I'm afraid I didn't tell you quite everything that happened."

"Wait a minute. What is this?" Kirsten spoke very slowly, and Dugan could sense her anger building. "What are you saying?"

"Everything happened the way I told you. I did nothing, except foolishly go into that . . . that place, and order a beer. But there was something I found out later, after I was arrested." He stopped, sipped some of his scotch, then looked first at Kirsten, then Dugan. "The waitress was underage. I don't know how old, maybe seventeen or . . . whatever the law is up there. They questioned her, and then they let her go."

"How do you know that?" Kirsten snapped out the question.

"The police station there was very small and when she was leaving she passed right by me. She stopped and whispered to me. She said she was sorry, but she'd had to say what she said to them, because they told her otherwise she'd be in big trouble. She . . . she was crying."

"Crying, hell," Dugan said. "What was that little . . . what was she talking about? She had to say what?"

"When she told me, I had no idea. But later the police took me in a room and told me what she said I did. They read her statement to me from one of their reports. They showed me where she signed it. They told me—"

"Bishop," Dugan said, his voice very soft, "please, what did the *girl* say?"

"She said I . . . well . . ." His voice trailed off and he was staring down at the table in front of him. "I can't say it. I mean, maybe I could if . . ."

"I'm staying right here," Kirsten said. She sounded disgusted now, on top of being angry. "You haven't been honest with me . . . with us. I don't know why I expected a priest to be any different from my other clients, but I did. Anyway, dammit, you have to face this." Her voice rose a notch. "You have to say what she said. You can't keep dodging around, for God's sake. I don't care if you're embarrassed or—"

"I think he's got the point," Dugan said, then turned to the bishop. "So, what did this girl tell the police you did?"

"Well, like the other women working there, she hadn't been wearing anything above her waist, as I told you, and she said . . . she told the police I offered to give her money if . . . if I could touch her breasts, and more money for . . . for . . . a blow job. Those are the words they read to me. I've never used that expression in my life. And she told them she said yes, and that I fondled her breasts and then she . . . she did . . . what she said I asked for, and that I paid her." He took a deep breath then, and gulped more of his scotch, and Dugan was glad he'd given it to him. "The police said that this was a very serious crime because she was a minor." He slapped his hand on the table and looked up, and there was some spark—finally—in his eyes. " 'I didn't do that!' I told them, 'not any of it!' " Then he sighed, and his remembered outrage seemed to evaporate and his voice dropped back to a monotone. "They knew I was telling the truth. They knew what they'd done was wrong, encouraging that poor girl to lie."

"Did they know you were a priest?" Dugan asked.

"No. Nothing in my wallet said I was a priest. My friend Bud says priests should make sure their Roman collars show up in their driver's license photos, in case they get stopped, but I never do. I don't want special priv—"

"Okay, we got it," Dugan cut in, thinking Kirsten might slug the poor guy if he started telling how honest he was. "How about getting back to the point?"

"Sorry. I told them I was a university professor, which was true. But I was from the States, and I don't think they were interested in getting me into big trouble. They mostly wanted enough evidence to get that tavern closed. They kept urging me to call someone, so I called—"

"Larry Candle." Kirsten's voice came from across the room and startled Dugan. He hadn't even noticed her get up from the table. "Larry Candle," she repeated, leaning forward now, staring at the bishop. "You called him and you never knew that all he did was call your brother." She paused and took a step back toward the table. "Or were you lying about *that*, too."

"Lying? I'm not . . ." The bishop stood up, his face turning red. But that didn't last either, and he sat back down. "I haven't lied to you. Not once. I've omitted some things, but I haven't lied."

"And I suppose you think there's a difference?" Kirsten was pressing awfully hard, and Dugan wished she'd back off a little.

"There *is* a difference," the bishop said. "But I can understand how you feel. If . . . if you want to quit helping me, I understand that, too. Just send me your state—"

"I didn't say anything about walking away. Besides, how can I quit the case now? I've wrongfully fled the scene of a crime, on your behalf. I've stood eyeball to eyeball with a professional killer that somebody sent to Walter's cottage, and who must be out there right now, doing what he can to identify me, so that he can make sure I'm not around to identify him. It's not as though—"

"What killer?" The bishop seemed confused. "You didn't tell me you saw anyone."

"There really hasn't been time, has there? Anyway, I'm not

quitting this case. And I guess it's true that you didn't know Larry Candle called Walter, because Larry says Walter frightened him and warned him not to tell you or anyone."

"I knew only that Larry took care of it right away—or at least I *thought* it was Larry who took care of it—because a little after noon the next day the police told me the charge was frequenting a house of prosititution or something like that, and they were dropping it, and that I could leave. I got the impression someone might actually have come to the police station personally on my behalf, but later, when I tried to thank Larry, he didn't want to talk about it."

"Because he didn't have anything to talk about," Kirsten said. "All he did was call exactly the wrong person, the dumb little—"

"Wait! That's not fair." Dugan was amazed to find himself defending Larry. "How was he to know he shouldn't call Walter?"

"No one in his right mind would call somebody like Walter Keegan for help," Kirsten said. "Anyway, we still don't know for sure what Walter did. Maybe he called someone in Canada. Maybe he flew a man up there right away. My guess is he bribed someone, but he certainly got you out of there. And I'll tell you something else Walter got, too, I'd bet on it."

"Uh-huh," Dugan said. Kirsten must have reached the same conclusion he had, back when the bishop first started describing his interview by the police.

"I don't understand," the bishop said. "What else did Walter get?"

"Copies of the police reports," Dugan said. "He'd have wanted those for sure, even if he didn't know then whether he'd ever use them for anything."

"No way he doesn't have those reports," Kirsten said, "including the girl's signed statement."

"But she wasn't telling the truth," the bishop said. "If Walter makes the statement public, she'd admit—But she can't, not

159

now, not if she's the one who called me, and who . . ." He stopped. "And if the statement's revealed, the fact that she can't deny or verify what she said, that doesn't matter, does it? The damage would be done by then."

"Even if she were around now—which I'm sure she isn't," Kirsten said, "what good's a retraction so many years later? With the accused apparently having pulled some strings, maybe even bribed someone, to get the charges dropped in the first place?"

"You see? More reasons why I can't just tell everyone about my arrest."

"Yeah, so much for going public and letting it all blow over," Dugan said. "Not only you, bishop, but the cardinal and that whole conference of bishops would be publicly embarrassed. No more head of Catholic Charities for you. I mean, you'd have a helluva time just getting a job in any parish in—"

"Give him a break, Dugan," Kirsten said, "and keep quiet."

He thought that was a little unfair, given how she'd been hitting the poor man over the head pretty hard herself, but he stood up. He took his and the bishop's glasses—both empty again—from the table. "How about a refill?"

"Not for me," the bishop said. "And you're right. It's not just me anymore. I didn't do what that girl said, but I refuse to bring shame on the whole Church." He paused for a long time and Dugan wanted to fill in the silence, but didn't, and finally the bishop looked up. "I'm not very courageous, obviously, but one thing I'm not afraid to do is die, you know, and that's exactly what I'll do before I voluntarily let her lies be made—"

The phone rang.

It was a wall phone, and closer to Kirsten. She answered it and listened. Then she hung up again, not having said a word. There was a new worried look on her face. "Forget that scotch," she said, "and make a pot of coffee. That was Cuffs."

"And?" Dugan asked.

"And our apartment is under surveillance."

160

THIRTY-FIVE

need to sit up," the bishop said. For the second time in three days he'd been met in an alley and ordered onto the floor behind the front seat, while this strange man called Cuffs drove, starting and stopping abruptly, lurching around corners. "Please, I need—"

"What's the big hurry to sit up?"

"I've been down here at least fifteen minutes." He could hardly believe all this was happening, but the pains in his back and legs were very real. "And my muscles and joints are too old to—"

"Keeping you comfortable's not my job," Cuffs said. "Stay put."

But they'd made no sudden turns for the past five minutes or so, and he decided they weren't trying to evade anyone any longer. So he sat up in the backseat, permission or not.

To his surprise, all Cuffs said was, "We're almost to your place, anyway."

"I'm not going home," the bishop said. "Not yet."

"The hell you're not. Where you think you're going? Especially since I'm the one driving."

"I want to go visit someone, in a nursing home." He gave Cuffs the address, then added, "It's not far."

"I know how far it is, for chrissake. But we're not going there. Tomorrow I'll take you anywhere you want. Now we're going to that big old dump you live in, and you're gonna go inside and lock all the doors."

"Fine. Take me to the rectory. I'll take a cab to the nursing home."

"It's past ten o'clock. Those old people go to sleep right after supper."

"She's usually awake. Besides, she probably won't know I'm there, anyway."

"Well then, why the hell—"

"She's my mother, and I visit her." Tired as he was, he was surprised at the strength of the anger showing up in his voice. "Why should I explain—" He stopped, because by then Cuffs was making a turn in the direction of the nursing home. "Thank you," he said. "God bless you."

"She's your mother, for chrissake. You can cut out the God crap."

There were two of them. They were sitting in a light-colored Chevy Caprice, a four-door sedan.

Cuffs had told her he was sure they hadn't seen him deliver the bishop, but had shown up afterward. Looking down from their window, Dugan had said he couldn't be certain, but agreed they were probably the two cops from the playground. It seemed maybe Walter Keegan wasn't hurt so badly, after all, if he was already able to send someone to keep an eye on them. It couldn't be the gunman from Walter's cottage. He couldn't possibly have identified her yet. Besides, he would come alone when he came—and she was certain he would come.

The bishop had probably been through enough for one day, anyway, and she needed a break, too. She'd found herself more angry at him than he deserved. So she'd gotten him out the back door and into Cuffs's car, and Dugan had gone out the front way.

The idea was that Dugan would hurry along the sidewalk in the same direction the Caprice was facing. Maybe both men would just sit tight in the car, but probably one of them would follow him. In the meantime, in the alley behind their apartment, Cuffs and the bishop would be headed in the other direction.

Dugan had insisted on wearing his tan trench coat. "Maybe they'll think I'm out on a flashing expedition."

"Don't let on that you know they're watching," Kirsten had said. "And if they stop you, please, don't mouth off. Okay?"

"Would I do—"

"Yes." She'd closed the door pretty abruptly.

Now, with both men gone, she grabbed her jacket and the cell phone, and went up the back stairway one flight. Ownership of the top-floor apartment gave them the right to build a deck on the flat roof, but so far they hadn't gotten around to it. She went to a corner at the front of the building and, crouching in the dark, raised her head above the low parapet wall and looked down on the street. The Caprice hadn't moved, but now the driver was alone.

Ten minutes later Dugan came strolling back along the sidewalk with a newspaper under his arm, and a man in a White Sox cap trailing twenty yards behind. Dugan disappeared from view as he got close to the building's entrance, and the man in the Sox cap walked on past and got into the Caprice. She waited, giving Dugan time to get up to their apartment and turn off the lights. When he joined her on the roof, he was still wearing the trench coat, and he had a plastic insulated mug in each hand.

"Coffee?" he said, holding out one of the mugs.

"Not yet." She stuffed the cell phone in his coat pocket. "That's your two friends, right?"

"Yep."

"Hold on to the coffee for me." She started across the roof toward the stairs.

"Where you going?"

"Just watch." She pointed back toward the front of the building. "There won't be a problem," she said, "but if there is, call nine-one-one."

She went all the way downstairs and out into the alley. Her indirect approach had been *too* indirect. She'd gone to an awful lot of trouble to plant a falling bird in Walter Keegan's cottage, only to have the hit man pretty much blow away her chances for a reaction from Walter that would tie him to the bishop's stalker. In fact, if she hadn't been in the way, the man would have waited in the dark, Walter would be dead, and that might have solved the problem once and for all. On the other hand, the man might still have been there when the bishop showed up, and he'd have killed the bishop, too.

At the end of the alley she turned right and walked toward the street in front of their apartment. The truth was—like it or not—she hadn't wanted to confront Walter Keegan directly, not unless she was very certain she had to. That feeling hadn't gone away, but how she dealt with it was about to change.

When she got to the corner the Caprice was still there, facing away from her, down the block to her right. There was, as usual, lots of traffic on their street. Drivers headed for nearby night spots were scouting out parking spaces, and taxis were cruising for fares. She waited near the corner until she spotted a cab with no passengers approaching on her side of the street. She started walking toward the Caprice, keeping an eye over her shoulder on the cab. She had one of her Wild Onion business cards in her hand.

As the cab drew close to the rear of the parked Caprice, she stepped out into the street, waving the card. "Taxi! Taxi!" The cab stopped with a sharp squeal of its tires, and she opened the rear door. "Hold it a minute," she said.

Cars were already piling up behind the taxi and, when she left the door open and didn't get in, horns started blaring instantly. She stepped quickly along the street side of the Caprice

164

until she was just ahead of the driver's door and then, keeping her face turned away from the driver, jammed the business card down under his windshield wiper.

The cab beside her was easing forward and the cabbie was hollering, "Hey! Close fuggeen door or get een cab!"

So she got in and they drove off quickly, followed by a string of cars. She didn't turn to look, but doubted the men in the Caprice would bother following. Even if they did, they'd want to retrieve the card first. Or she hoped they would, anyway. And if they'd been sent by Walter Keegan, they'd realize the message on the back of the card was for him, even though his name wasn't on it. All it said was: *Yellow Bird Falls. Don't Miss It. Call Me.*

Like it or not, it was time for a more direct approach.

Cuffs walked the bishop all the way down to his mother's room, but waited out in the hallway. Even though it was late, she was sitting up in a chair by the window. He didn't bother to switch on the light, but her head moved and he could tell she heard him. "Hi," he said.

"Hello," she answered, and there wasn't the slightest hint of recognition in her voice.

"It's me," he said. "Peter." He kissed her lightly on the forehead, then sat on the edge of her bed. "How are you feeling?"

"I'm not going," she said. "I just don't enjoy that anymore."

He'd long ago given up asking her to explain anything. "I can't stay long," he said. "Do you want to pray with me?"

"No." The answer was firm, but it didn't mean she understood what he was asking.

"Our Father . . ." he began.

She stared at him.

"Say it after me, Mom. Our Father . . ."

"The frosting's on the pumpkin," she said. "The fodder's in the shack."

He'd long ago given up crying over her, too. She just was

the way she was. "Who art in heaven," he said. Maybe some tiny part of her knew, at least, that there was someone paying attention to her. And maybe not. "Hallowed be thy name . . ."

She stared down at the white blanket that lay across her knees, occasionally picking at it, while he continued the prayer.

". . . and deliver us from evil."

"From evil," she said, not looking up. "That Walter's a mean one. You be careful, Peter."

"Mom?" He leaned closer to her. "What—"

"And not only poor Walter, y'know." She lifted her head and looked out the window, as though seeing something in the darkness outside. "Deliver us from evil, there's so many mean ones out there." Her head sank again, her chin nearly touching her chest.

He sat in silence, not wanting anything he said to pull her mind somewhere else. Moments passed, though, and he finally said, "Mom?" She didn't move, and he was suddenly afraid. He knew her heart was so weak she might slip away at any time. He knew it, but he wasn't ready for that. Not now, not yet. "Mom?" he begged. "Please?"

She raised her head and looked right at him. "No thank you," she said, smiling the same gentle smile he'd known all his life. "I just don't enjoy playing bingo anymore."

He stood up and held out his hands, palms down, above her head. "May almighty God bless you . . ." As he whispered the words of blessing, he traced a cross in the air over her. ". . . forever and ever. Amen."

She was asleep, breathing in and out in a soft snore, by the time he kissed her on the forehead. He wondered what dreams would visit her, whether Walter would be a part of them. And who else? *And not only poor Walter, y'know.* He stared past her, out the window. *Deliver us from evil, there's so many mean ones out there.*

He turned and went to rejoin Cuffs Radovich, a man more

than familiar with the "mean ones out there," perhaps one of them himself. It struck the bishop, suddenly, how having such a man on his side was at once both disturbing . . . and comforting.

THIRTY-SIX

Kirsten had gone only a few blocks in the cab with the "fuggeen door" and then walked back home. When she got there Dugan had wanted to talk. Now it was Saturday morning though, and she couldn't recall anything beyond dropping into the chair by the living room window and telling him to talk fast or . . . or something.

She hauled herself out of bed and by eight-thirty she was struggling with a cheese and chopped pepper omelet, and was delighted when Dugan came into the kitchen just in time to see her finally fold it over successfully.

"Good work," he said, "although this will make two fat-laden breakfasts in two days."

"I know, but it helps me think."

He poured coffee, laid plates and utensils on the table, and put bread in the toaster. "I carried you to the bedroom last night."

"Really." She slid half an omelet onto each plate.

"Yep. And if we keep this up I'll never be able to do it again."

"Let's worry about that after breakfast." They savored a few bites in silence, then Kirsten decided to get started. "Now we know," she said, "why Bishop Keegan can't tell all."

"Or *won't*, anyway."

"Right, and it's his call, not ours. But if he won't reveal his secret and eliminate the hold Walter has over him, that leaves the question we never got back to last night. What does he have that Walter wants?"

"Or *someone* wants, anyway."

"It's Walter," she said. "Maybe along with someone else, or on behalf of someone else. But what does the bishop have that they want?"

"And," Dugan waved his fork for emphasis, "who hired someone to kill Walter?"

"That question just gets us sidetracked."

"A hell of a sidetrack, though. Especially since the guy almost killed you."

"Coincidence. No one knew I was there."

"Someone knows now."

"But not Walter. And all the man I ran into knows is what I told him—that I'm the cleaning lady."

"There's no way he believed you. Any hit man who sees you and actually thinks you're a cleaning—"

"Don't be an elitist."

"What?"

"You're saying that someone who provides domestic services has to look a certain way."

"Put it this way." Dugan added more coffee to each of their mugs. "The hit man is probably an elitist. He didn't believe you. Period."

"As I said, the whole issue gets us sidetracked."

"I agree, but it's still a hell of a side—"

"C'mon, Dugan!" She didn't want him dwelling on the hired killer, even if she couldn't chase the man out of her head, awake or asleep. "What is it the bishop has?"

"Maybe nothing. Maybe someone's just got a grudge against him."

"But the calls say that they *want* something from him."

"Well, maybe it's not a thing. Maybe it's a decision he can

make. Maybe some property owner—one of those big donors, let's say—wants Catholic Charities to buy *his* piece of property, for an orphanage or something, instead of somebody else's."

"See?" Kirsten said. "That's exactly the kind of thinking we need. You're good at this."

"You think I'm right?"

"Not a chance."

"Me, neither," he said.

"But it's still the kind of thinking we need."

"I agree," he said. "Besides, you don't want me thinking about that hired killer . . . or wondering what his policy manual says about witnesses."

Since it was Saturday, the diamond shop was open and Mark Brumstein's receptionist would handle any calls to Wild Onion, Ltd., and contact Kirsten right away. By eleven o'clock, when Dugan left for his office, there'd been no calls from anyone.

At twelve, the phone rang. It was Cuffs. He'd be sticking with the bishop all day. "Some kinda ceremony for schoolkids on the West Side this afternoon," Cuffs said. "A couple hours in church, a reception after, then I take him home again." He paused. "Nobody's called him, threatened him, tried to kill—"

"Whatever it is they want, they don't seem to want him dead," Kirsten said. "Just keep staying close whenever he's out. And hey, have a fun afternoon in church."

"I don't care where he goes," Cuffs said. "Church services . . . cocktail parties . . . to me they're all the same thing."

"Oh?"

"Yeah. People gettin' together with a buncha other people they don't really like so they can all bullshit each other for a while and then go home." He gave a snort that might have been a laugh. "As for Pete, though, I'm gettin' to kinda like—"

"Pete?"

"Yeah. Pete."

"Most people call him Bishop."

"Most people don't know their ass from a stop sign," Cuffs said. "The official title is Your *Excellency*. I asked him and that's what he said. Then I told him I'd be damned if I'd call him that."

"I'll stay with Bishop. He seems satisfied."

"That's your business. To me he's Pete, and whether he's satisfied or not is his own goddamn problem."

"Call me if there's any news." She hung up, then recalled Cuffs starting to say he was "gettin' to kinda like" the bishop. Extraordinary. She almost called back to follow up on that, but figured he'd deny he said it in the first place.

She did make a call, though, and was happy to hear a woman answer. "Johanna Gage, please," Kirsten said.

"This is Johanna."

Kirsten identified herself. "My husband and I met you last night, remember? At the cocktail party?"

"I remember you. I . . . well, I suppose you're aware that . . ."

"That Dugan had already met you? Oh yes, he told me," Kirsten said. "I must say, you did a nice job of keeping that to yourself."

"Thanks. Bishop Keegan acted as if he'd never met you before, and it seemed best to follow his lead." She paused. "Well, did you . . . um . . . enjoy the party?"

"Yes." Kirsten decided to get to the point. "I'd like to talk. Can we get together?"

"Well, I . . . I suppose so. Maybe sometime next—"

"Why not lunch?" Kirsten said. "Somewhere near your place? I could meet you in an hour."

THIRTY-SEVEN

Kirsten was good at catching people off-guard and convincing them they wanted to do something they didn't know they wanted to do. Of course, she got lots of practice. Usually on Dugan.

She let Johanna pick the restaurant. It was just west of Michigan Avenue, near Bloomingdale's. There were thousands of shoppers spending their Saturday wandering the Magnificent Mile, and about half of them—apparently blind to the outrageous prices—had chosen the same spot, and were there ahead of Kirsten. Johanna, though, had somehow managed a booth in a back corner, where Kirsten found her waiting, along with a glass of Pinot Grigio for each of them.

They told each other what nice outfits they had on, agreed to be on a first-name basis, and ordered.

"I went ahead and ordered the wine. I hope you like it," Johanna said. "By the way, lunch is on me. My husband and I live nearby, and he comes here quite often when he's in town. I join him occasionally, but he always has clients along, to talk business. Everything's business with Gerard. He . . . anyway, we run a monthly tab and they'll just add this on."

"Thank you." Kirsten had intended to pick up the check, but Johanna's comment did give her a conversational opening.

"And what does your husband do? From last night's conversation, I take it he lived in South Africa for a while?"

"Yes, we both lived there for years."

"And do you go back often? Last night he seemed very knowledgeable about—"

"Darling Gerard loves an audience. He's such a . . ." She didn't finish, and Kirsten was certain it wasn't a term of endearment she left out. "Well, then we lived for a time in Australia."

"My, sounds like you're with the State Department or something."

"Oh, no. Gerard's involved in . . . international trade. Various things."

"Fascinating. Like what things?"

"Oh, in South Africa it was . . . I guess paper, mostly." She drank some of her wine. "And in Australia . . . um . . . gold, and paper there, too . . . whatever."

"Oh." Johanna didn't seem to have much of a handle on her husband's business, but Kirsten wanted to get closer to home, anyway, and to find out what help she might be. "And you? she asked. "How long have you been with the archdiocese?"

"Well . . . I'm not really *with* the archdiocese, at all. That is, I'm not an employee."

"You're not?" Kirsten stopped her jaw before it fell too far open. "Aren't you . . . I mean, my husband . . ."

"Yes, I know, and I suppose it was unfair of me not to correct him."

"So you're *not* the bishop's secretary?"

"Hardly. I volunteer in the office. I'm good at organizing, and I've taken over much of the business-type things . . . what an executive director would do, if they had one. Bishop Keegan is in charge, of course, but we work closely together. There was even talk of hiring me, but I don't want that. My husband's been . . . quite successful. I like my freedom, and— The point is, the archdiocese operates on a tight budget and Bishop Keegan and I share the same secretary, who's on maternity leave just now. When your husband called, the bishop was busy and I took the call."

"You're kidding," Kirsten said, and couldn't keep herself from smiling. "I don't believe this." The waiter appeared with their lunches, both salads. He poured a second glass of wine for Johanna. "Just wait till I tell Dugan."

Johanna frowned. "I'm sorry," she said, between sips of wine. "I really should have corrected his mistake."

"Are you kidding? This is great. We were just talking about jumping to conclusions about people, based on—"

"Excuse me," Johanna said. "I'm a bit pressed for time and you wanted to discuss something. You said it had to do with Bishop Keegan."

"Oh. Sorry." Kirsten set her fork on her plate and tried the wine. "Mmmm, very good," she said, noticing that Johanna was well into her second glass. "Dugan said you had an interesting conversation."

"I suppose so. I did tell Bishop Keegan about it. He said it was fine to talk to either of you. But he didn't say about what. He's not always very . . . communicative. But he's a sweet man."

"You think he's in the wrong job, though, right? Dugan told me that."

"Well, I . . . it's not that he doesn't do well at it. I think he could do just about anything he put his mind to. I mean only that it's obvious to anyone with half a brain that he'd be happier as a teacher." She dabbed her napkin to her lips, then laid it down and looked directly at Kirsten. "I like Bishop Keegan, and I'm worried about him as . . . as a person."

"Do you have any idea what . . . might be bothering him?"

"You know, your husband asked me to think hard about that, and I have." Johanna leaned forward across the table. "Would you like to hear what I've thought of so far?"

"Sure." Johanna seemed the kind of person who liked to figure things out.

"I don't think it's job stress or overwork, not even with this new commission he's in charge of. I know the bishop quite well and I'm convinced he's . . . afraid. I think if it was his health or something like that, he'd have mentioned something. My guess is someone's deliberately frightening him." She sipped her wine. "Am I right?"

"Actually, I'm not at liberty to say." Kirsten took a bite of her salad. "But why do you think that?"

"Otherwise, why hire someone like you? I wondered at first if it had anything to do with Catholic Charities. But I think not. We're a pretty open operation. All the major issues are discussed among staff. And frankly, the big decisions are all made by the cardinal."

"You really *have* been thinking," Kirsten said, to encourage her to go on.

"So I keep asking, why would anyone want to frighten him?" Johanna furrowed her brow. "I can't imagine him ever having harmed anyone. So I was thinking maybe someone is trying to scare him into giving them something. But he has no money or property that I know of, not even a car, and my guess is he gives away most of the little bit of salary he gets." The waiter poured her another glass of wine and Johanna smiled up at him, then sat back and frowned at Kirsten, looking rather sheepish. "So . . . I haven't gotten very far. But do you think I'm on the right track?" When Kirsten said nothing, Johanna added, "I'd really like to help."

"That's what I wanted to find out." Kirsten smiled. "If you think of anything, anything at all that you think might be helpful . . ."

"Oh, I'll call. But it would help to know if I'm even thinking in the right direction, or . . ." Again Kirsten didn't respond, and Johanna frowned. "I understand you can't talk about it, but you *will* let me know if I can help, won't you?"

"Of course."

"Thank you." Johanna picked up her fork, then suddenly checked her watch. "Oh my! You stay and finish your lunch. But I have to run. Darling Gerard will be into one of his classic snits."

Johanna hadn't even touched her salad, but she obviously wanted to go. Kirsten finished her wine and they walked out together. She had a few ideas that she wanted to pursue before dinner. She and Dugan wouldn't have the whole afternoon together, as they'd planned.

Lucky for her, Darling Dugan wouldn't know a "classic snit" if it tripped him on the street.

THIRTY-EIGHT

I f the call had come on the private line in the bishop's room, he'd have missed it. Confirmation was at 3:00, and he was headed out the door, with Cuffs waiting out front to take him to St. Agatha's.

He ran back to take the call. "This is Bishop Keegan," he said.

"Yeah." The voice was hoarse, but recognizable. "It's your favorite brother."

"Walter? Is that you?"

"You got some other brother I don't know about? Who do you think it is?"

"I . . . I'm sorry, I . . ." Walter's aggression still made him nervous, after all these years. No, not just nervous, but frightened. "How are you, Walter?"

"Maybe you been praying for me," Walter said, his sarcasm undisguised, "because I'm gonna survive."

"Um . . . I'm on my way out. Maybe—"

"Yeah, right. Very important guy," Walter said. "I wanna see you. How about tonight?"

"No, I . . . I'll be tied up until late." He needed time to think, talk to Kirsten.

"Well, tomorrow then. Seven o'clock. You free then? Or do I have to call the pope or someone?"

"No, no. Tomorrow's Sunday. That's fine. What hospital are you in?"

"I'll probably be outta here by then. But I'll call again and leave word. By the way," he paused, "bring your new lady friend along if you like."

"Lady friend? I don't—"

"Thought you were in a hurry," Walter said, and hung up on him.

Kirsten left Johanna on Michigan Avenue and took a cab downtown to Dugan's office. She had her own key and was letting herself into the suite just as Larry Candle was coming out.

"Leaving already, Larry? It's barely three-thirty."

"Hey, it's Saturday P.M., y'know? Nobody wants to talk business. Besides, I gotta go pick up my daughter. It's my visitation weekend and we're going shopping for stuff for Indian Princess. That's in two weeks."

"Good." She had no idea what he was talking about. "Have a nice time."

"You know what Indian Princess is, right? It's this program where groups of fathers and daughters go on campouts over the weekend. Great opportunity to get to know each other in a different environment than usual, y'know? We're really looking forward to it. At least I—"

"Larry."

"Yeah?"

"You're standing right in the doorway."

"Oh. Sorry." He stepped aside to let her in, but kept on talking. "You should meet my daughter, though, she's—" Just then Dugan came into the reception area and Larry stared at him as if he'd had a sudden inspiration. "Hey, Doogie pal, you guys oughta have a kid, y'know? You both got a lotta class. You'd be a great father. You and me could take our daughters to Indian Princess together and—"

"You're gonna be late, Larry," Kirsten said. "Good-bye."

"Oh, yeah. 'Bye."

He was finally gone, and she followed Dugan back toward his office. "Does he still call you that?" she asked.

"What? Oh, you mean *Doogie?*" Dugan glanced back at her over his shoulder. "Yeah, I guess he does. I don't really notice it anymore."

"How could you possibly . . ." But she dropped it. "Anyway, I need to use a phone, and maybe spend time on the Internet. You're not ready to go yet, are you?"

"Nope." He stopped and pointed to his right. "Try Fred's office, although his computer's probably never been used before."

She was just logging off, at about five o'clock, when Dugan appeared in the doorway. "Ready to go?" he asked.

"Yep." She grabbed her jacket and they left the suite. "I called Johanna Gage and we had lunch." They stepped into the elevator. "She wants to help."

"Does she know anything about what the hell's going on?"

"She thinks someone's trying to scare the bishop into something, and was more interested in bugging me about whether she was right than anything else. A couple of things she said were interesting, though, and I've been trying to follow up on them."

"Get very far?"

"Nope. I did get hold of the bishop for a minute and he verified what she said about her work at Catholic Charities. I'll tell you about that later." She'd wait for just the right time to tell him how wrong he'd been. "I also called that investigator you're supposed to be giving work to, Clayton Warfield."

"Guy with the broken finger."

"I'm sending him on a field trip. And I have some travel in mind for you, too."

"Really?" The elevator stopped and they stepped out. "Where to?"

"Let's talk about it later," Kirsten said. "As Larry Candle says, 'It's Saturday P.M., y'know? Nobody wants to talk business.'" She nodded and waved to the security guard. "Including me," she added.

"Me, too. Let's head for some place cheap but romantic for an early dinner. After that, if you've reminded me to go easy on the cheap wine, we could go home and fool around a little."

"Great plan," she said. "Larry's right. You got a lotta class, *Doogie pal*."

THIRTY-NINE

S aturday night Charles Banning stayed home, hoping to hear from the man from Miami, but by midnight there'd been no call. He started paging through the directory for a number he was surprised he didn't know by heart. That's when the phone rang.

He let it ring three times and then, more from a habit of deceit than anything else, he feigned grogginess when he answered. "Hullo?"

"We need to meet." The voice was weak, but it was Walter Keegan.

"I agree," he said. "My office, Monday. That is, if you're out of the hospital."

"I'm not. Someone will bring you here."

"I told you from the start, all meetings are when and where I—"

"Not this one. You're coming here . . . partner. Go look out on the street."

"What are you talking about?" But he was already leaning forward, looking out the window.

"You see a light-colored sedan? Right in front of your place?"

"There's one pulling up now." He felt his pulse rate rise. "Yes, it's stopping."

"Be down there in five minutes, partner. We need to—"

"Hold it right there." Another round had just begun, and he had to attack or get knocked on his ass. "My name is Charles Banning. I'm speaking with Walter Keegan of the Chicago Police Department." He kept his voice clear and level, as though speaking into a recorder. "We disagree about when and where to meet. As a compromise, I agree to meet at your suggested location, but at my—"

"What the hell are you—"

"Shut up, Keegan." He was pumped. "I'll meet you at five in the afternoon, tomorrow. Where are you?"

"My people will pick you up right there at one o'clock, you sonovabitch, no later."

"Thank you. And . . . if that car is still out there ninety seconds from now, I'm calling nine-one-one."

"Cocksucker," was all Keegan said, and then hung up.

He checked his watch and went back to the window. At seventy-five seconds, the sedan drove away.

More than pumped now, he was charged. Who needed coke? But then again, why not?

Ten minutes later he was humming with an internal current that pulsed so fiercely he wondered why he couldn't hear the buzz. Even the phone number he'd forgotten suddenly flashed into his mind, and he tapped it out.

"Discreet Consultations," the woman purred. "How may we be of service?"

"It's Chuckie. I want my mommy." He recited his code number. "I need to talk to my mommy. Hurry up."

"Of course, darling. I'll get her."

There was a click, then a new voice. "Yoo-hoo, Chuckie?" Pretending she was calling out. "You'll have to wait, honey. Mommy's in the tub."

Ah, one of his favorites.

Already standing, he switched the phone to his left hand. "Please, Mommy. I can't wait." Whining. Holding on to himself. Bouncing on one foot, then the other. "I have to go, real bad."

"Well . . . okay. You can come in. But remember, Chuckie darling, noooooo peeking."

FORTY

S he'd love to make the trip herself, Kirsten had assured him the previous night, but she had to go with the bishop to meet Walter on Sunday evening. Both travel agents she spoke with told her that on such short notice, and having to change planes and all, you just couldn't get way up there and back in one day. Be lucky to do it in two.

She said she had a strong feeling time was getting short, so she'd called a friend who had a friend who had a pilot's license.

Now, Sunday morning, the weather looked good and Dugan was trying to convince himself that a flight in a small, private plane wasn't such a bad idea. Exciting, actually—especially on someone else's nickel. He got to tiny Palwaukee Airport, about thirty miles due north of O'Hare—where the *real* planes fly out of, he kept thinking—just before dawn. The pilot was a solid-looking guy named Bob with a square face and close-cropped graying hair—and even a leather bomber jacket, for God's sake.

Bob was all business and exuded self-assurance, and they were up in the air in fifteen minutes. The plane was a four-seater, but there were just the two of them. Bob obviously thought it important to explain why they were taking the route they were, so he droned on about wind velocity, cloud cover, altitudes, temperatures, and other information Dugan missed because he was busy looking out the window. He did hear, though, that they would touch down in Green Bay to drop off a package and then pass over Sault Sainte Marie and bear east to North Bay.

"A touchdown in Green Bay," Dugan said. "Not easy for a guy from Chicago."

"Shouldn't be any prob—" Bob stopped. "Oh, a joke, right?"

From then on, there wasn't much conversation to distract him from his sight-seeing. He felt more like a kid than he would have admitted. They made their stop and took on some fuel or whatever, and the weather was perfect, bright and clear—until right at the end. About a half hour out of North Bay they hit clouds, then wind. When the rain came and started freezing up on the windows, the muscles around his heart froze up with it. Out of the corner of his eye he studied Bob, but couldn't find a trace of concern. That helped, a little.

The landing was pretty good, considering how hard the wind was blowing and how close the ground was before he could actually see it. Then they slid sideways on the slick runway for what seemed like about two miles before they got straightened out. Bob seemed to enjoy the experience, though. "Makes all that training time seem worthwhile. But hey, skies are clearing over there," he continued, pointing to their right, where Dugan saw nothing but more clouds. "By this afternoon we should have smooth sailing. Trip home will take longer, but you'll love night flying."

He'd called the City of North Bay Police Department from Green Bay, and Inspector Bill Joplin was friendly as hell, explaining more about procedure and the Canadian Freedom of Information Act than he wanted to know, and then told him that for an incident outside the city of North Bay he'd have to contact the OPP, the Ontario Provincial Police.

So he made that call and the OPP seemed eager to help, too, but said he'd have to wait until Monday to pick up police records. He'd expected that, and had arranged with Bob to stay over and return the next day if absolutely necessary. But he put some pressure on and finally got through to a Corporal Wise, who sounded more British than Canadian. Corporal Wise relented and said he'd direct "my chap on duty" to take care of him—if he complied with all the requirements and if there *were* any records.

He rented a car at the airport and drove to the west edge of town, where the North Bay Detachment of the OPP worked out of a red brick building. When he said he was there for records, the desk sergeant told him to come back tomorrow. But he invoked the name of Corporal Wise and, after a sad shake of the sergeant's head, got sent down a hall to a small, windowless room.

Kirsten had left it to him and he decided on an approach that was straightforward—or at least partially straightforward— so he stepped up to the chest-high wooden counter and described the incident in question as a bar fight and identified himself as representing one of those arrested. "I'm his attorney," he said, handing his card to Corporal Wise's "chap on duty," who turned out to be a round-faced, pink-cheeked young woman named Inspector Dockery. "Or is it solicitor here in Canada?" he asked.

The inspector smiled at him across the counter. "Either one is fine, sir," she said. "We watch your TV shows, you know. So we're familiar with the language."

He decided she wasn't kidding him at all, just being nice. "Anyway, I'd like the police reports," he said. "It was at a place called Yellow Bird Falls."

"I'm very sorry, sir, but I'm not supposed to give out records on the weekend."

"But Corporal Wise said he'd get someone to help me today."

"Well . . ." She looked around the room, as though she

wanted to help, but just couldn't. "I'm sure Corporal Wise told you that, but he's a bit . . . well, absent-minded sometimes, and he didn't mention it to me. If you'd come back tomorrow, I—"

"Excuse me." He leaned forward and lowered his voice, even though no one else was in the room. "You see, my client has made a proposal of marriage," he said, "to a . . . well, a *very* wealthy woman." He'd dreamed up a number of different scripts for the *modified* part of his straightforwardism, and decided on this one after he saw Inspector Dockery. "The woman's family is quite protective of her, and we just found out they hired a very expensive private detective agency to do a background check of him."

"Really?" She seemed at least slightly intrigued by his far-fetched tale, so maybe her TV watching included soap opera.

"Oh yes. You see, although my client was arrested after the fight, the charges were eventually dropped. But his recollection of the event is, at best, a bit cloudy. He thinks he may have been charged with . . . well, with frequenting a house of prostitution. You can see how—"

"Bawdy house," she said. "A common bawdy house."

"What?"

"That's what we call them here . . . bawdy houses."

"Oh. Anyway, we don't want to be surprised by what some private investigator might turn up, so . . . I really need to see those police reports. And every minute counts."

"I understand," she said, "but—"

"This detective agency they've hired is famous for being thorough, so my client, Mr. Peter Keegan, has to assume they'll find out about his arrest. He has to decide, immediately, whether to bring the matter to his fiancée's attention himself— defuse the bomb, you understand—and how best to do that, if necessary."

"Peter Keegan," the clerk said, as though concentrating on the sound of the name. "I'm afraid you need signed authorization from Mr. Keegan. Also, we're only required to keep records seven years, so how would you know they haven't been destroyed?"

"I wouldn't," he said. "But I do have an authorization." He showed her the letter they'd stopped by the rectory to pick up, signed by Peter Keegan with no mention of the *bishop* part. "And here's his driver's license with his signature and his picture on it, and my driver's license with my picture, and my attorney registration card, all of which you can copy for your records." He laid everything out of the counter, then paused for breath. "So, the file?"

"I'll . . . okay, I'll see what I can do." She seemed suddenly nervous—even guilty, maybe—which he didn't understand, and didn't like at all.

He sat down to wait, but in a surprisingly short time she was back with a thin manila folder. "This is the only part of the file which relates to your client."

The folder held a single typed page. The police had responded to a complaint of: *Drunks fighting, Yellow Bird Falls Saloon.* Lots of people were arrested, because this page related to: *Arrestee No. 11: Peter Keegan.* Under charges, it said: *1. Attendance/Common Bawdy House:* and below that: *2. Poss. Addl. Chgs., see below.* There was a space for a narrative report, which was blank except that in the center someone had stamped: *CLOSED: N.F.A.R.* The signature at the bottom of the page was: *S/I Robt. Crenshaw*

"Those letters mean no further action required," she explained, but she had no idea who Robert Crenshaw was, other than that he'd obviously been the supervising inspector. She checked a roster book behind the counter and there was no one by that name listed any longer. She photocopied the report.

He took the copy, paid the five-dollar fee, and then—as though he'd just thought of something—he pointed to the upper right corner of the page. "Look," he said. "Here, where it says page one of four pages. You don't know what happened to the other three pages, do you?"

"Oh, I never noticed that," she said, obviously quite surprised. "I know there was just the one page when—I mean . . ." She didn't finish.

"And," he asked, "how long ago was that?"

"Was what?"

"When the other man—I suppose it was a man, right?—when he came in and asked for this report."

"Oh," she said. "I . . ." She sighed. "Maybe three, four weeks ago."

"And did he have a written authorization?"

"Yes . . . well, he showed something to me. And we're required to keep them for our records. But we got to chatting. I remember he was very talkative. And after he left . . . somehow I couldn't find the authorization."

"Not to worry," he said. "But now we can assume the woman's family has the report. So my client will have to break the news right away, before they do. You're sure the other three pages weren't there."

"Oh yes, sir." She lowered her eyes, then looked up again. "I suppose," she added, "you'll be reporting me."

"Reporting? Oh, you mean for giving out my client's report, and not belong able to prove you had authorization? Why would I do that, when you've been so nice?"

She smiled. "Thank you."

Oh," he said, "one more thing. That bar. Is it still there?"

"Seems to me there *is* a little tavern out that way. But it has a different name, and I can't think . . ." She cocked her head and squinted her eyes, trying to remember. "It's like . . . P. J.'s or something."

Actually, it was P. K. and Bobby's, and the only customer in the place was out cold, his head resting facedown on a table in the booth closest to the door.

The bartender was a huge man whose shoulder-length gray hair could have used a shampoo, but he was pleasant enough and seemed happy to have someone conscious to talk to. He didn't have a clue who P. K. was. "But the Bobby part," he said, "that there's Bobby Crenshaw, what bought the place when old Harrington couldn't make a go of it. Bobby came inna some money—inheritance or somethin'—quit the OPP, and bought this here saloon. Spruced it up a bit and give it a new name. Kept me on, he did."

"So you were the bartender before he bought it?"

"Hell, yes. I about grew up here. I was a big ol' sumbitch, only seventeen and still in the ninth grade—or maybe it was the eighth—when Harrington hired me to keep the peace around here. Spent a lifetime, good days and bad, in this old shack."

"How about the days when it was a topless bar?"

"Hell, you heard about that? Bottomless, too, some of the dancers. Didn't last more'n about eight, ten months. Those was pretty good days. I thought it was great, especially at first. All them tits and ass and all hangin' out all over. I was goggly-eyed for weeks. But then I got kinda used to it, y'know, every day like that. So when they made Harrington cut that shit out—Bobby bein' a copper an' all, he was a part of that—it didn't really bother me none." He ran the rag over the bar. "Course, these days, I wish I'd of had a camera back then, kinda help me relive old times."

"And Harrington sold to Crenshaw after that?"

"Yeah. Lotta folks didn't like it much when Harrington hired them there young girls to parade around bare-assed. But hell, wasn't no other jobs for 'em. They could all use the money, and I think a awful lot of 'em got a kick outta showin' off their stuff, too. Hardest part was keepin' out them underage girls."

"Really?"

"Hell, yes. They'd lie about their age to get the job. Fact, what finally shut the whole thing down was when they caught

one of them underage girls for sure. Bunch of them fuckin'
Indians and all got into a fight and the coppers came and arrested everyone but me, and this here waitress turns out too
young and Bobby says she said a customer gave her money for
a blow job or something. I didn't see nothing like that, but I'
spose it coulda been. Anyway, that gave folks the excuse they
was lookin' for. Town council talkin' about shuttin' us down,
and other folks talkin' about hellfire and burnin' up the place
and all. Harrington pissin' and moanin' how he couldn't make
a go of it without the naked girls. 'Course, his biggest problem
was he was a drunk. Then, like I say, Bobby come inna some
money all the sudden—didn't take that much is my guess—
and bought out ol' Harrington."

"Bobby around today?"

"Hell, no. Time went on, Bobby got to be a drinker hisself.
That's what did him in. Goin' on three, four weeks, now. Got
stinkin' drunk and went out wanderin' in the woods in the
middle of the night in a storm and fell off the bluff into the
river. Busted his head open on them rocks and then drowned
on top of it. This here place is mine, now. He left a will and
all. Good thing for me I was in hospital gettin' my appendix
took out when he done it. Otherwise people mighta thought I
got him drunk and—"

"What about the girl?"

"Huh?"

"You know, the underage girl?"

"Oh, Cassie? Backwoods girl, that one. Tiny little thing.
Shy, kinda cute. Had a touch o' Indian blood in her, they say,
which I say is why she got a little thick around the ass after
while. But she always had a real nice pair of—"

"What I mean is, where is she now?"

"Hell, nobody knows. She took to drinkin' hard, too. Used
to come and go, and finally took up with Bobby hisself. Ol'
Bobby, he come to love that girl. They was real close. I know
he was thinkin' of changing his will, but he never got to it.

Then, about the time he drowned hisself, she just up and dis-appeared. The cash what was in Bobby's hidin' place under the floor here disappeared, too. I never told no one. Guess she was entitled. I'm thinkin' Cassie'll show up again one day. Not till the money runs out, though."

Dugan finished his beer and laid a twenty on the bar and left. He was thinking Cassie wouldn't show up again one day at all. Not ever.

FORTY-ONE

They picked him up Sunday afternoon and took him to the hospital. The room was on the top floor and Banning thought it looked more like a hotel suite than a hospital room.

Walter Keegan was fully dressed—a tall, muscular man in a custom-made suit—even though he looked weak as hell. The two sat down in easy chairs across from each other. Banning began by congratulating him on surviving the attack, looking for any hint that Keegan suspected him of sending the hit man. But all Keegan would say was that he wasn't hurt so bad, and he was ready to push his brother harder now, looking forward to his cut of the deal.

"Good," he said. "Your share here is a lot of money. Even these days, even after you pay the taxes."

"Taxes?" Keegan first seemed amused by the very idea, then just as quickly turned mean. "Just forget the fucking superiority bullshit with me, okay?" He crossed one leg over the other and fingered the sharp crease in his pants leg. "I don't need that. Not from a guy got his hands in the same stinking pile of garbage as me."

Banning smiled. He hated this creep who dressed like some

debonair TV super-cop and thought like a street punk. Why do guys like him—

"What're you shaking your head about?"

"Just thinking." He hadn't realized he was shaking his head. "Most people expect men like your brother—priests and the like—to be different. Not interested in things like money. But I know better. Everyone's the same. Everything's a struggle." He was just making talk now. Actually, it was the courage to engage in the struggle that set men like himself apart from—

"Hey!" Keegan startled him again. "You wanna sit around and space out every two minutes, do it on your own time."

"I'm looking at the big picture," he said. "It concerns me. Your strategy isn't working."

"That's fucking bullshit. I told you, Peter's always been easy to scare. Christ, when we were kids he was afraid of our old man, a two-bit piece of chicken shit on his best days. Then he goes off to the seminary and gets himself fucked up even worse. Scared of the fucking pope now, I guess, and the cardinal and all of 'em. Scared of everybody. 'What'll people think?' That's one of his goddamn theme—"

"I didn't ask for his life story. I said it's taking you too damn long."

"Well, too fucking bad, Mr. Big Picture." Keegan stuck a huge, unlit cigar in the corner of his mouth. "I'm the one's got what's gonna do the trick, and I know how to use it. I've moved into phase two, so don't get antsy. Christ, you—"

"You said that before, said he'd cave in right away, and I agreed on a bigger share for you. That was Wednesday night. Now it's fucking Monday and here we are, still in some so-called phase two." He paused, then added in a lower tone, "I want this over with, you understand? Soon."

"Listen up, Charlie boy." Keegan thrust his face forward, and the cigar bobbed up and down as he spoke. "You gotta learn to stop talking to me like I'm some kind of fucking employee. We're *partners,* you and me."

"Then I want the rest of that report, partner. I can speed things up."

"What you can do is *fuck* things up."

"I won't do anything without checking with you. I just want a copy of the hooker's statement, that's all."

Keegan shook his head. "How stupid you think I am? You got page one, and that's all you're gonna get. I told you that Wednesday." Keegan paused. "And the next fucking day, guess what? Someone tries to gun me down."

This is what Banning had been expecting, and he was ready with outrage. "That's why you called me, then. Jesus, you actually think . . ." He stood up and stared hard into Keegan's eyes. "Look. You want your share, you get the job done. Meanwhile," keeping his voice low and steady, "I'll show myself out."

The cigar in his hand now, Keegan grinned like a wolf and shrugged his shoulders. Banning turned and walked slowly out of the room.

He took a cab home. He'd learned two things. First, Keegan knew nothing, and couldn't afford to act on mere suspicion. Second, he was as determined as ever not to turn over the police report. Banning had gone up after the original himself. He'd been furious when it wasn't there, and almost stirred up new problems for himself. But he'd handled it.

And he'd handle Keegan, too.

FORTY-TWO

At 6:30 Sunday evening, Kirsten picked up the bishop and drove to Area One headquarters. That Walter was already out of the hospital surprised her, but his choice of a meeting place didn't. At Fifty-first and Wentworth Avenue, Area One was just over five miles south of the Loop, in the heart of the South Side ghetto. Far from prying eyes, and at the same time easy to get to—right alongside the Dan Ryan Expressway. And, of course, a police station was Walter's turf.

The moment she turned into the drive off Fifty-first Street, an unmarked squad car appeared directly in front of them, leading them into the crowded parking lot, and a similar car pulled in behind them. They drove right on past the main building itself, winding among rows of parked cars, all the way to the south end of the lot, where—in a three-car procession—they passed beneath the wide-open overhead door of another building, nearly as large as the police station itself.

They might have been in the repair shop of a large and bustling automobile dealership, except they were working on a Sunday evening and the vehicles perched up on lifts, or sitting in diagonal rows along the walls with their hoods propped open, were all police vehicles. There were marked and un-marked patrol cars, squadrols, police department tow trucks, even a couple of small blue buses—maybe for hauling prisoners, or for carrying groups of cops to crisis locations.

The air was heavy with the smells of gasoline and grease and engine exhaust, and there were lots of men in dark blue coveralls, coming and going, calling to each other above the din of revving engines and whining power tools. As far as Kirsten could tell, not one of the men paid them any attention or even noticed the three cars passing by.

There wasn't much time to look around, though, as the lead car drove on and turned left into the last of three empty repair bays at the very far end of the building, just short of another open doorway. She stopped and thought for a few seconds, until the bishop said, "I think they want you to pull in beside them."

"Right. And then the car behind us—the one with Walter in the passenger seat—will park in the bay to our left," she said. "Cozy." She glanced back over her shoulder. "But you know how women are. We get a little nervous in auto repair shops."

"Well, I—"

She hit the gas hard and shot straight ahead, then braked and skidded to a stop directly below the open overhead door, half in and half out of the building, at enough of an angle so cars couldn't pass through on either side. "It's a woman thing," she said. "We hate being closed in among so many men." She hit the button that locked all the doors. "Keep your window closed," she said, and then lowered hers about an inch.

The driver from the car behind them appeared and glared down at her. "I guess you think that's some kinda goddamn cute trick, huh?"

"Watch it," she said. "There are clergy present."

"Right," he said, "and you—"

"Tell the acting chief that if he wants to talk he should come and get into the backseat here, alone," she said, "and we'll go for a drive."

"Look here, you—"

"Tell him if he's afraid to be alone with his own brother, he can stick an extra gun in his belt. And you guys can follow along behind." She closed the window.

"Kirsten," the bishop said, "are you sure—"

"I'm not sure of anything," she said. She'd just interrupted the bishop, the same way she'd interrupted the cop, and with the same sharp edge to her voice that she wouldn't ordinarily have used with him. But she had to keep her game face on, even though she felt a trembling in her arms that she hoped wouldn't show when Walter joined them. That is, *if* he—

The rap of a ringed finger on her window made her jump. It was Walter. "Let's go," he said. Despite his hulking size, he looked pale and drawn, not at all healthy.

She unlocked the back door and, once Walter was inside, she drove out the rear gate of the police lot. Determined not to be the first to speak, she drove up Wentworth Avenue, turned onto Fifty-first Street, and headed east—away from the Dan Ryan.

"It's good to see you up and about, Walter," the bishop said, obviously unable to stand the silence. "How are you feeling?"

"Just dandy, brother." He sounded, though, as if he'd just run up a flight of stairs. "Never been better."

Kirsten said nothing. She was busy beating back the strange mix of intimidation and anger that surged inside her at the mere sound of Walter's voice, filled with meanness and cynicism that even his fatigue didn't cover up. She glanced several times in the rearview mirror. There was a car following them.

"They're back there," Walter said. "Be happy. You won't have to drive me back from wherever we're going."

"We're not going far," she said. "Maybe just a drive through the park." She paused. "You wearing a wire or anything?"

"That's ridiculous."

"Then tell me. Yes or no."

"No. Why would I be?"

"I don't know," she said. "And I don't know why you asked for this meeting, either."

"Walter," the bishop said, "why are you doing this? You're having me followed, threatening me. Why?"

"Those are serious charges, Peter," Walter said. "Maybe you oughta call the police." He coughed—or maybe it was a laugh—then added, "You two don't mind if I light up a cigar, do you?"

"No," the bishop said, "I don't—"

"I mind," Kirsten said, "very much."

"Well, then," Walter said, "here's Washington Park. Pull in and stop somewhere. We can talk outside the car and I can smoke my cigar."

She turned right, onto the curving park drive, but didn't stop. "Compromise," she said. "I'll drive slow. You open the window and blow all the smoke outside."

Washington Park was an urban oasis of grass, trees, and playgrounds, a mile long—north to south—and a half mile wide. It wasn't the safest place in the city for a trio of white folks to gather after sundown to chat, but—with two out of the three of them armed, and a carful of cops nearby—that wasn't why Kirsten didn't want to stop. The main thing was, she didn't want Walter out of the car.

"Fair enough," Walter said. He lowered the window and lit his cigar. "See how easy I am to get along with?"

"Aren't you going to tell me why you're doing this, Walter?" the bishop asked. "I thought that was why you wanted to talk to me."

"Why keep accusing me? Maybe I just wanted to have a conversation with my big-shot brother who thinks he's too good for me. Maybe—"

"I don't think I'm too good for you," the bishop said.

"He is, of course," Kirsten said, "but that's not the point. I *know* you're the one behind his being threatened. So skip the denials. What is it you want?"

"Well, well, Petey boy, congratulations. You got yourself a big-mouth woman here." Kirsten heard him draw on the cigar and exhale—the smoke must have gone out the window—before he went on. "I wanna know, Peter, who sent the goon after me," he said. "I wanna know how it happened you showed up just about the same time. And I wanna know why your ex-cop lady friend showed up, too."

"I wanted to see you," the bishop said. "I only—"

"Wait, Bishop." Kirsten pulled to a stop on the side of the road. Walter didn't seem inclined to get out, but still she left the car in drive, with her foot on the brake. She'd warned the bishop not to give out any information, to say as little as possible. She tilted the rearview mirror until she saw Walter's face in it. "I don't know how many ex-cop women your brother knows, but if you're suggesting I showed up at your place, you're crazy." Accurate, yes, but still crazy. "The bishop drove out to see you. When he got there you were unconscious, and bleeding. He didn't see who shot you. He didn't see any other man. Your brother saved your life, Walter. He could have turned around and driven home. He could have let you die, and let the stalking and the threats die *with* you, but he didn't."

"Well, isn't he the good boy, then? Peter was always a good little boy. Took care of his mother. Obeyed his father." Walter's voice was softer now, but more hostile and sarcastic than ever. "My father, too. But the asshole never took the strap to you, did he, Peter? He wouldn't, of course, because your mother woulda called the cops on him, or worse. Too bad your wonderful mother didn't care if the asshole tore *my* skin off."

"But that's not fair," the bishop said. "She's your mother, too. She adopted you. And she tried—"

"Bishop, please," Kirsten said. "Ancient history isn't what's important here." She knew, though, that that wasn't true. The past these two men shared was very important, to both of them. Just as the past her own father shared with Walter was important to her—more important than she wished it were. But she wanted to hear from Walter himself.

"Your mother was never my mother," Walter said, "whatever piece of paper some two-bit judge signed. My mother's dead. I almost died with her, and any decent father would've taken good care of a son who almost died at birth. But not the asshole. No, the asshole decided it was *my* fault, like I killed her on purpose, or something." Walter paused and leaned forward toward the bishop. "I say a prayer every day, Peter. You know that?"

"That's . . . that's good, Walter," the bishop said.

"Yeah. And here's what I say: 'Dear God,' I say, 'don't ever forget the asshole. Just keep holding his skinny butt deep down in hell . . . until I get there.' That's what I say. You like that prayer?"

"No, I—"

"Anyway, like your lady friend says, that's old business." Walter sank down again into the backseat. "I wanna know who sent the goon after me. Was it you?"

"That's crazy," the bishop said. "I had nothing to do with that."

"I didn't think so. But I wanted to hear you say it. Just to be sure. 'Cause, you know, good little boys never lie."

Kirsten saw Walter shift slightly in his seat, and almost simultaneously heard him open the door beside him. But by that time she'd slammed the accelerator to the floor and the car was sliding and squealing onto the asphalt of the park drive. She immediately slowed down again, though, not wanting the cops in the other car to get nervous and interfere.

"What the hell you doing?" Walter obviously didn't want out badly enough to risk a dive onto the pavement, even at just fifteen or twenty miles an hour. Not that he sounded particularly afraid, either. "Stop the car."

"No," Kirsten said. "The meeting's not over just because you got your chance to toss a few one-liners at your brother. There's that other item on the agenda. So let's get to it. Why the threats? What do you want from the bishop?"

"I don't know about any threats, and I don't want anything," he said.

"Not good enough." She knew there was a reason Walter set up this meeting. He was tough and slick, but certainly no genius. Maybe he wasn't certain, now, how to make his demand. "Besides, your brother and I have talked it over," she said, "and he might just give in, to put an end to this." As if giving in ever put an end to blackmail. "So what do you want?"

"I don't want anything," Walter repeated. "But . . . put it this way." He paused. "Suppose somebody—not me, but someone else—wanted something from Peter. Suppose they offered a good price, but Peter—always the obedient son—wouldn't sell. Suppose this someone wanted whatever it was real bad, bad enough to cause the holy one here some serious damage if they didn't get it." He paused again, and she was convinced he was trying to be careful as he spoke. "And let's say I was to accidentally hear about it," he said. "And Peter's my half brother, you know, so I wouldn't want him to have a problem. You follow me?"

"It's not that complicated," she said.

"So I call him up and arrange to meet him and warn him about this problem I heard about, and he brings you along, which is—"

"You said to bring her," the bishop broke in. "You specifically—"

"Which is—like I was gonna say—what I told you to do. And now that I got a chance to see what a hotshot helper you got here who left me her business card, I don't need to be bothered with the whole thing anymore." He tapped her on the shoulder. "So stop the car."

"Not yet," Kirsten said. "There's—"

"I said stop the car, goddammit." Now he *was* anxious to

get out. "Or I wave my hand and you got cops all over you."

"And what do they do," Kirsten said, "since we've committed no crime?"

"What do they do? They drive me away from here, and then they make sure you spend the next twelve to twenty-four hours sittin' around some place looking at your shoes. And if you think that can't be arranged, you—"

"Fine," Kirsten said. He was right, and she stopped the car. "And your brother thanks you for all your help. Good-bye." The unmarked squad car was pulling up beside them.

"Yeah," Walter said. He opened the car door, then leaned forward and laid his hand on the bishop's shoulder. "And if what I accidentally heard is right, I'd say make the sale, little brother. Make the sale. 'Cause otherwise, you know what's gonna happen."

"I *don't* know," the bishop said.

"Oh, I think you know, all right. What's gonna happen is you get dragged down off that high, clean pedestal you been sittin' on, down into the mud with the rest of us pigs." Walter got out of the car and leaned over, his face close to the open rear window. "You two have a nice day," he said, then blew a thick cloud of cigar smoke into the car and walked away.

"For the record," Kirsten said, "it's eight-seventeen P.M. Walter just filled my car with foul-smelling smoke." She reached down to the floor of the car. "And I'm shutting off the tape."

FORTY-THREE

Kristen drove out of the park and took Fifty-fifth Street east. Neither she nor the bishop had said anything by the time she'd turned north on Lake Shore Drive, and she was beginning to think they might get all the way to the rectory in total silence.

She was determined not to start the conversation, not to steer it one way or the other, but finally she couldn't wait. "Tell me," she said, "what you think about all that."

He didn't answer at once. Then he said, "No matter how hard I try, I can never seem to get through to Walter."

Not the sort of response she was looking for. "You know, Bishop," she said, "sometimes you make me so angry I could scream." So much for not steering the conversation.

"What? I don't—"

"Walter Keegan is *not* hard to 'get through' to. Walter Keegan is mean, cruel, and a goddamn liar." She knew she should shut up, but couldn't. "You want to beat yourself up about your own failure not to 'get through' to a man whose hide's so thick a damn hit man's bullet wasn't able to penetrate to a vital organ. It's as if you want to concentrate on yourself—even if it's your own failure—rather than on reality." She glanced over at him, but he was staring straight ahead. "You are a good person, I

204

know that. But not perfect. You have all sorts of faults. Even if you don't lie, you don't always tell the truth. You get scared sometimes, and that makes you act like a child. You try to hide and hope difficult situations will just go away. Then, when they don't, you focus on 'poor you,' instead of getting on with what has to be done."

"Well, I—"

"No, there's more. You love to sit back and have other people do things for you. You have desires and curiosities—like about sex—you don't like to admit to." She hit the brakes and barely avoided slamming into the car in front of her. "You do stupid things and then you . . . well, in other words, you're like the rest of us—like Dugan, and me, and Larry Candle, and even like Walter. Like all of us, dammit."

"I know all that . . . or at least I think I do."

"But I don't *want* to talk about you. What I want to do is figure out how much of what Walter said is true." She shook her head. "So, with all that out of the way, what do you think?"

"I don't believe him when he says he just overheard something."

"I don't either. I can't believe he even expects us to," she said. "But he says someone wants to buy something. What's that about?"

"I really don't know. I don't own anything worth all this."

"There must be something. A valuable book, maybe? An antique gold chalice?" And then she remembered. "Or what about that land your—"

"My God! That's why Walter said 'obedient son.' My mother's . . . did I tell you my mother inherited some land in Wisconsin years ago when her sister died?"

"You told me it's in trust and you're the trustee. Does someone want to buy—" She stopped. "Wait, one thing at a time. First, who knows about that property?"

"I really don't know. It's certainly not a secret. Many of my friends know, I'm sure. I've talked about it often . . . and what to do with it. Some people at the chancery office probably know. My friend Father Bud Burgeson knows, certainly."

"He's the one—he and his twin brother—who went on the trip to North Bay with you?"

"Yes. He knows, and his brother, Kenny. He's a lawyer and I even spoke to him once about possibly donating it to some children's home or something. Let's see . . . the cardinal knows, or at least I'm sure I've mentioned it to him. Larry Candle probably knows, and—"

"Does Walter know? Have you talked about it with him?"

"Yes. Years ago. He got very angry and walked out on me when I showed him the trust, and how it leaves the land entirely to me when our mother dies."

They'd gotten off Lake Shore Drive but were still several blocks from the rectory. She pulled to the curb and stopped. "So there could be . . . what? A dozen people who know about your mother's property?"

"Probably. Three or four years ago I had it appraised and it wasn't worth much. So the appraiser would know. I'd say a dozen is a conservative guess."

"Okay, so tell me more about that property," she said, "and who it was who recently tried to buy it from you."

FORTY-FOUR

There's nothing incriminating on that tape. Maybe he's telling the truth," Dugan said, although that seemed pretty unlikely to him, too. Kirsten dropped the minicassette back into her purse. He'd gotten home very late from Canada and she'd been gone when he woke up this morning. Now she'd appeared unannounced in his office—with Walter on tape and with lunch—and they were sitting at his desk eating sandwiches and sorting out possibilities. "Walter must have a million sources of information. Maybe he's not involved at all, but just heard something—like he says—and wanted to warn his brother."

"Uh-huh, brotherly love. And maybe the bishop has no reason to be afraid of him. And maybe he's not a cold-blooded killer who drove my dad off the force and into an early grave. And maybe—"

"Stop! I give." Dugan rolled up a potato chip bag and tossed it in the wastebasket. "Although, do you think maybe you're letting your own feelings influence you? I mean . . . just a tiny bit?"

"No," she said. "It's Walter who went up to Canada, or sent someone, when Larry called him. It's Walter who has the whole police report that includes the girl's statement, Walter who sent goons to scare the hell out of Clayton Warfield, not to mention harrassing you a bit, and Walter—"

". . . and Walter who's threatening the bishop. I give. With someone else, probably. Or maybe in competition with someone, or else the hit man at his cottage had nothing to do with this, and that's hard to buy. Anyway, whoever they are, they seem to want something the bishop has, except he hasn't got anything worth extorting him for."

"That's what he thought," Kirsten said. "But last night when Walter said he wouldn't sell because he was an obedient son, it was like a lightbulb lit up in his head. A few months ago someone asked him about buying his mother's property."

"What property?"

"Vacant land she inherited years ago. In Wisconsin, way up near the Michigan Upper Peninsula, about three hundred fifty acres. He says what isn't woods and swamp is rocky and no good for farming. His mom had this dream that it be used for an orphange or a summer camp for kids. It's in a trust and he's the trustee, so he could sell it, but he didn't need money and didn't want to act contrary to his mother's dream. So he said no. They came back again later, with lots of facts and figures on land values in the area, and said the buyer might go as high as a thousand dollars an acre. He was surprised at the offer, but he just repeated the land wasn't for sale. He really hadn't thought about it since then."

"It sure sounds like that could be it," Dugan said. "Except. . . ."

"Except what?"

"Well, almost every Sunday in the *Tribune* you'll find ads for land like that. 'Hunter's paradise,' or some such description, which means 'lousy soil, out in the middle of nowhere, and no developers are interested.' I think you can get it for four, five hundred dollars an acre, max. Why would someone want to pay way more than that, and try to force a sale by extortion and blackmail, not to mention mur—" He stopped when he saw her staring at him. "What?"

"You never told me you were looking for property in Wisconsin."

"Well, not seriously, you know. But every so often, after I've put in six ten-hour days in a row, I get to thinking I'd like a getaway spot, somewhere—"

"That would be so cool." She shook her head. "But we'd never go. It's too far."

"Nice dream, though, isn't it?" He'd never mentioned the idea, because he knew it was silly. "Anyway, maybe there's oil or something on this particular piece."

"Did you ever see an oil well in Wisconsin?"

"I've never been way up there. Who knows?"

"If there were oil, everyone would know it by now—like Exxon and Amoco and friends. I searched on the Internet. I even sent Clayton Warfield up there to look. He's no expert, but he can't see any excitement about land values. Not much farming; lots of rocks and some swampland, like the bishop said. Finding good well water without having to dig too deep seems to be a major problem for people who want to buy land."

"It's all we have to think about, though," Dugan said, "so let's figure it's worth a whole lot to someone for some reason. Who wanted to buy it?"

"He doesn't know who. The contact was through a broker."

"So we ask the broker," Dugan said. This investigating stuff was pretty easy, actually. At least when people weren't shooting at people, or strangling them.

"The bishop asked," Kirsten said, "but the broker had been contacted by a third party and didn't know who the actual buyer was."

"So . . . we *still* ask the broker," he said, feeling he was really getting into the game now. "He might even be in on it."

"How do you know the broker's a man?"

"Intuition," Dugan said. "Anyway, did you get his or her name?"

"Of course. You met him a few days ago," Kirsten said. "In fact, he took your card and promised to get in touch with you."

"Charles Banning," Dugan said. "Wants me to donate to Catholic Charities."

"You got it." Kirsten stuffed the remains of her lunch back in the bag it came in and tossed it across the desk toward him. With one smooth motion he caught it and banked it off the wall and into the wastebasket. "You're good at this," she said.

"I practice."

"No. I mean at helping me."

"Oh. Well then, try this suggestion: a real estate developer and philanthropist like Banning is unlikely to be conspiring with Walter Keegan to blackmail his brother."

"That's what the bishop thinks, too," she said. "Of course, we don't know a thing about the man, except . . ."

"Except you probably think he looks as shifty as I do. That's not enough."

"No, but there's something else—something I didn't tell you before. Right from the start I had Cuffs trailing Walter. The very night the bishop first came to our house, Walter made a stop at the building where Banning lives. Of course, there are seven other apartments in the building, but one was vacant. And when you eliminate the elderly widows and the people who were out of town . . ." She reached for the phone. "Anyway, Banning's the next step."

"Wait a minute," he said. "If he's crooked, you don't want to let him know you suspect something. But he already wants to sign me up as a donor, so maybe you should let *me* talk to him." He paused, certain she'd object.

She didn't.

"I can tell him I'm considering a donation to Catholic Charities," he said, "and while we're talking, I can just . . . uh . . ."

His mind was blank. "Well, I'll figure out some sneaky way to bring up the bishop's mother's property."

"Actually, I think that's a great idea."

"Really?" He couldn't believe she was agreeing.

"Really." Kirsten stood up. "Meanwhile, I have to run."

"Oh? Where . . ." But she was gone.

Great idea?

What the hell? Had he just been talked into something? Or was she trying to humor him again, keep him busy, so he'd stay out of the way and not worry about her.

When she left Dugan, Kirsten made the ten-minute walk through the Loop to her own office. She wasn't sure why she'd wanted to maneuver Dugan, and not just flat-out ask him to meet with Banning. Just to stay in practice? Or was it really that important that he *offer* to help, rather than her asking? Whatever it was, it probably said something about her maturity, or their relationship, or something.

At her office she went to the computer, logged onto the Internet, and checked her e-mail. There was nothing but junk, but that reminded her to check her ordinary mail and her phone messages. No surprises there, either. She wandered around her little two-room suite, straightening things up. Sometimes she was tempted to give up her office. But she liked having it. She kept all her records here—actually, all in one file drawer. Still, it showed she was running a real business.

There was a benefit in having a place of business that was separate from the rest of her life, because she tended to mix the two things together more than she ought to. Dugan had a different attitude. He worked longer hours than she liked, but he didn't bring work home and, of course, he *never* asked her for help or advice with his law practice. She, on the other hand, seldom came here to her office and often asked Dugan, one way or the other, for assistance.

It wasn't as though she couldn't make it on her own without him. She knew very well that she could. If it were just an extra brain or an extra pair of feet that were needed, she could hire someone—on a case-by-case basis, or even as a permanent employee. After all, she used Cuffs's services from time to time.

No, she didn't *need* Dugan's help. She *wanted* it. She enjoyed thinking things through with him, arguing with him. She enjoyed *being* with him, dammit, and why—

Beep!

The electronic burp made her jump a foot, and a nasty little note on the computer screen told her there'd been no activity and the damn thing was going to disconnect her from the Internet if she didn't stop dreaming and get down to business.

She stared at the monitor screen. Okay, smartass. You did market values pretty well last Saturday. But that's pretty mundane. Let's get creative.

Too many hours of creativity later, she had a backache, blurred vision, and just a hint of what it was she might be looking for. "And 'good-bye' to you, too," she said out loud, and shut down the PC.

She stood up and stretched, then paced around her little office a couple of times. Finally, she picked up the phone and tapped out her landlord's number.

"Brumstein and Brumstein Wholesale Jewelers, Inc."

"Hi. It's Kirsten. Mark still there?"

"Sure. It's Monday. He'll be here till the last starstruck, betrothed-over-the-weekend, two-income couple has left."

"I'm on my way. I don't need an engagement ring. Just half an hour of his time."

FORTY-FIVE

When Banning returned Dugan's call and said he had a dinner engagement that evening, Dugan was ready. "I'm tied up at seven, myself," he said, "but how about a drink before that?"

Dugan didn't want to leave a lot of time, in case the encounter didn't go well, so they met in the lobby of the Palmer House at 6:15. They rode the escalator up one long flight to the mezzanine level, where a waiter in a white shirt and a black bow tie greeted them as soon as they stepped between a couple of huge potted plants and into the bar area.

"My usual spot, Max?" Banning said, pressing something into the waiter's hand.

"Certainly, Mr. Banning. Follow me."

Dugan might have been impressed—mildly, at least—except that that was so obviously the point. There were about a dozen little round tables in the roped-off area to the right of the bar itself, and most of them were empty. They did get seated at a table far away from anyone else, though.

Dugan deliberately ordered first. "Any beer you have on tap," he said. Then, after Banning ordered a Dewar's on ice, he reversed himself. "Hey, that's a good choice, Charlie," he said. "I'll have the same."

Banning seemed to like that.

"So," Dugan said, "you're really sold on Catholic Charities, huh?"

"Well, I truly believe that those of us who've been blessed with material wealth have a moral responsibility to help people less fortunate than we." It sounded like a canned speech already. "Catholic Charities has one of the lowest administrative cost ratios of—"

"Administrative cost ratios?" Dugan asked.

"The percentage of income devoted to central administration as opposed to direct client intervention programs. Not that there aren't others who do well, also. The Salvation Army, for example. But I'm a lifelong Catholic myself—although not much of a churchgoer, I'm afraid." He gave a sort of just-between-us-guys wink. "So CC's an excellent choice if you want to maximize the use of your tax deductible contributions . . ." The man droned on, while Dugan wondered how he could steer the conversation to land in Wisconsin. Surely there'd be some opportunity if he paid attention. ". . . great opportunity," Banning was saying. "So what about it?"

"Um . . . what about what?"

"What about you? Wouldn't you like to join us in—"

"Oh, well, whaddaya call it, CC, sounds great. But you know, Charlie, I'm not really in your league." He watched Banning's self-satisfied smile grow wider. "I mean, guys like you are mega-bucks. Me, I'm just a personal injury lawyer, and my—"

"Well, we all start somewhere, don't we." It was a statement, not a question. "But I imagine you're moderately successful. In time, and with aggressive investments, you'll—"

"Say, Charlie, now that you mention it, let me ask you about that. My portfolio is starting to grow a little and . . . well, a charitable giving program is one thing on my agenda. But besides that, I'm looking to diversify, get into some deals with really major return possibilities. Maybe real estate development." He paused for a sip of Dewar's, then leaned slightly forward. "Everyone knows you're a heavy hitter in this town, Charlie. Maybe you've got an idea for me."

The suggestion that he might come up with an idea for Dugan seemed to appeal to Banning. "Well," he said, "was there anything in particular you had in mind?"

"Actually, I was reading . . . but wait a minute." Dugan leaned back in his chair and shook his head. "Damn! I apologize, Charlie. I'm the one called you to discuss Catholic Charities. Then all the sudden here I am, trying to pick your brain, and take advantage of your special knowledge and expertise. It's like meeting a gastroenterologist for a drink and then asking him about your bellyache."

"It's not an imposition. It's what I do. And as for free advice . . . if there's some deal we can work on together, I'm sure you'll want it to be one that's financially advantageous to both of us."

"Yes . . . certainly." Dugan stared down at his glass, rotating it slowly on the tabletop. "The thing is, I read something recently, not sure where, about resort property."

"Resort property?"

"Yeah. About these savvy investors who are buying up vacant land, way out in the country. They get it pretty cheap, then develop it as hunting and fishing resorts, but upper echelon. Sometimes they're near Indian reservations, you know, where there might be gambling casinos?" He sipped some scotch. "So I was just wondering . . ."

"Is that so?" Something new showed in Banning's eyes. Was it suspicion? Or was he just thinking? "Are you talking south," he said, "like maybe North Carolina? Tennessee?"

"No, my guess is that'd be too expensive. I was thinking upper midwest. I don't know, Minnesota, maybe. Or Michigan. Or how about northern Wisconsin?"

Banning stared at him. "Northern Wisconsin? I've really

never had any reason to look into land values or development possibilities up there." He made a point of checking his watch. "But I'll ask around. See if I can find you someone who has. Meanwhile, I have to run." He stood up. "Let's stay in touch."

"For sure," Dugan said. "Have a nice evening."

FORTY-SIX

I couldn't agree more," the bishop said. "We *all* find these meetings difficult. But, really, what's the alternative?"

"Hell, that's easy," Bud said. "The alternative is a world without these darn, depressing cluster meetings. Or, as the Bible calls it, 'the Promised Land.'"

It was past ten o'clock Monday night. He'd presided over a meeting of the priests of all the parishes in his geographical "cluster." With all of them badly overworked, the exchange of ideas he'd tried to foster was constantly sidetracked by words of discouragement and frustration. That was nothing new. But he kept holding these meetings. Communication was crucial. Now he was exhausted, and Bud was driving him home.

Undoubtedly, Cuffs Radovich was following them, but Bud wouldn't know that, wouldn't even dream of it. That his friend had no idea something terrible was happening to him seemed strange. And sad, actually. He'd always considered the ideal life as one so open and honest that you wouldn't care if the whole world knew every single thing you did. What freedom! But here he was, still a slave to a sordid little secret that threatened to tear him apart. Even this man who'd been a close friend for over forty years, and who knew about the incident itself, didn't know that it was creating havoc after all this time.

When he'd decided he had to do something about the threats, he'd known it would be terribly painful to reopen that scab, even to tell the very people he'd hired to help him. Kirsten was right when she said the reason he'd blurted out part of the story in that very first telephone call was to keep himself from backing out. Now she and Dugan knew the whole story, and in a way this made him feel nearly as close to them as to his longtime friend. They knew the stupid, shameful thing that had started it all: how a supposedly mature, respected spiritual leader had crept into that sad, shabby tavern where women with no futures got paid to parade naked in front of men— men like him.

To whatever extent it was sinful, the deed was long forgiven, he knew, but it could never be undone. Despite how carefully he'd guarded his secret, hoping it was buried for good, Kirsten and Dugan knew now what even Bud didn't know—how it was rising to the surface, threatening to humiliate not only him, but the cardinal, the conference of bishops, the whole Church. And they never once blamed him. Oh, Kirsten could get angry if she caught him—still fearful—holding back something or trying to avoid reality. But for the impulse that initially took him into that degrading place, no blame.

More important, they believed what he said about the wait-ress—poor girl. He agreed with them that she had to be the one who'd called him—God rest her soul. She'd spoken of "Bobby" protecting her and Dugan had learned that Bobby was the policeman and that the waitress had later become his girl-friend. Now they were both dead. He shuddered when he thought of Dugan's finding her body. The papers said she'd been struck on the head with a blunt object several times, then apparently strangled.

It meant a lot that they believed him when he said that what she'd told the police were lies, because what he said was true, and his fear had convinced him that people would never believe him, and—

"Wake up, Peter." Bud whacked him on the shoulder. "I said your guy's way back there now."

"Gosh, Bud, I'm sorry. What's that again?"

"I was saying that bodyguard of yours got stuck back at the last light." Bud was adjusting the rearview mirror. "He's way behind now and—"

"You mean you *knew* he was there?"

"Of course. I saw him drop you off before the meeting, and I see you keep checking to see if he's back there. And if you don't mind me saying so, I'm not so senile I can't tell something bad is going on, something that's got you scared to death. So if you ever wanna tell me . . ." He paused. "Anyway, what do you think your guy would do if I hit the gas and tried to lose him?"

"I've spent several days with him. I *know* what he'd do. He'd catch you. And when he did, he'd lean down and poke a huge finger in your face and warn you—to put it in his own language—that if you try any shit like that again, he'll tear your ass off."

The traffic light ahead had only just turned yellow, but Bud slowed to a stop. "Jeez, Peter," he said, "I never heard you talk like that. When whatever's goin' on is over . . . you oughta write a book."

"Bud," he hesitated, "do you remember my telling you about what happened after . . . after you and Kenny left me up . . ." He stopped.

"Up in North Bay, you mean, after we came home? Sure I remember, but . . . my God, Peter, does that have anything to do with—"

"No. No, it's not that. I just mean . . ." He knew he shouldn't have mentioned it. "I mean that I'll tell you about this too, sometime."

They drove the rest of the way in silence.

When they were stopped in front of the rectory, he opened

219

the door. "I'm afraid I'm not very good company these days. But thanks . . . for everything."

"Hold on a second," Bud said, and he twisted around in the seat to look out the rear window. "Your guy's not there. Maybe you oughta wait here in the car until he shows up."

"Oh, don't worry," he said, but he wondered himself why there was no car visible behind them for more than a block. "Sometimes he's around, but you just can't see him." He got out of the car. "Besides, it's not that big a deal, anyway."

Even as he pushed the car door closed, the window was sliding down. "I'll stay here," Bud said, "till you're inside."

"You don't have to—"

"Hey! Would you get your tail up the sidewalk so I can go home and go to bed?"

So he hurried up the walk. If the truth were known, he was scared. He obviously hadn't realized how much he'd gotten used to Cuffs being nearby, either right with him, or hanging somewhere around the edges wherever he went. Where was he now?

At the top of the steps he turned and gave a little wave, then watched Bud drive away. It was only eleven o'clock, and everything was fine.

Except the light—the one high above the front door. It was out again. Or maybe *still* out. He struggled to get his key in the lock. Hadn't he checked that light after they replaced the fuses last week? He opened the front door, then stepped inside and closed it behind him.

It was very dark. He saw nothing, heard nothing . . . and knew at once that he was not alone.

"Your friends aren't much help, are they," the voice said.

There were other words, too, he knew, but they seemed so far away. Not as real, somehow, as the chill of fear that broke over the backs of both his hands. He saw a vague outline of a man, but then his legs went limp, and he was heavy, and collapsing, and then his forehead crashed against something very, very hard.

FORTY-SEVEN

L ate Monday night Charles Banning took his drink—ginger
ale, no bourbon—into the library, where he spread a well-
worn map across a smooth, mahogany table and stared at it
for . . . What? the hundredth time? It still told him only what
he already knew. Unless Liberty's Champions got the land they
wanted, and he got their money, he'd lose everything.

Liberty's Champions. Whether they had the guts to ever
move beyond their rhetoric and war games, they'd proven right
away they had money. What hadn't become clear until too late
was just how loose a grip they had on reality.

He'd met with two of their leaders in secret and made a deal,
unconventional to say the least, but one that would net him
enough to cover his loans that were closest to default. Keeping
them anonymous, he'd find the land, advance expenses and the
cost of options, and make the purchases to create a large
enough tract. They established a guaranteed fund from which
whatever purchase prices he could negotiate were to be paid.
Then, once the land was transferred to them, all the money
left in the fund was his.

Maybe he shouldn't have assured them so strongly that he
could put together a tract large and remote enough to serve
their purposes. But what should he have said, that he *might*

be able to put a deal together? That kind of weaseling response was beneath him. Besides, they were to blame for the whole fuckup, not him. He began where they suggested—undeveloped land, way up in northern Wisconsin. Difficulties arose at once: property tied up in trusts and too many small-town lawyers and too many owners with irrational expectations. There was even talk of some Canadian conglomerate looking at the same region. But if that was ever more than a bullshit rumor, it was over now.

He'd told them he'd have to look elsewhere. Minnesota, maybe. But for Liberty's Champions—"Liberty's Crazies" would be more accurate—there was no elsewhere. They'd become obsessed. Divine power had chosen a special place for them, and they *would* have it.

So he'd continued the search, putting in long hours personally. Then something said in one of those goddamn calls from Liberty's Crazies narrowed his focus. Poring again over hundreds of pages of tract sheets, surveys, and title records, he discovered a large section of land owned by one entity, a trust. Just the size and type of location the assholes were looking for.

Better yet, when he found out whose trust it was, he realized he'd gotten the sort of break that hard work and true genius often combine to produce. Land like that was obviously of no use to a senile old woman, or to a bishop, either, if she were to die. So a deal was inevitable. He cooked up a story about his "buyer" that he thought would appeal to the bishop and made an opening offer, not far below the going rate for similar land. When the answer was no, he wasn't surprised. He was familiar with greed. A week or two later he'd tried again, this time with appraisals of the land and the surrounding area . . . and a significantly higher offer.

No sale, though. Not at any price.

That's when he'd arranged to meet Walter Keegan. He'd known within thirty minutes that the man had criminal tendencies. Keegan was smooth and sly—if less intelligent than he thought he was—and a vein of greed ran deep inside him. The fool had finally been stupid enough to reveal the hold he had over his half brother. Of course Banning wished he had the complete report, including the girl's statement.

But even that didn't matter anymore.

He reached out and patted the telephone as if it were a living thing, a tiny pet anxious to obey its master's will. This morning his phone had done exactly what he wanted it to. It had brought the man from Miami back to him, and he was putting the man to good use. Right now, possibly. He'd know tomorrow.

There'd been one other call today that had made him curious. Why would a guy claim it was urgent they meet at once, if all he wanted to do was give away money? Turns out it wasn't generosity, after all, but just one more problem. One more problem that he'd handle.

Now it was nearly midnight and he sat and sipped plain ginger ale and wondered whether he should dip into his stuff, to celebrate his new plan that—

The phone rang.

The caller didn't identify himself. Or was it *her*self? He could never tell. They always used a low, hoarse voice, almost a whisper. Fucking paranoids.

"It won't be long now," he promised.

"No, not long. We have decided."

He didn't like the sound of that. "What do you mean?"

"You have two more weeks."

"Don't be absurd." Banning was suddenly angry—rightfully so. "I'll do what—"

"Two more weeks." The voice was barely audible, but the menace—and the madness—came through. "While your promises continue, the conspiracy spreads like a fungus. Our nation's leadership has lost its senses, our government has come unhinged." The odd rhetoric was familiar by now, the terminology repetitious and tiresome. "We will no longer wait, and

thus contribute to the annihilation of individual freedoms."
There was a pause. "A firm committment on the land. Two
weeks or . . ." another pause, ". . . or else we take other appropriate action."

" 'Other appropriate action'?" He put sarcasm, even con-
tempt, into his voice. "Who else will you people run to? I'm
the only—" The line was dead.

When he set the receiver down, it was slick with perspira-
tion. He stood up and walked across to the revolving bookcase.

Fuck Liberty's Champions. Without him what would they
do, put an ad in the paper? *Wanted: Isolated tract of land. Must
be large enough to train an army of divinely inspired assholes who
plan to take over and save everyone's freedoms while the whole
goddamn country goes down the toilet.*

Besides, he was going to meet their fucking deadline, maybe
beat it.

FORTY-EIGHT

The bishop found himself sitting on the floor, his back against the wall. Still in the rectory entrance hall, he was sure of that, even though he couldn't see anything. It must have been the voice that woke him up, the sound of it coming at him gradually, as though from far away. He could hear, but he couldn't concentrate on the words. Strangely enough, he found himself embarrassed and struggling to recall whether he'd ever fainted before in his life—as if that were really important.

Even those thoughts quickly disappeared, though, as waves of pain swept through his head. He must have slammed it against the edge of the table when he fell. He instinctively reached up to touch it, and was horrified when he felt warm, sticky blood. But he also felt some kind of cloth, a blindfold wrapped around his head. That startled him and he dropped his hand at once back to his lap.

". . . a bump on the head," the voice was saying. A man's voice, the one he'd heard before he blacked out, not at all comforting. "You'll survive."

"No," he said. "I'm bleeding. It's bad."

"Bad? You don't know bad." The voice chuckled. "Maybe a little blood will wake you up. These people you're depending on, they can't protect you."

"Who are you?" he asked, remembering suddenly that he ought to try to make the man talk.

"I'm no one. Just a messenger."

"What's your name? What do you want?"

"I'm a messenger, and here's the message. Call a man named Charles Banning. Tell him you've changed your mind." He spoke in a monotone, as if the words were memorized. "You've decided to sell the property. He'll know what you mean. He'll remember."

"I don't understand. You'll have to explain more clear—"

"Shut up!" The voice was mean, then sighed and continued as before, as though reciting. "Do as I say or the world will know what a pervert you are. Fooling with a poor little girl. You have forty-eight hours to contact this Banning person. Otherwise, the world will know what kind of nasty things you do when no one is looking."

"Please, what's your name?" He tried to stand, but the movement sent fresh pain through his head and he gave up. "Why are you doing—"

"I'm a messenger."

"But I need . . . I need a doctor." He knew his job was to get the man to be more explicit, but he just couldn't do it. He was too tired . . . too afraid. He felt the man move quietly by him and open the door. "I'm bleeding. Please."

The blindfold was yanked from his head and the door closed again, softly. He struggled to get to his feet, ignoring the pain this time. Finally he was standing, one hand propped against the wall to keep his balance, the other hand clasped to his forehead . . . where the worst pain was, and the blood.

His head was spinning wildly. He was terribly afraid and was sure he was about to vomit. He imagined he heard someone coming, someone who would help him. But he was falling again, was on the floor.

He called, "Please! Please!" But fear had taken his breath away. He couldn't get the cries to come out very loud.

And besides, he knew there was no one to help him.

FORTY-NINE

Cuffs had told her there'd be plenty of places to park at eleven in the morning and he was right. The whole block was marked *No Parking, School Zone.* So that's where Kirsten and Dugan sat and waited.

In a few moments he came out of the rectory and tried to fit himself into the backseat. "Jesus," he said, "can't you afford a bigger car?"

"We could go inside," she said, "but you said you'd rather talk in the car."

"Right," Cuffs said. "Too many goddamn women—a cleaning lady and a cook and God knows what all—comin' and goin' in there. Just now there's a mean-looking nun going through boxes and boxes of old toys and junk, checkin' everything against a mile-long list and gripin' about there used to be five skateboards and now there's only three, for God's sake."

"Ah," she said, "finally." So whoever left the note on the mannequin in the rectory must have walked away with two skateboards, including one with the bishop's fingerprint on it. "I'm so glad you said that, Cuffs."

"Right," Dugan said, and she knew he understood, too. "The bishop wouldn't be likely to remember handling it when they were sorting out toys for the sale."

If Cuffs was mystified, he didn't show it, and didn't even ask what they were talking about. "You listened to the tape I gave you, right?"

"We did," she said, and took the cassette player from Dugan. She pushed rewind, watched the numbers race backward, then hit stop and then play.

She and Dugan had listened twice already, and she didn't miss what she was looking for by much. There was a door closing, and then just noise, and finally a man's voice: *Your friends aren't much help, are they.* She stopped the tape.

"Well," Dugan said, "I guess the guy was right about that."

"Bullshit," Cuffs said. "What he was right about was that a little bump on the head was all Pete really—"

"Pete?"

"That's what he calls the bishop," Kirsten said. "So . . . go ahead."

"I'd have gone after the guy," Cuffs said. "But Pete goes down the second time and I think maybe he's really hurt worse and I better see about him." He stared at her, as though challenging her to disagree. "I'd make the same damn choice again."

"Fine," she said. "What I'm second-guessing is my initial decision to wire him and have you keep your distance. He could have been badly hurt. He could have—"

"That 'coulda been' stuff is crap, too," Cuffs said. "He wasn't hurt bad. He fainted and bumped his head and it bled a little. I don't blame him, but he was mostly scared to death, on top of bein' exhausted and stressed out and all. Change your mind if you want to, but you're the one told me anyone wanted him dead they coulda killed him a month ago. This *messenger* creep sure didn't try to lay a finger on him. It's obvious what they want is that . . . property . . . or whatever."

She wasn't surprised Cuffs didn't ask what the property was. His approach to his work was simple: you do your own damn job and you mind your own damn business. "And you didn't see the guy," she asked, "or his car or anything?"

"Nope." There wasn't a hint of apology or regret in Cuffs's voice. "He didn't see me, either. When Pete—"

"I just can't get used to your calling him Pete," Dugan said.

"Yeah? Well, we all got our hang-ups. Anyway, he went to that meeting and he said that'd take a few hours and his friend Burgeson would give him a ride home. Nobody's gonna bother him when he's around people, so I drove back to the rectory."

"Why?" Kirsten asked.

"I was thinkin' it's a good chance to go look around the place—it's big and old, and I wanna see where the weak spots are. He gave me a key a couple days ago. The other two priests are out of town, there's no live-in help, and the guy who answers the phone and door leaves at nine o'clock. So after he's gone a few minutes I let myself in. I'm just startin' to look around and I can hardly believe it when I hear somebody picking the lock on the back door by the kitchen. So I hid in the dining room. It's just one person that comes in and he's too quiet to some dopehead rippin' the place off. He went down the hall toward the front, and then I couldn't hear anything. I knew he must be just sitting and waiting for Pete."

"You could have grabbed him right then," Dugan said, "and we could have—"

"Uh-huh. Yeah, I go after the guy and maybe he's a pro, and maybe I have to shoot him. Then he's either dead or not, and either way we got cops all over and lots of explaining to do. Or maybe I take him easy and he's some nobody who's gettin' paid to scare Pete and doesn't even know who he's workin' for. So we got him for breaking and entering and we're nowhere."

"You're right," she said. "So go ahead."

"So I let him settle down and I sneak out. I made it back before the end of the meeting and followed Pete and this Burgeson guy for a while when they left. I listened in and the mike was working fine. And lemme tell ya, that Burgeson guy's a bright guy—even if he *is* a priest. Caught me behind 'em, figured out why I was there, and wondered what I'd do if he tried to shake me." He paused. "Pete was so damn surprised he started cursin'. I think he forgot he had the wire on."

"That's hard to believe," Dugan said.

"No, it happens a lot," Kirsten said. "Leave it on a person a while and pretty soon they get used to it and don't think about—"

"Not that," Dugan interrupted. "I mean I can't picture the bishop cursing."

"Well, he did, dammit," Cuffs said. "Talkin' about kickin' ass, or something. I didn't give you that tape yet. Here, listen for yourself." He gave her another tape and grinned. "Actually, though, he was just kinda qoutin' *me*."

"Anyway," Kirsten said, "get back to what happened."

"So after the meeting I followed for a few blocks and then I ditched them and drove like hell back to the rectory again and parked in the alley. I'm hiding at the side of the building by the time they get there. When Pete goes up to the door, I run around and go in the back and wait in the kitchen. I got the headset on and I hear Pete sayin' his head's bleeding, but he sounds okay. I decide I won't go for the guy until he finishes whatever he wants to say and we got it on the tape. But I have to be careful because by now I'm sure he's not just some mope."

"Not a bad decision," Kirsten said, and Cuffs's total lack of response told her he'd reached that conclusion without her help. "It just didn't work out quite right," she added.

"Not my fault," Cuffs said. "Anyway, when I can tell the guy's ready to go I'm on my way down that hallway in the dark and remembering how Pete said he's bleeding but thinkin' he's not hurt bad. Then I get to the front hall and goddamn if he's not falling down again, cryin' or moanin' or something. And . . . well, at that point it's the hell with the other guy."

"Right," Kirsten said. She thought Cuffs maybe waited a little too long before he started down the hallway, but kept quiet about that. It was a judgment call, and she hadn't been the one having to make the judgment. "And the doctor says he's fine, right?"

"Sure. I took him to a doc I know can keep his mouth shut. Washed off the blood, closed up the cut, and gave him some pills. I told him he shouldn't come back here to the rectory afterwards. He should just drop out of sight. I'd hide him somewhere, but . . . y' know . . . even people like him, religious people, they think they gotta *act* tough even if they don't really feel that way." Cuffs was shaking his head, and Kirsten guessed he was secretly admiring the bishop's decision. "So anyway, that's what he did." He opened the car door. "That's the whole story. I'll stay here with him till I hear different."

She watched him head up the sidewalk to the rectory door. "Funny thing," she said, "I think he actually *admires* the bishop."

"I'm not sure admiration's the right word," Dugan said. "But he calls him Pete, and now he says he's got him using street talk. Cuffs probably thinks he's the bishop's *mentor*."

The medication the doctor gave him had dulled the pain in his head to a manageable ache. He'd slept a little, too, a rare blessing these days. When he called and said he'd slipped and banged up his head, the cardinal suggested he take the rest of the week off. The fact was, though, he had too much work to do to take time—

The intercom phone beside his bed buzzed. "This is Bishop Keegan," he said, out of habit.

"Who *else* would be ans—" There was a pause. "Anyway, it's me, Radovich I'm still downstairs if you need me."

"Thank you," he said. "I'm going to take a nap and . . . well, after that I . . . wonder if you'd mind—"

"I know," Cuffs said. "You wanna go visit your ma. What the hell, I said I'd be around, didn't I?"

"Yes. I mean, thanks, I guess." But Cuffs had already hung up.

He lay down on the bed and maybe he fell asleep and maybe he didn't. Awake or asleep, though, he kept hearing his mother's voice—very soft, but clear—as though it were floating through the air, looking for him. *There's so many mean ones out there*, she kept saying, *so many mean ones.*

FIFTY

Kirsten sat and thought awhile, even after Cuffs was back inside the rectory. Finally, long after Dugan had rewound the tape, she pulled away from the curb. "I guess someone wants to buy that land pretty badly," she said.

"Uh-huh." Dugan's tone said she was stating the obvious.

"So, when you think about it, darling, what has to be done is simple."

"You're using the 'd' word again."

She hadn't even noticed, but didn't say so. "He insists on keeping his arrest secret. So, short of us finding out who's blackmailing him, and silencing them somehow—not much of an option given the deadline—what's left but to sell?"

"He won't like that opinion. You're the one who told me he doesn't believe the property's his to sell, that he owes it to his mom to try to use it the way she wanted to."

"I didn't sign on to make him happy." She turned south onto LaSalle Street. "By the way, should I drop you at your office? Or . . . how about Manny's?"

"Not a fair choice," he said. Which was exactly why she'd suggested it. Manny's was an old-style cafeteria surrounded by cut-rate clothing stores, about a mile and a half southwest of the Loop, and she knew he couldn't pass up the best corned beef sandwiches this side of the Alleghenies.

"Lunch it is," she said. "So, let's say he sells the land. What's the problem? Not what his mother wanted, but she won't know it's gone. He keeps his secret, and gets more money than he needs to take care of her until she dies. Then, if there's anything left, he can use it to help poor kids somehow, which is basically what she wanted."

"Uh-huh. And the next time brother Walter and this Banning guy want some—"

"Banning might be just a middleman, not involved with any threats."

"No? Then when I asked him about land in three different states, why did he only hear 'northern Wisconsin'? And why'd he tell me he'd never investigated land there, and then run off and leave a perfectly good glass of Dewar's untouched?"

"Good point, but . . . that voice on the tape, how would you describe it?"

"Male," he said. "Maybe a slight Spanish ac—Your hit man?"

"I'd bet on it. So if the bishop's 'messenger' was sent by Walter, why is it the same man who tried to kill Walter?"

"Damn. Well, whoever the hell it is, the next time they want something, they'll be back. And with blackmail, there's always a next time."

"Unless someone steps in," Kirsten said, "to make sure there isn't."

"Oh. And how does this someone do that?"

"We're under a forty-eight-hour deadline now, but after the property's sold, it shouldn't be hard to find out who bought it. Even if it's bought and sold again over and over, as I think it would be, through a string of . . . what is it you lawyers call them?"

"Straw men, they called them in law school. I hated that property class; my C minus was a gift. Since then, the closest

I've been to a real estate deal was when we bought our place, and I was way too busy to go to the closing of that one."

"I remember it well." She'd always suspected the real reason he didn't go was because everyone there would know he was an attorney and still had no idea what was going on. "Anyway, sooner or later, whoever *really* wants the bishop's mother's land, say some mining or chemical company or something, will take title to—"

"Mining or chemical company? What's that about?"

"Ideas I got from the Internet, trying to find out what would make land like that so valuable to someone. For example, environmentalists and industry have been fighting for years over sulfite mining in Wisconsin, but that's south and west of the bishop's land. Then there's the constant search—wherever there's vacant land—for every sort of mineral and chemical: coal, silver, gold, diamonds, oil, natural gas, chromium . . . and lots of stuff you and I never heard of."

"I'm not sure I ever heard of sulfite, actually," Dugan said. "But *why* it might be valuable to someone seems less important than who the someone is who's putting the squeeze on the bishop."

"And the final owner who wants to use the land might never have heard of the bishop. Before them, though, there'll have been the original buyer, and along the line a series of those straw . . . straw persons." Kirsten said.

"You figure once you have all the links in the chain, you'll find out which one made the big bucks, which would be the one behind shaking down the bishop."

"Right." She'd been over this in her own mind a dozen times, but wanted him to think it through with her. "There's another problem, though. Even after he sells the property, they'll still want to keep him quiet about *why* he sold."

"Okay," he said, "and they'll still have his secret to hold over him."

"But what if he changes his mind, stops caring if people hear about his arrest?"

"That's possible, I guess." He spoke slowly, and she could tell he was hooked, trying to figure out where she was going with this. "But why would he?"

"It's possible. That's what counts," she said. "And the buyer knows that, too."

"So let's say he sells, then later starts yelling about how they only got the property by extortion, or whatever. So what? What's sold is sold. He'd have to go to court to try to undo it. That'd be tough to do, and it could take years. They can ride out his accusations, discredit him as a desperate man who's been living a lie."

"You know?" she said. "That's an interesting thought."

"What is?"

"What you said: 'What's sold is sold.' Trying to undo a sale would be . . ." She decided to get back to her point. "Suppose the buyer has something to hide besides extortion." She didn't care now how obviously she was leading him. "Something so damaging that he can't take a chance on riding it out if the bishop talks."

"Something like murder?"

"Uh-huh."

"Then they have only one choice," he said. "First, they have to get the land."

"And then?"

"And then they have to silence him—permanently."

"Exactly," she said. They were headed south on Clinton Street. Traffic was light, and they'd make it to Manny's before noon. "And there is . . . well, one other thing to think about, darling."

"Will you stop using that word?" he said.

"Why do you—"

"Forget it. What's the other thing?"

"Whoever it is must know by now that we're helping the bishop."

"Right. That is, they know *you* are, anyway," he said, and— He stopped. "You mean they might decide they have to deal with you the same as they do the bishop."

"Well, not *exactly* the same," she said. She turned west onto Roosevelt Road, just around the corner from Manny's now. "If they decide to get rid of us, they don't have to wait until after they get the property."

He sighed. "Why do you keep saying *us*? You're the one he hired."

"Yes, but we're a couple." She turned north on Jefferson, passing Manny's on their right.

"Hey," Dugan said, "you went right past an open space."

"There's a parking lot in the back."

"I know, but I've never seen a vacant place on the street here in my life," he said, "and you just blew it."

She kept going, around the corner onto Taylor Street, then into the little parking lot behind the restaurant. She could smell corned beef—or imagined she could, anyway—and knew Dugan would rather concentrate on whether to get the kreplach or the matzo ball soup with his sandwich. But there was one more thing. "We're a couple," she repeated, "and besides that, you've been with me all morning."

"I agree on both counts," he said, "but—"

"Remember that Chevy Caprice?" she asked.

"The one out in front of our place a couple of nights ago?"

"That one," she said. "It kept going east on Taylor when I turned in here." Circling the parked cars, she eased back out of the parking lot exit and stopped. "Look," she said, and pointed to their right, where the Caprice was disappearing around the corner a half block away, going south.

"Damn," he said. "Not a coincidence, I guess."

"I spotted them two blocks after we left the rectory." She

turned left and at the corner swung north on Jefferson and picked up speed. "We'll get Italian sausage sandwiches at Al's," she said. "The one on Ohio Street. They drip all over your clothes, but they're delicious."

"It's on Ontario," he said, "not Ohio." He was twisted around in his seat, looking out the rear window. "Al's is great for Italian sausage. But hell, for what might be my last meal, I'd have preferred corned beef . . . and Manny's matzo balls."

FIFTY-ONE

A fter lunch Kirsten went to her office. There was just one phone message and, when she tapped out the number, they put her through immediately.

"Organized Crime." There was an audible wheeze when he inhaled. "Acting Chief Keegan."

"You called me."

"I wanna talk."

"Fine. I can meet you at—"

"Now. Here, downtown. I'll have someone waiting for you. You'll be searched, by a female. No recording devices," another wheeze, "like you probably had when you wouldn't talk outside your car. They'll take you to the canteen. I'll meet you there."

"Who's gonna search *you*?"

"Nobody."

"And why should I jump when you say jump?"

"Because you and me understand each other. And because it's in the best interest of your client."

Half an hour later she and Walter Keegan were sitting at one of a dozen small round plastic-topped tables in a dismal space about the size of two classrooms, on the top floor of Central Police Headquaters, Eleventh and State. They each had a cup of foul-tasting coffee from one of the vending machines that stood in a row along the north wall. The other machines dispensed soda, candy, sandwiches, snacks, hot chocolate . . . even cigarettes. On the table beside Keegan's cup was a blue-covered loose-leaf notebook.

There were three other people in the room. Two overweight black women and one emaciated Hispanic man, all in civilian clothes with ID badges, all sitting apart from one another and staring nowhere in particular. A patch on the man's shirt said *Maintenance.* One of the women was smoking a cigarette, and coughed repeatedly.

"I thought this was a smoke-free building," Kirsten said.

"It is."

"Oh." She waited, watching how the woman lit one cigarette from the stub of another, and how all of her large, round body parts shook in unison whenever she coughed—which was about every ten seconds. Walter just sat there, saying nothing. They were playing a male game, she decided. See who can outwait the other. But she was a female, so . . . she stirred her coffee with a wooden stick.

"That coffee's black," he said.

"So?"

"So there's nothing to stir."

"So you win the game." She stood up. "I'll see myself out."

Keegan sipped some coffee and looked up at her. "You don't like me."

She sat down. "I despise you. I don't trust you. I suppose you could say if I hated anyone, it's you."

"Because of your father."

"No. Because of you. What you did to him. What you're doing to your brother. What you've done through the years to—"

"Shit. I might have been saving your old man's life. You weren't there. You only know his version."

"Right. And he's . . . he wasn't a liar."

"No, he wasn't. Not that bad a copper, either. But he had a blind spot; a fatal flaw, you might say." She stood again, and he grinned up at her. "You don't wanna hear it, do you? Fine. So let's talk about my wonderful little brother."

She sat down. "Talk, then."

"Here's what I think. I think you came to my cottage and put that fucking bird in the fuse box. I think you were there when I came in the front door. I think you saw the greaseball prick . . . excuse me, the perpetrator who tried to whack me. I—"

"You have a lot of thoughts, but we were going to talk about your brother."

"Little Peter. A prince of the church."

"He's a bishop," she said. "Prince is a term for cardinals. I heard it in a movie."

"What's the difference? He'll make cardinal if he has his way. That's why he sucks up to everyone." Keegan started to cough then, and his hacking reminded her of the smoking woman. She looked around and saw that neither of the women was in the canteen anymore. ". . . identify the fucker for me," Walter was saying.

"What?"

"The fucking hit man, I want you to identify him for me. You got a better look at him than I did."

"You're kidding. You as much as killed my father, for God's sake. Why would I help you, even if I could?"

"Because, like I said earlier, it's in the interest of your client. The bastard's a pro, and I got a book of photos here he might be in. You identify him, and I'll tell you what I know about what's going on with Peter. It's a trade. If it helps you get him out of it, fine. If not, fine." He paused and fought off another fit of coughing. "I want the shooter. I want the bastard that sent him, too. But I want the shooter first . . . real bad."

241

"What if he's not in there?"

"Then you got nothing to trade. I think he's a spic. He might be in the book."

"Suppose I ID him and you catch him. Then you'll want me to come in as a witness, and I already told the police I wasn't—"

"I find out for sure who it is, there'll be no need for witnesses. Believe me."

"If I do pick someone out, how do I know you'll tell me the truth in return?"

"When you hear what I got to say, along with what you must already know, you'll know it's true. You can do whatever the hell you want with it."

"And if I point to someone, how do you know *I'm* telling the truth?"

"First, because some of these assholes in here I know it can't be. If you pick one of them . . . Anyway, you won't do that. I been asking around. One of your old man's disabilities got passed along to you."

"Oh?"

"Yeah. You have a hard time with a flat-out lie."

"That the fatal flaw you mentioned?

"Nope."

She decided to drop it. "Okay," she said, "open the book." He did, and she turned the pages. Each page held six photos. It didn't take long. She stared down at the page in front of her.

"Well?"

"Him," she said, and tapped her finger on one of the photos.

"Okay." She thought maybe he smiled, but he coughed again, and she couldn't really tell. "You're sure, right?"

"Yes," she said. "Now, your turn."

"Like I say, some of this maybe you know already, but I'll give it all, so you can tell I'm telling the truth. Peter's mother—"

"Your mother, too."

"Bullshit. Peter's mother has a big chunk of land in Wis-

242

consin. I'm talking huge, like three, four hundred acres. It's mostly woods and swamp, but bits of it are leased out to farmers even though the soil ain't worth shit. It's in a trust, now, and Peter's the trustee. He can do whatever he wants with it."

"You've seen the trust?"

"Years ago he showed me. All I remember is it goes to him when she dies. Just him, not the two of us. So much for the 'my mother, too' crap."

"Maybe she had a plan for the property," she said, knowing this was true, "and didn't think you'd—"

"And maybe she didn't give a shit about me." He sipped his coffee. "Real estate guy named Charles Banning wants the property and the bishop won't sell, not at any price. Banning knows I'm Peter's brother and came to me for help."

"Wait. Why does Banning want the property?"

"He doesn't want it himself. He's buying it for someone else. The buyer wants it, real bad. Banning says the buyer put up a million dollars and—"

"A million dollars? You gotta be kid—"

"Banning says the buyer put up a million. Banning buys the property for whatever he has to pay, eats all the expenses, and pockets the rest. Property ain't worth shit at market rates, so Banning figures to make a bundle. The deal stinks like dead fish, but he has his own blind spot, which is he needs money . . . bad. Anyway, he tells Peter some rich guy who's dying wants to buy the land. But Peter won't sell."

"And who's the dying man who'd pay a million for land like that?"

"I said that's what Banning told Peter. It's really a militia organization called Liberty's Champions. I checked and it's a real group. Sound like a bunch of half-asses, but the million's real, too, sitting in a real bank. I saw the proof, an escrow agreement. Anyway, they want a headquarters, a training ground. They're fucking crazy, Banning says—not that he isn't—and they think God chose this special place just for them. Like the new Israel, or something. They don't want anyone to know it's them until they got the deed in their pocket. They're big on secrecy. Loony bastards."

"So, when he couldn't get your brother to sell, Banning came to you. You knew about the phony arrest in Canada, and—"

"I knew I saved Peter's ass is what I knew. Now it's payback time. All I'm doing is putting a little squeeze on him. Just reminding him he's not really so far above the rest of us. Gets way up there, thinks no one's lookin', and whips out his . . . well, anyway, there he is, messing with a young girl like that."

"I have a copy of the police report." She caught his eyes widen, just a bit. "Doesn't say much."

"I know, not the one page I left there. But I got the statement. Did you ask him what his little whore said? What she told the—"

"She was a waitress. Just a girl. The cops threatened her." Kirsten sipped her coffee and found it as as foul-tasting cold as it was hot. "She's dead now, anyway."

"What?" She'd swear his surprise was genuine. "What makes you think that?"

"I think . . . I *know* . . . she lied to the cops about what happened up there. She came into town for some reason. I think she might have been ready to retract her statement. Run a check on a Jane Doe, last Friday, at the Moonglow Motel."

"I'll look into it." He wasn't good at hiding his thoughts, and again there was surprise, even admiration, in his eyes. "You been working at this. But I have her statement. I'm the only one's got it. An original, signed by her. And it's enough, even with her dead. Peter'd be finished. Spent his whole life kissing ass, and for nothing."

"And you have your people threatening your own brother, terrifying him? How can you do that?"

"Half brother," he said. "And as for terrifying him, I'm just giving him a dose of reality. It's only his own guilt and his own phony self-righteousness that makes a ten-year-old blow job a big deal in the first place. I'm not hurting him, not even touching him. Earning my cut from Banning, that's all." He paused. "Thing is, Banning's—"

"Wait. Not hurting him? What about his head? What about last night?"

"Last night what?" He stared at her. "I know you were at his place this morning, and I know you shook off my guys. Assholes. What happened last night?"

She told him, saying nothing about the tape, or about Cuffs being nearby.

"Not my people," he said. "I started to say Banning's turned out to be more wacko than I thought. I think he's decided to cut me out. I think he's the one who hired the spic here." He tapped the book of photos. "I'm watching my— Hold on. Tell me what the guy looked like. Last night, I mean."

She gave him the bishop's vague description. "It could have been the same guy, sure," she said. "But it could have been one of a million other guys."

"Maybe." He crushed the paper cup from his coffee, then leaned toward her. "We've done our trade. Tell Peter to sell the property. Tell him to sell to Banning and his buyers, or else he's gonna have to go out and find himself a real job."

"You mean you're going to keep after him? You're—"

"Looks like I don't need to. Seems Banning has his own intimidator now. But I'm still the one with the damaging proof. And even Banning's smart enough to know I still got my cut coming if Peter does the deal. And if he doesn't? I'm out some money, and Peter sees a lot of himself on TV and in the papers. Wouldn't surprise me he blew his brains out—if he's got the balls to do it—when it hits the fan. And it will, believe me, if he doesn't sell."

"You'd do this, to your own brother?"

"Now more than ever," he said. "Why the hell you think I'm telling you all this? I wanna move it along. Maybe you noticed the spic left me with a little trouble breathing. I don't know

245

yet how far I'll be coming back. Meanwhile I want that asshole shooter while I'm still able to walk. Whatever happens, I don't get free room and board for the rest of my life for sittin' on my ass, like Peter. My share of the money from Liberty's Champions will help me enjoy my golden years."

"You are truly despicable," she said.

"Thank you." He stood up. "My part of the trade was to tell you what's going on. I didn't say it wasn't gonna keep going on."

She stood, too. "One more thing."

"You got enough to let Peter—"

"Not about him. About my father. What blind spot were you talking about? What fatal flaw?"

He laughed. "Got to you, didn't I?" He pulled a huge cigar from his pocket and stuck it, unlit, in the corner of his mouth. "Maybe blind spot's not the right description. Maybe more like a nervous disorder."

"Oh?"

"Yeah. When it got right down to life and death, he didn't have the nerve to make sure he took out the bad guy before the bad guy got him."

"Maybe he wanted to be sure the guy he was facing was really a bad guy, before—"

"Same thing." He pulled the cigar from his mouth and flashed one more ugly grin. "Same . . . fucking . . . thing." He turned and walked out of the canteen. The emaciated Hispanic man left, too, and the bulge over his right hip showed he was carrying a pistol under his maintenance worker's shirt.

Kirsten was the only one left in the room. She sat down and stirred her cold black coffee. There were tears in her eyes and she didn't know who they were for, or even whether they were tears of pain . . . or rage.

FIFTY-TWO

So Walter claims the buyer's not some terminally ill tycoon at all, but a nut-case group called Liberty's Champions." Dugan shook his head, which didn't make things fall together any better. They were in Kirsten's office, Wednesday, the day after her meeting with Walter Keegan at Eleventh and State. "I don't suppose," he said, "that you called Park?"

He knew she would have. Parker Gillson was her best research tool. Ex-newspaper and radio reporter, friend of anyone who knew anything, Park could learn more about any person or topic in twelve hours—according to Kirsten—than most people could in a week. Of course, Park was also an investigator for the Illinois Supreme Court's agency that polices lawyers for ethics violations, which made Dugan a little wary of him.

"I only called him yesterday, so he hasn't had much time. But he says there's an organization called Liberty's Champions all right," she said. "Apparently started in Texas, a radical right-wing militia group. He says it's hard to pin down how many there are, but they talk big on the Internet, and they show up at rallies here and there around the country. They're antitax, antigovernment, and pro–automatic weapons for everyone—except the feds, I guess. They have ties to Nazis, the Klan, Aryans, skinheads—all the geniuses of the world."

"A fun group," Dugan said. "But do they have a million bucks to throw around?"

"Park doesn't think so. They're under scrutiny by the FBI, the ATF, and recently the IRS. He doubts they've ever had twenty thousand in the bank."

"They probably don't believe in banks," he said, "except as places to rob to get money for guns . . . or land."

"No sign of that. Unless some goofy right-wing tycoon recently dumped it on them, they have no real money. People mixed up in groups like Liberty's Champions tend to live on the margins of society. Most of them work sporadically, at best. I mean, look at the Unabomber, or the guys who did Oklahoma City."

"Right. And would you take a check from people like that?"

"If I have my way, the bishop will. But it'll be a cashier's check, drawn on a downtown bank. Not something that can be faked."

"So, regardless of where it comes from, the bishop gets the money, and—"

"Actually, his mother's trust gets the money," she said, "and Liberty's Champions get a deed to the property."

"To set up their worldwide headquarters, or—"

"Or transfer it right away to someone else who put up the money," she said.

"Well, whoever it is, a thousand an acre makes three hundred fifty thousand. A nice piece of change. Of course, if the bishop knew who it was who'd pay more, he could skip Banning, and make the markup, too."

"Even if he cared about profit, if his secret got out it wouldn't be worth it to him," she said. "Anyway, I think Walter's telling the truth about Banning lying to the bishop about the buyer being some dying man."

"I agree. Like I told you, he definitely lied to me about not having looked at Wisconsin land values. Too bad, too. The bishop seems to like him. Apparently he worked hard raising money for Catholic Charities."

"The bishop doesn't know him well, and tends to see only the best in people. Park says anyone could raise funds for infant nutrition centers. They're an easy sell, about as uncontroversial as . . . well, as food for babies."

"You put Park on Banning, too?"

She smiled. "He first attracted attention in his late teens, as a Golden Gloves boxer. Strong, quick, great instincts; but he lacked discipline and faded away. He made it through college at U of I, Circle Campus, supporting himself doing collection work for a group of bookies on the Near West Side."

"Ah, a working man. Maybe still with a few connections."

"Very possible. But today he's basically a lone wolf in a commercial real estate business dominated by a dozen big partnerships. He's got an image of himself as a mover and shaker that he's bought into big time, but Park says it's a delusion."

"He's got an expensive apartment. Must be doing something right."

"Five years ago he was running a string of slum buildings on the West Side. Sleazy and small-time. Had a wife then, too, who was his partner in the business. She died in some sort of freak skiing accident in Vail or Steamboat or somewhere. There were a couple of huge insurance policies on her life and both companies balked a bit about paying out. But with no real proof he was involved, they settled up. Pretty soon he was plowing large amounts of cash into a couple of very risky deals. He manged to attract some investors, and pretty soon—with great luck and a boost from a couple of well-placed aldermen— he turned over some hefty profits for himself and a few clients."

"Moving him to sleazy and big-time. And making him the new wonder-worker for a while, right?"

"With people flocking to him. He's still convinced he's a genius, even though his more recent deals haven't worked out.

In fact, Park thinks he's close to going under. The take on the street is that his word doesn't always match reality."

"And that's among real estate developers," he said, "whose bread and butter is making things look different than they are."

"Isn't that what they say about lawyers?"

"And lawyers don't make the money developers do. Life's not fair." He paused. "So maybe the buyers picked Banning to do the deal because they know he's a crook."

"Agreed," she said. "And the million dollars Walter says Liberty's Champions put up is sitting there, waiting for a deal. So I called Banning. First he acted as if he could hardly remember mentioning the property to the bishop, but then he said he'd get back to me today with whether his buyer is still interested, for three hundred and fifty thousand. Even if there's no million, anyone who can ante up three-fifty right away has a lot of cash sitting around somewhere."

"Or a great credit rating," he said.

"Maybe we'll find out if it's Liberty's Champions or not. I suggested that if there's a deal we close in escrow, but Banning says that if there's a sale, he's sure his buyer will want to send someone to town, to close the deal in person."

"Doesn't make sense. A buyer who insists on anonymity, yet doesn't want to to close in escrow?" He looked at her and shook his head. "The idea of a face-to-face meeting stinks even worse than the rest of this whole thing."

"I know, and—" A buzzer announced that someone had entered her waiting room. "That'll be the bishop. Assuming he accepts my proposal, you and he have work to do, including meeting with a *real* lawyer."

"And your proposal is . . . ?"

"My proposal is, bad odor or not, we go right along with their program." She smiled. "Sort of."

FIFTY-THREE

Not long after Dugan left with the bishop, Charles Banning called Kirsten back and said his buyer still wanted the land and would pay three hundred fifty thousand dollars, but only if the sale was concluded within five days. They agreed to meet at the bishop's office the next morning to plan a meeting to close the deal.

Then she called Johanna Gage. "I'm sorry to bother you, but it's an emergency. Can you come to my office right away? It involves the bishop."

When she got there Johanna was obviously upset. "I knew there was something wrong," she said. "I never believed that story about how he tripped and hit his head. He's in danger, isn't he? And I want to help."

"I know you do," Kirsten said, "and I suppose I shouldn't have kept you in the dark so long. You were right about someone deliberately frightening him." She paused. "Bishop Keegan's tied up right now and I need help with a couple of decisions, from someone who's an insider at the chancery office." She leaned forward across the desk. "If I share some things with you, Johanna, can I depend on you to keep them absolutely confidential?"

"Well, I . . . that is, of course you can. I just want to help."

"Okay, then. In a nutshell, it's land they want. The land's in a trust and the bishop's the trustee. Some people want to buy it and he told them absolutely not. Now he's being threatened with very serious consequences unless he sells."

Johanna stared at her, clearly at a loss for words. "Well . . . why doesn't he go to the police?"

"I can't tell you why. It's just not . . . not something he wants to do."

"My God," Johanna said, "you make it sound like . . . well, like blackmail or something."

"Whatever it sounds like, he's decided to give in. He's selling the property."

"Giving in?" Johanna's eyes widened. "Why that's . . . that's awful."

"Maybe, but that's his decision. He and I are meeting Charles Banning tomorrow morning."

"Good heavens," Johanna said. "Charles Banning? I've never liked that man, frankly, but is it he who's threatening Bishop Keegan?"

"Banning's the broker for the buyers. We're meeting with him—and possibly some representatives of the buyers, too—tomorrow morning to talk over specifics on how to close the deal. He won't tell me who they are, but I've discovered that it's a radical right-wing militia group. The kind that advocates violence and white supremacy, among other things."

"My God!"

"Apparently they want the land for a headquarters. Anyway, whether Banning personally knows anything about the threats I'm not sure, but I don't trust him, and I sure don't trust any representative of his buyers. I'd like to keep the bishop's exposure to any of them down to a minimum. That's where you can be of help."

"I'll do whatever I can."

"First, there's this preliminary meeting tomorrow morning. Obviously, we don't want anyone else in the chancery office to know what it's about. Then, if the meeting goes the way I hope it does, we'll get the closing on the sale over with right away. I'll have more control over things if I choose the location, and I'd like to do the closing at the chancery office, too. Banning's buyers, though, might feel that's too public. I'm wondering, in the evening would they have to sign in with a security guard?"

"Theoretically, I guess. But a person could sign any name they want. Nobody checks IDs." Johanna obviously agreed on Kirsten's choice of location. "Charles knows that building, and the kinds of tenants there are. The chancery office takes up the entirety of several floors. Most of the rest are ad agencies and PR firms, architects, designers, even a few theater and entertainment people. Lots of creative types. People are always coming and going in the evenings. You don't even have to sign in until eight o'clock or something."

"Security guard all the time, though. Right?"

"Sure, but unless you're *terribly* strange or dangerous-looking . . . Actually, security there's a little lax. It doesn't matter much to the people in the chancery office, though, since the office closes at five. It's rare that anyone's there past five-thirty."

"No one works late?"

"Almost never. It's a rule. The cardinal wants to hold on to quality people and, since the pay's not that great, he recently directed that no one—priest or lay person—is allowed to work after hours or on weekends without his personal approval."

"So, if we want to meet Banning there after hours, would the bishop have to ask permission?"

"If he did, he'd have to ask himself, because the cardinal's in Rome."

"And no one else is likely to be around by, say, six-thirty?"

"Only if they get permission from Bishop Keegan. But no one will ask. That's one rule they all love to keep."

"Good," Kirsten said. "Let me tell you what I have in mind.

I only need you for the preliminary meeting . . . tomorrow morning."

The bishop left his mother's room and walked to the little parlor by the front desk where Bud Burgeson was waiting for him. "Gosh, Bud, it's past seven-thirty." They headed for Bud's car. "Too late to meet the rest of the guys for dinner now. Sorry."

"Hey, what are friends for?"

He knew how hard Bud worked at his parish, and he'd hated asking him to do something like this on a Wednesday, which was Bud's day off, too. In fact, he really hadn't wanted to see anyone, but Bud had insisted on picking him up and taking him to meet their friends for dinner. Dugan had encouraged him to go. He said there was nothing more to be done until morning, so why sit around by himself and worry? Cuffs would have driven him to the nursing home if he'd asked, maybe even gone out to dinner. But he needed a break from Cuffs.

Bud drove out of the nursing home lot. "What would I rather do," he said, "than spend precious moments of my waning years driving you to see your sainted Irish mother? I bet she thought you were the occupational therapist, wanting her to go play pinochle."

"It's bingo," he said.

"What?"

"It's bingo they used to try to get her to play, not pinochle. And it's been a year since they tried."

"Anyway, it's just a Wednesday. I got nothing else to do except sit around in some comfortable restaurant with a handful of guys I've known for forty years or so, and knock down a couple dry martinis and a juicy steak."

He knew Bud was trying to get him talking, but he couldn't think of anything to say. He'd stayed too long with his mother. She hadn't recognized him at all, just sat in her chair fingering her rosary beads and mumbling. As he listened, he suddenly thought he heard her asking over and over for some water, but when he held the glass to her lips she just smiled and shook her head. Then she began again, repeating unintelligible phrases, and he finally realized that each phrase ended with *Walter*. A string of words, then *Walter*. Again, then *Walter*. She was praying for Walter. Or she wasn't, and it was his own overactive imagination.

"Right, Peter?"

"Um, sorry."

"I was saying," Bud went on, "those other guys actually carry on conversations. Very hard on the ears, you know, all that camaraderie and laughter, when I can be sitting here with you, and . . ." An ambulance screamed up behind them and Bud pulled to the side to let it go by. "Anyway, Peter, you know I'm just kidding. How about we just pick up a pizza and go to my place and watch *The Magnificent Seven* on tape?"

"You must have seen that movie a dozen times."

"Two dozen, probably. A classic."

"You know," the bishop said, "when this is all over . . ." But he just let it go.

"Right, when this is all over. Whatever *this* is." Bud reached over and patted him on the shoulder. "And, is it coming close to being over?"

"Yes. It'll be over by Friday morning. That much I finally decided on today. What no one can tell me, though, is just how much will be over."

FIFTY-FOUR

The chancery office opened at nine, but Kirsten arrived promptly at eight and Johanna met her and walked her back to the bishop's office. Dugan had described the office for her, but—maybe because it didn't seem to match the man— she was still surprised it was so large and luxurious. There was an antique walnut desk which alone would have filled up her office wall to wall, and beyond that a couple of huge windows looking out high above Huron Street. Three comfortable-looking chairs faced the desk and, to her left as she entered, a coffee table and a small sofa. The wall to her right was lined with bookshelves on either side of a closed door. On a small table near that door was a tray with a carafe and several cups. Despite all the furniture, there was plenty of open space.

"The bishop went to the men's room. He's a nervous wreck. I set everything up myself. That's fresh coffee there, on the table," Johanna said. "Do you think there'll be more than one person from Liberty's Champions with Banning? Because I could drag in another—"

"He said maybe they'd come, but he wasn't sure. So forget it. Or they can sit on the sofa." She paused. "What about you? You all set?"

"Oh, yes. I've been practicing my lines."

The bishop came into the room, then, and Johanna left them alone.

"So," Kirsten said, "you're still comfortable with yesterday's decisions?"

"Yes," he said. "My mother had her dream, but this is . . . for the best."

"Father Burgeson took you to see her?"

"Yes. I tried to tell her, but I'm sure she didn't understand. She was praying for Walter and I don't think she even knew what she was saying. Sometimes I wish she—"

"Fine." She wished she hadn't brought it up. "We need to get ready."

Shortly after ten Banning arrived, full of smiles. He was tall and broad, as she'd remembered. But this time she noticed how large his hands were, and she guessed he'd put on weight recently because his suit, an expensive blue pinstripe, was a little too tight. He also looked like he could use a good night's sleep, and his eyes never seemed to fix on any one thing, just kept skipping around.

"Help yourself," Kirsten said, gesturing toward the coffee.

He poured himself a cup and settled into one of the chairs near the bishop's desk. He'd just taken a folder from his briefcase when Johanna appeared at the door.

"I'm so sorry, Bishop Keegan," she said, "but His Eminence . . . I told him you were in conference, but he insists on seeing you at once. Apparently that group from Ecuador is arriving early, and . . ." She carried it off perfectly, well aware that the cardinal had left for Rome several days earlier.

"Gosh, Charlie," the bishop said, "I'm awfully sorry. Looks like I'll be busy all morning." He stood up. "But I've talked it all over with Kirsten here. She has my complete authority. Whatever she says, goes."

"Well," Banning started, "I . . ." But the bishop was gone.

She was happy to see the confusion that passed across Banning's face, but he recovered quickly, reminding her that his buyer wanted a face-to-face meeting right away to close the deal.

"That's fine," Kirsten said, "but I'm still puzzled. Don't real estate closings involve lawyers and title companies and documents sliding back and forth across the table for signatures?"

"This one's different, my dear." Banning's condescending smile nearly made her throw up. "You needn't apologize for being confused."

"Different how?" She smiled sweetly back and wanted to smack him one.

"For a transaction like this, all I really need is the bishop's signature on a document that assigns his mother's interest in the real estate in her trust to me. Then I can deed the property out of the trust to my buyer, and he can pay the bishop. That would be it."

"Great. So why a meeting? Why not just have the bishop sign the document and have someone deliver it to you and pick up the money?"

"My buyer—"

"Ah, the mysterious dying man."

"My buyer is . . . quite cautious," Banning said, ignoring the obvious implications of her comment, "and is sending a representative to witness Bishop Keegan execute the assignment of interest." He slid a sheet of paper from the folder in his hand. "Here's a copy."

She took the document. "One page?"

"You can have a lawyer review it. When we meet, Bishop Keegan will sign the original of that, and then," he handed her a second sheet from his folder, "I'll execute this deed to the property to my buyer."

"And pay the bishop," she said.

"Yes. You and he demanded a cashier's check for one hundred thousand dollars payable to Mrs. Keegan's trust for the first installment of the payment. As you know, that check's already been placed with her bank, with instructions to deposit it into her account at the opening of business on the day after the closing, unless I advise the bank differently. I trust—"

"Yes. I left a message on your voice mail last night. We've seen the check, the instructions, and . . ." she smiled again, "and that notation on the check that says it was purchased by Liberty's Champions."

"So," Banning said, ignoring any implications of that statement, too, "once the bishop assigns the trust's interest in the property to me, and I deed the property to my buyer, my buyer will give the bishop cash for the final installment and—"

"Cash? Two hundred fifty thousand dollars? I don't believe this."

"Look," he said, his expression finally showing that he acknowledged the oddity of the whole business, "none of this—the desire for secrecy, Liberty's Champions, payment in cash—none of it makes sense to me. I'm just the broker of the . . ." He paused, and sighed. "If Bishop Keegan objects to any of this, I'm instructed to give him this message." He took another sheet from his folder. "Here are the words, exactly: 'If the transaction doesn't go through as described, the alternative we previously discussed will occur.'" He folded the paper in half and looked up at her.

She stared back. What was there to say?

"Perhaps you know what that means," Banning said. "As for me, I don't want to know. Obviously, there must have been contact between my buyer and the bishop, contact of which I am unaware." He slipped the paper back into the folder. "You know, I'm sorry to have gotten mixed up in this in the first place. I'm willing to go through with it, because it appears there would be adverse consequences for the bishop if I don't. But if you tell me diff—"

"Oh no," Kirsten said. "He's going ahead." Banning was not one of the better liars she'd run into. And it seemed not to occur to him that the circumstances were too bizarre for her to believe he didn't know more than he was admitting.

"The fact is," Banning continued, "I don't like being misled. I tend to be rather sentimental, and that story about a man with a terminal illness really tugged at my heartstrings." She nearly gagged, but again Banning seemed not to notice the obvious. "When I saw that notation on the cashier's check, I naturally assumed Liberty's Champions was some entity owned by my client, and gave it little thought. Then I received your message, telling me that's the name of some sort of militia group."

"Yes." She waited.

"I questioned my buyer about that, and . . . well, I'd been given false information. However, the Constitution doesn't restrict the right to purchase property to those with whom we agree. So, as long as they have the money . . ."

"Yes." She sighed. "What else?"

"As I said, the final installment will be in cash, to be delivered to the bishop personally." He looked up. "And there's to be someone else at the meeting, also."

"You're right about that," Kirsten said. "Me."

"I've been assuming that. But my instructions are that the bishop's brother is to be there, also. Walter Keegan." He looked up at her. "Apparently, this Walter is a police—"

"I know who he is." This was more surprising. Probably Walter's idea. He didn't trust Banning, and insisted on being there.

"The money will be in fifty- and one-hundred-dollar bills, and the bishop will have ample opportunity to count it." He paused. "My buyer's representative is flying in this afternoon. The exchange will take place tomorrow. I'll have to let you know where and—"

"No. I'll tell *you* where," she said, putting an entirely new, hard edge to her voice, "and I'll tell you when."

He stared at her. "I don't agree."

"You have no choice. It'll be right here," she said, pushing hard, watching the anger flare up in his eyes. "Six o'clock this evening. Or else no deal." She stood up. "If there's nothing else . . ."

"He won't want to meet here." Banning's voice had a tough, harsh tone now, too. "And his plane's not even due in till five-thirty."

"Seven then. Seven-thirty at the latest. But here . . . or no-where."

"Let me talk to Bishop Kee—"

"Take it or leave it, Mr. Banning. You heard the bishop. What I say, goes." He stood then, too, but said nothing, ob-viously surprised by the sudden turn in their conversation. "We'll be here," she said, "until seven-thirty. Otherwise, tell Liberty's Champions there's no sale and they can go through with whatever other plans they have. Period."

"You don't know what—"

"Oh, but I *do* know. I'll see you to the door, Mr. Banning."

At the waiting room, the receptionist gave Banning a cute little wave good-bye and pointed the way to the elevators.

Back at the bishop's office, Kirsten went to the window ledge behind the desk. There was a phone there, hidden by a stack of books. The receiver was off the hook and she replaced it. She walked to the door beside the table with the coffee service, opened it, and stepped into a small conference room.

The bishop sat alone at a table that was empty except for a telephone. He managed a thin smile, but looked too tired to get up.

"I kept trying to remember to speak loud enough," she said. "Were you able to—"

"Yes," he said, nodding toward the phone. "The intercom picked up everything."

"You probably could have heard through the door if you'd sat right by it," she said, and suddenly thought of an answer to one more question that had bothered her for days.

"Anyway," he said, staring down at his hands in front of him on the table, "I . . . I guess I'm still not absolutely sure we're doing the right thing."

"Yeah? Well, I'll let you know if I'm ever *absolutely* sure of anything."

FIFTY-FIVE

At 6:45 that evening Dugan left Cuffs in the lobby and rode the elevator up to the chancery office. He joined Kirsten and the bishop, the three of them as ready as they'd ever be.

Seven o'clock came and went.

At 7:15 the phone rang and he picked up.

"They're on their way up." It was Cuffs. "Just two of 'em. Banning and that asshole Walter Keegan."

Dugan was surprised. "What? Only the two of—"

"Is that what I said, for chrissake?"

"Wait there and watch for a third."

"What the hell's he look like?"

"I don't know. Might not even be a *he*, might be a she."

"Shit, I'll call if anyone heads up that the guard here doesn't know."

"Right. And remember, stay right there until Kirsten or I call and say differently. Or the bishop. No one else."

"Hey, goddamnit, you told me that five times now."

"Sorry," Dugan said. "Oh . . . does Banning have a—" But Cuffs had hung up.

"So just Banning and Walter?" Kirsten asked.

"Right."

"I hope we aren't making a mistake," the bishop said. He sat down behind his desk, then stood up again. "Are we certain what we're doing is legal?"

"We've been through all this," Kirsten said. "Dugan says it's not a crime."

"Trust me," Dugan said. "Lawyers know these things." He headed out to open the door to the suite. "Civil fraud, maybe," he called over his shoulder, "but not a crime." Uh-huh. No way they could go to jail for it. Not a chance.

By the time he got to the reception room, Banning and Walter Keegan were already waiting outside the glass doors to the suite.

Dugan had never seen Keegan before, but even under the dim after-hours lights in the corridor he looked like a cop. And not Officer Friendly. He had the same arrogant, world-weary look on his face as those two who'd approached Dugan in the playground a week earlier. Keegan looked twice their age, though, and far from healthy. He was a large man in a custom-made suit and a silk tie more expensive than any Dugan owned, but his shoulders were hunched forward like a man struggling with asthma or emphysema.

Banning's pinstripe was rumpled, and he looked nervous and unhappy, despite the phony smile on his face. A small fabric duffel bag—maybe big enough for two six-packs—hung by a strap over his shoulder. That was good, since Dugan didn't think a quarter million in hundreds and fifties would have fit in his pockets.

He unlocked the door with the bishop's key and pushed it open. "Gentlemen," he said, and stretched out his hand. "Can I help with that bag?"

His greeting and his offer were both ignored. He relocked the door and nobody said another word as they walked down the hall.

The bishop was standing beside his desk. He looked as nervous as Banning, actually, and his suit was equally wrinkled.

"Good evening, Charles," he said. "Hello, Walter."

"Good evening, Bishop Keegan," Banning said. "You haven't changed your mind again, have you? You still want to sell your mother's property?"

"Of course he does," Walter responded. The sarcastic tone came through, despite his shortness of breath. "Always a smart boy, that Peter. Obedient boy." Walter stopped just inside the office, moved to his left, then leaned back against the wall beside the open door. A cop. Even if it was clear he shouldn't have been up and around.

Kirsten was standing, too. "Where's your buyer?" she said, facing Banning.

"I received a last-minute call," Banning said. "A change of plans."

"A change?" the bishop asked. "What—"

"The whole reason for a meeting," Kirsten said, "was your buyer wanted someone to be here."

"Same thing he told me," Walter said. "But so what? How else is a low-life cop ever gonna get inside his important brother's classy office? Right, Petey boy?"

"Walter," the bishop said, "you're welcome here any—"

"I take it," Kirsten said, "the deal's still going ahead."

Banning patted the bag at his side. "I have the money here. And . . ." taking a sheet of paper from his jacket pocket, "the assignment of interest for your signature." He unfolded the paper and held it out toward the bishop, but Kirsten intercepted it.

She glanced at it, then passed it to the bishop. "It's the same as what we've seen," she said. "You can sign it." She turned back to Banning. "After we count the money, of course."

"My job," Dugan said, glad to have something to do.

Banning gave him the little duffel bag. It was plum-colored, apparently brand new, and had L. L. BEAN imprinted on one side in block letters. Dugan dumped the contents onto the bishop's desk, and everyone but Keegan sat down.

There were twenty-five wrapped packets of one-hundred-dollar bills, and he counted a hundred bills in each packet. It took just about a half hour, and he didn't notice whether anyone moved or said a word the whole time.

He stacked the money carefully back in the bag and zipped it up. "Two hundred fifty thousand dollars," he said, looking up at Kirsten. "No fifties."

"Now, Bishop, if you'll just sign that paper," Banning said, "we can be on our way."

The bishop signed and Banning put the paper back in his pocket. "I'll send you a photocopy." He turned to Walter. "Let's go."

"Get out of here," Walter said.

"What?"

"I said get your tired ass outta here. I got things to talk over with my favorite little brother."

"But you . . ." Banning paused, apparently saw it was no use arguing, and turned to go. When Dugan started after him, he turned back. "I can find my way," he said.

"I'll have to get the door. It takes a key, even from the inside."

They went back down the hall and when they got to the reception room, Dugan had a vague impression something was different. But he unlocked the door and pushed it open. Only then did he realize that the lights beyond the glass doors were out, and the corridor was pitch black.

He leaned out and looked both ways. "I guess it's—"

The right side of his head exploded in pain, and he may actually have seen someone, or not. But he was falling and falling, as though the floor were a long, long way away. And then there was nothing at all.

FIFTY-SIX

The simplest plan is best. Kirsten always knew that. But it was when Dugan had said "What's sold is sold" that she'd known what had to be done. Turning a sale around wasn't going to be easy. So let them try, if they dared.

It would have been a surprise if Banning's buyer had actually shown up and been identified for certain. She'd never really counted on that. The thing she really didn't like, though, was Walter's staying behind in the office.

"I thought you'd stick with Banning," she said, "to make sure you get your cut of the deal."

"Anything I got coming I'll get. Banning knows that." Walter moved to one of the chairs and sat down. "But I got a feeling there's not gonna be any cut."

"Oh?"

"Banning's an idiot," he said. "And on top of that he's too damn desperate for money to think straight even if he wasn't an idiot."

"What are you saying?" the bishop asked.

"I'm saying I saw that paper he had you sign. An assignment of interest, for all the property in the trust. That's great. But I talked to a lawyer. How does Banning know there's any real estate still left in the goddamn trust for him to deed to someone else?"

"He did a title search," Kirsten said. "It showed there's been no transfer of the property."

"You mean there's been nothing recorded," he said. "And no transfer up to when? Yesterday? This afternoon?" He smiled. "Besides, you're too smart to let Petey boy give in to blackmail that easy. I got an idea some shit'll be hittin' the fan pretty soon. 'Cause I think they're gonna find out there's no property there."

"But Walter," the bishop said, "how did—"

"Quiet, please," she said. "Let's hear what he has to say."

"I figure you dumped the property outta the trust. Sold it or something. Banning and these Liberty's Champions people will find out right away, of course. They can sue you, my lawyer says, with a dead-bang winner of a fraud case. But for what? A lawsuit drags too much out into the open—like who the buyer is, and other things Banning doesn't want out—without being sure Peter could get the land back and resell it to them, even if he wanted to. They get nothing from a suit but head-aches."

"And their money back," Kirsten said, figuring there was nothing to lose now, "which your brother'd be happy to give them, anyway."

"So I'm right," Walter said.

"Mostly," she said. "But there is some land still in the trust. Ten acres, tucked in between national forest on one side and, on the other, the land the bishop deeded out of the trust this morning."

"I asked if you could sell it that fast. The lawyer said it's possible, but only to someone who's already done their own title search, or who's willing to take your word that there's no problem with the title."

"Actually, the buyer's a matter of public record, or will be by morning. It's the Worldwide Trust for the Preservation of

Plains, Forests, and Wetlands. They got about three hundred forty acres, 'restricted to recreational use only, in perpetuity,' the deed says—or something like that." Kirsten smiled. "They have pretty good lawyers of their own, and they're well-protected under the terms of the deal."

"What'd you do, Peter? Give it away?"

"No," the bishop said. "The price was three hundred dollars an acre."

"And you," Walter turned to her, "you figure why would they want to make his arrest public now. There's no land left for him to turn over. Besides, they don't have the really damaging evidence."

"Because," Kirsten said, "you have it." Lightning flashed beyond the windows; then a roll of thunder. She checked her watch. "I wonder what's taking Dugan so—"

"She's got you taking a big chance, though, Petey boy," Walter said. "They might try to flush you down the toilet anyway. Out of anger, or revenge."

"I know that's possible." The bishop moved over to the window behind his desk. "Now I just wait, I guess." He leaned forward as though trying to look past his reflection and out into the night and the rain that was slapping in huge sheets against the glass.

Kirsten picked up her purse from the desk top and went to stand beside him. "We've talked it over from every angle, you know." And they had, a dozen times, but she knew he wanted to hear it again. "They're not going to reveal your arrest." He didn't answer and she wanted to reassure him, wanted to take his arm. But she didn't.

"But you and your lady friend cheated them," Walter said. "At the very least, they'll be screaming for a refund, you know."

"I'll give them their money back."

"Of course. But only, Petey boy, only if you still have the money to give."

She'd feared this, when Walter stayed behind. She took the

bishop's arm. He stared out the window, scarcely breathing, until finally he said, "What do you mean?"

"Well, little brother, I got what you want. The original, and there are no copies. I don't care about the cashier's check. You just give me that two-fifty in cash and the police report's yours. Right now. And something else you'll get, too."

The bishop finally moved, turning very slowly away from the window to face his brother. "My God, Walter," he said, "a few days ago you were on the edge of death. Look at you. You might be dying right now. I can't believe you're saying this."

"I can," Kirsten said. "Greed gets to be a habit hard to break. But," looking at Walter, "what's the something else?"

"A promise," he said. "A promise that Petey boy won't be bothered by Banning. I'll handle him my own way. For my own reasons."

"Where's the report?" Kirsten was certain Walter intended to *handle* Keegan, whether the bishop agreed to his deal or not. "And how do we know—"

"No," the bishop said. "All my life I've protected my good name, at any cost. Not just for my sake, but for the Church. I thought *later* maybe I could let go of everything, even that. But now I see how wrong that is, Walter. You've shown me there's no difference between now and later. We hold on—not just to physical things, but anger, greed, even reputation—thinking later we'll let them go, later we'll set ourselves free."

"Forget the bullshit," Walter said. "Just make the deal and let's move on."

"No. You can't move on. Because you can't let go, Walter, can you? I don't know whether it's greed, or a desire to hurt me and get back at me, but you've held on to whatever it is so tight for so long that now, as late as it is, you can't let it go." He turned back to the window and stared at the rain being driven against the glass. "You've woken me up, Walter. I do want to move on. So . . . there is no deal."

"Bishop," Kirsten moved closer, both now facing the window, "are you sure?" She took his arm. "If it's the money you're—"

"It's not the money. It's my life. I'm not going to spend one more day of my life holding on to something that can so easily be taken away. Let him do whatever he—"

"Shut the fuck up! Everyone!" A man's voice, from the office doorway. "And don't anybody fucking move." A familiar Hispanic accent. " 'Cause anybody moves," he said, "they fucking die."

FIFTY-SEVEN

D on't turn around, Bishop Keegan," she said, her hand still on his arm, her voice loud enough for everyone to hear. "Do whatever he says."

Facing the window, she saw the reflection of the man in the doorway. The same leather sport coat he'd worn at the cottage. The same automatic, with the same silencer. Now he was shoving Banning, hands clasped to his head, into the room ahead of him. He seemed very calm, considering he had four people to keep an eye on.

Four people. And Dugan?

She yanked hard on the bishop's arm and pulled him down with her to the floor, the desk between them and the hit man. She expected a shot then, plowing into the massive desk or exploding through the window. But there was no shot. This man was cool, not wasting rounds.

"Stay down, Bishop." She kept her voice loud, all the while fumbling in her purse for the Colt .380. "You haven't seen him, and he doesn't want to kill a bishop for no reason. He'd have the whole world—"

"Shut up, bitch," the man said. "You, copper, toss your gun over here." She heard Walter's weapon hit the floor. "Good. Now both of you get over by the desk, where they are."

"He's got my *gun*, Peter," Walter said. His *gun*. A message more for her than for the bishop? "This guy's good. And it's me he wants, little brother, not you or—"

"Shut up," the man said. "And move, like I said."

Now or never.

She raised up, fired, dropped down again. But the man wasn't where his voice had come from. He'd already moved off to the side, coming toward the desk, the barrel of the automatic sweeping around, trying to cover everyone at once. Not quite as sure of himself just now. She raised the Colt again and—

The bishop stood up right in front of her, facing the gunman. "Please," he said, "don't hurt any—"

Two more shots exploded in the office. A gun with no silencer. She never figured Walter for just one weapon.

Time slowed down.

She reached out to grab the bishop, saw the hit man diving toward him, too. Another shot, and the lights went out at the same time. The man was screaming. He must have been been hit, but he was on the floor beside her now, wrestling with the bishop. She stepped back, didn't dare shoot in the darkness and confusion.

Suddenly the lights went on again. Across the room Walter stood watching, one hand still on the wall switch, his small backup revolver in the other. His breath seemed shallow and labored, his chest and shoulders heaving.

But the hit man was on his feet now, too, holding the bishop in front of him as a shield, his right arm wrapped tight around the bishop's neck, forcing his chin up, pulling his head back. His gun wasn't in sight, and his right hand was a mass of blood, running down his wrist and onto the bishop's shoulder. But his left hand was working just fine. It held a knife, a gleaming five-inch blade up against the taut white skin of the bishop's throat, just above his Roman collar.

The room was very quiet. Banning was backed against the wall to her left, hands still on his head, mouth wide open.

Walter and Kirsten held their stances, weapons extended. The man hadn't shot Banning out in the hallway, so he must be Banning's man. But what had happened to Dugan?

"Away from the switch," the man said finally, "or I slice the windpipe."

Walter lowered his hand. He smiled a vicious smile at Kirsten. "I need to save my breath to kill this bastard," he said. "So you explain things."

She turned her head. "He means either one of us can bring you down," she said. "And if you hurt the bishop, we both—"

"Shut up. This is what you will do," the man said, "or this one dies a painful death. The woman puts her weapon on the desk where I can reach it. And you Walter Keegan, you throw yours to the floor, over here."

"No!" The bishop's voice was strained. "He'll kill you, Walter, if—Aaah!" His cry of pain came out a harsh, throaty gasp.

A two-inch line of blood appeared where the knife had slid just under the skin below his ear. "You see?" the man said. "Very painful." He moved the knife again, just slightly, and the bishop writhed. "But enough. No one needs to die. I will let him go once I am out of here." He nodded Kirsten's way. "You, cleaning woman. Gun on the desk."

She never believed he wouldn't kill Walter, and her too, even before he announced that he recognized her. But she couldn't watch that blade slice through the bishop's throat, and there was a chance the man might actually let him go. She laid her gun on the desk and stepped backward.

Still holding the bishop between him and Walter, the man closed the knife with a flick of his wrist, dropped it into his jacket pocket, and picked up the Colt.

And as he did, Walter dove for the door. The man fired once, left-handed. Plaster tore away from the wall, but Walter was gone.

"Keegan!" the man yelled. "Walter Keegan!"

"Whadda you want, greaseball?" Walter wasn't far away. "You're already dead."

"Wrong," the man said. "It is your brother who is dead. Unless you throw the piece in here, and come in after it. Your life or his." A pause. "And believe me, amigo, I will shoot him sure as fucking shit."

Kirsten knew then that he would, and knew that Walter knew it, too.

"Walter!" the bishop yelled. "I'm not afraid to die. Call the police. They'll catch him."

"You see what courage your brother has, Mr. Brave Policeman? You should see how hard he's shaking, and how he has already peed in his pants. But still, he is brave enough to die for you. So are you the coward in the family? Throw your gun in here, and then come in. Or will you run? Let your brother die to save your tired ass?"

"Fucking greasy spic," Walter called. But silence followed that, and then his hand appeared and his gun flew into the office and landed on the floor.

"Let me see *you* now, asshole copper. Or are you pissing in *your* pants, too?" Walter didn't appear, and the man kept it up. "Bad po-leece man, huh? Gringo pussy! Fucking no-balls coward! This skinny-ass priest has more courage than—"

Walter came in on the run, charging straight toward where the man held the bishop.

But the man moved away from the bishop, back and to the side. Walter stumbled, veered toward him, and the man opened fire with Kirsten's .380. The first slug buried itself in Walter's chest, the second tore into his throat. But Walter—or his body—wouldn't stop. His momentum carried him into the man, drove him stumbling backward toward the huge walnut desk.

The last thing she heard as she dragged the bishop out of the office was the sickening thud of bone against solid wood.

FIFTY-EIGHT

She'd grabbed her purse but Dugan had her cell phone and there wasn't time to find an office phone and call Cuffs, or 911. Unlike Walter, she had no backup weapon and no choice but to run, dragging the bishop along with her, afraid any second the hit man would appear behind them. Even worse, though, was the fear of what she might find at the door to the suite.

But there was nothing, nobody—alive or dead—in the reception room. And no one coming after them yet. Not the hit man, not Banning. What did that mean?

The door to the corridor was unlocked, but the only light was what little spilled out from the reception room. "Hurry up!" She pulled on the bishop's hand like an impatient mother.

And like a stubborn child, he held back. "I have to help Walter," he whispered. "He saved—"

"Yes. He saved your life." She kept tugging. "And he's dead."

"But maybe he's just—"

"No. He's dead."

"My God!" But he gave up resisting. "There's a corner up ahead . . . to the right. The elevator's just beyond that."

She pushed him past her and followed him. Once they turned the corner the darkness was impenetrable, and they felt their way along the wall to the elevator doors. "I told myself I'd buy a little flashlight," she whispered, "back when I was hiding that bird in—"

"Here's the button," he said. She heard the elevator motor start up, happy he'd interrupted before she spoke Walter's name.

"You go down," she whispered. "I'm staying."

"But you can't—"

"I'm staying. Dugan's here somewhere." The elevator stopped. "Cuffs is in the lobby. You . . . damn!"

"What's wrong?"

"The doors, for God's sake. They're not opening." She tried to pry them apart, but it was useless. "Walter was right. This guy's good. The exit lights, the elevator door . . ." She grabbed his arm. "Where are the stairs?" she asked.

"Stairs?"

"There have to be fire stairs. Where are they?"

"I . . . I think there are two sets on each floor. One farther along this way. And one back at the other end, past the chancery office."

Pulling him with her again, she felt her way along the wall to a door, turned the knob, and pushed. There was light beyond the door, and for an instant she dreaded what she might find. But there was nothing, just an enclosed landing, a stairway turnaround with the downward flight on the right. She tried the knob from the inside and it didn't turn. A sign on the door said: *No exit from stairway except at first floor.*

"Okay, Bishop. Twenty-seven flights down and no way out till you get to the lobby. Can you do it?"

"Of course," he said. "But not without you. Come—"

"Wait." There was usually a pack of Wrigley's spearmint buried in her purse and she fumbled around until she found it. Only three sticks. She tore them all open and popped the gum into her mouth. "Tell Cuffs," she said, at the same time chewing furiously, "that if the elevator stays jammed he can come in this way." She ripped half the wad of softened gum from her mouth and jammed it into the spring-latch hole. "Now go."

"But . . ."

"Please. I have to go help Dugan." She pushed him gently toward the stairs and pulled the door closed. When she pushed it open again he was gone.

Why was there no sound of anyone coming after them? What hope was there of helping Dugan?

Hurrying back the way they'd come, she turned the corner and saw dim light coming from the reception room of the chancery office. There was no one in sight. Running now, she stopped just short of the glass doors, then leaned forward carefully and looked inside. The room was empty, but she could hear someone pounding, or—

Then a gunshot, from somewhere inside the office suite. She stood still, scarcely breathing, suddenly aware how much her jaw ached from chewing so hard on the rest of her gum. She waited. How long? Ten seconds? No more shots. Just that muffled banging or pounding. How long would it take the bishop to run down twenty-seven flights? How soon could Cuffs get up here?

And what had happened to Dugan?

The pounding hadn't stopped and she finally realized it wasn't from inside the chancery office at all, but from the darkness farther down the corridor. Like someone stamping their feet. She ran that way and the noise grew louder. The corridor dead-ended at a door, the other fire exit.

She turned the knob with her left hand. The noise stopped. Easing the door just slightly ajar, she spat the rest of the gum into her right hand and jammed it into the small hole, then shoved the door open.

A duplicate of the other landing. But in this one Dugan sat on the floor and stared up at her, wide-eyed. His knees were pulled tight to his chest to avoid the opening door, his hands stretched above his head and cuffed to the banister. Her cell phone was on the floor, crushed. The right side of Dugan's face was swollen and purple, and there was blood on his ear and down the side of his neck. But he was alive, and conscious, and the look on his face had already turned to relief.

She stood looking down at him, speechless, for God knows how long, until finally he opened his mouth. "Well," he said, his voice strained and hoarse, "it sure took you long e—"

Two hands slammed into her back, nearly lifting her off her feet, driving her into the landing. She teetered toward the stairs to her right, grabbed the banister to keep from tumbling down, and smashed a knee into Dugan's chin. By the time she regained her balance and was able to twist and look, the steel door had been pulled closed again. She wondered if whoever it was realized that the latch hadn't snapped into place.

Dugan was coughing and gagging uncontrollably, choking on something, and she dropped to her knees beside him. He gasped, then spat out a mixture of sputum and blood. "I was doing fine," he said, "until—"

"Until you bit me in the knee." More blood oozed from the corner of his mouth and she wiped at it with her thumb. "Stay here," she said, and didn't need the look on his face to tell her how dumb that directive was. She eased the door open, just a crack.

Someone was in the corridor, down by the entrance to the chancery office, coming her way. It was Johanna, with a gun in her hand.

"Is that you, Kirsten?" Johanna called, but softly.

"Yes."

"I thought so. I saw him push you into the stairway." Johanna stopped just a few feet short of the door, and Kirsten didn't open it any wider. "It was Charles Banning," Johanna said. "But he's gone now, on his way to the elevator."

"What are you doing here, Johanna? How did you—"

"I hid in the cardinal's office when everyone went home. I

wanted to help, only . . ." She took a deep breath. "I heard shooting and I was afraid. But then I snuck to the bishop's office and looked in. I saw Charles Banning shoot that man, the one in the leather jacket. He was unconscious and Charles killed him. Why would he do that? Anyway, Charles is gone now."

"No," Kirsten said. "The elevator doesn't work." She could see past Johanna, to where Banning was coming down the corridor their way, a gun in his hand, too. Maybe in the dark he hadn't found the other stairway. Or maybe he'd heard their voices and . . . "Banning!" Kirsten called. "That man. Is he dead?"

"Yes. I . . . he woke up. I was afraid he'd kill me, all of us. So I shot him. I . . . but, Johanna? What are you—"

"Johanna says you pushed me into the stairwell. She says—"

"What? I didn't push anyone." Banning's voice was twice as loud as necessary. "She's crazy." He kept coming toward them.

"Kirsten!" Johanna cried. "He has a gun, and he's the one who's crazy!"

Kirsten wanted to do something, but with both of them waving guns around, and both veering out of control, she stayed where she was, peering through the crack in the door. Where the hell was Cuffs?

"Please, Kirsten, help me!" Johanna said.

Banning stared at Johanna. "Why did you lie about me?"

"I didn't lie. You're crazy!"

"Shut up, both of you." Kirsten said. "It's over now. You're both safe."

"No. Look, he's coming at me." Johanna's voice was strained and hoarse, not much more than a whisper. "He's lost his senses. He's come unhinged. He—"

"Wait." Banning stopped, eyes wide, and Kirsten thought he *did* look crazy. "You," he said. "Your words. Your voice."

"Kirsten!" Johanna said. "Help me!"

"You goddamn bitch!" Banning's pistol hung down beside

his leg, as though he'd forgotten all about it. He stepped toward Johanna. "Liberty's—"

Johanna shot him. From ten feet away. Twice. Both bullets in the chest. Then a third shot, this one wild and into the ceiling. Mouth gaping, Banning sank to his knees, struggled to raise his own pistol, then toppled forward. His forehead nearly landed on Johanna's feet.

"Oh my God!" Johanna shrank back and the gun fell from her hand. "What have I done?" She turned toward Kirsten. "Help me, please."

Instinctively, Kirsten opened the fire door.

"Help me," Johanna said again, half-sobbing, half-speaking. "I didn't mean to hurt him, but he was . . . coming at me. He had a gun. He already killed—"

"All right, everyone! Freeze!" The voice boomed from far down the corridor.

It was Cuffs, moving their way, with the bishop behind him. Conflicting ideas tumbled in circles in Kirsten's mind, blurring into one another. She wasn't sure she wasn't spinning around herself.

"I'm so sorry." Johanna was sobbing. "I couldn't—"

"Save it, lady!" Cuffs again, no sympathy there. "You hear that?" He paused. "Cops are on their way. Better get ready." He backed up to the wall, his hands on top of his head. "Raise your hands, for chrissake," he said. "If they got any sense they'll take it slow. But God only knows what some charged-up asshole hero might do."

The bishop backed up against the wall beside Cuffs, his hands high in the air. Kirsten raised hers, too, and stepped out into the open.

At the far end of the dimly lit corridor, two uniformed police officers rounded the corner and came toward them on the run, weapons extended. "On your faces!" one of them screamed. "Get down!"

"What'd I tell ya?" Cuffs whispered, hardly moving his lips. "Dumb shits."

"On your faces, dammit! Or you're dead!"

They all obeyed . . . except Johanna, who was already on her knees, rocking side to side and sobbing.

FIFTY-NINE

T here's still the money," the bishop said. "It has to go back to Charles Banning's buyers—all of it."

Johanna Gage sipped on her martini. "Certainly," she said. "We all agree."

It was just past noon, Friday. Dugan was glad to be home, but his head hurt and he wished Kirsten hadn't insisted Johanna and the bishop come up for coffee or a drink. They'd spent all night and that morning with the police—being interviewed, sitting around for hours doing nothing, being interviewed again—and he had the feeling none of them had said any more than was absolutely necessary.

The investigators weren't totally satisfied, of course, even when they sent them all on their way. But there seemed no doubt that the hit man was the one Walter Keegan had described before, and was the one who'd shot him this time. All the witnesses said Banning admitted shooting the hit man, had been coming at Johanna with a gun, and was obviously out of control. It was hard to say she wasn't justified in killing him, even if her having taken one of Walter's weapons with her into the corridor was a bit surprising.

The investigators wouldn't tell them anything, of course, but Kirsten still had lots of friends in the department, and learned that preliminary tests showed that when Banning put a bullet in the hit man's head, the man was still unconscious and possibly already dead from a brain concussion. It was unclear, though, whether the cops thought it as significant as Dugan did that Banning had brought a gun to the closing.

And now, even though he was tired and his head hurt like hell, Dugan had made coffee and mixed a pitcher of martinis—which only Johanna went for—and was letting himself be drawn into yet another rehash of the events. This time it was about the money.

"I'm not sure I agree with you, Bishop," he said. "The cashier's check was earnest money. The bank was to hold it and deposit it into your mother's account at ten o'clock today unless Banning advised it differently. Now, though, like I told Kirs—"

"Let's not go into all that," Kirsten said, "at least for now."

"So by now it's already in her trust account," the bishop said. "But still, along with the cash, it has to go back to the buyers."

"Not necessarily," Dugan said. "Earnest money goes to the seller if the deal falls through and it's not the seller's fault." He knew these circumstances didn't quite fit that principle of law, but they seemed close enough, all things considered. "And as for the cash, a group like that—"

"They put up the money," the bishop said.

"Except that we've—"

"And they didn't get the property."

"But we've checked into them and—"

"You've told me what sort of people they are, but I still can't keep their money."

"Let me finish, dammit!" Dugan shook his head. "Sorry, Bishop, but you keep interrupting." On top of that, something about the look on Kirsten's face bothered him, and she kept staring out the window as though her mind were elsewhere. "I'm not saying you can keep someone's money just because they're a bunch of psychopathic radicals who advocate Nazism and ethnic cleansing and a violent end to the government and anyone else who disagrees with them. What I'm saying is . . . the money didn't come from them."

"I don't understand," the bishop said. "Why do you say that?"

"Because they've got nothing close to that. They've opened up their books to the government. It's a matter of public record."

"But that cashier's check, it identifies them as the purchaser of the check," the bishop said, "and Kirsten said Charles admitted—"

"How would Banning know where the money actually came from?"

"I don't know, but . . ." The bishop sighed. "I suppose, whoever it is, they'll show up to claim the money. And if they don't, I'll just have to find out who it is."

"You'll never find out," Kirsten said. She was still at the window, and looking down toward the street as she spoke. "I wouldn't bother trying."

"Why?" the bishop asked.

"Yes, why?" This was Johanna, who'd just poured herself a second martini from the pitcher. "After all, what Dugan keeps calling 'earnest money' was nearly a third of the purchase price. It wouldn't be honest to keep it. I'm sure Bishop Keegan will want to identify the rightful owner." She sipped her drink. "The fact is, Kirsten, I'm surprised and disappointed that you—"

"Oh, look," Kirsten said, pointing downward out the window. "The bishop's friend, Father Burgeson, just pulled up in a cab."

"Father Burgeson?" Johanna said.

"Bud's here?" The bishop stood up, obviously startled. "I wasn't aware he was coming."

"Well, he is," Kirsten said, "and he obviously wants you to come down there. He's waving his arms. You better hurry."

Dugan was already hustling the bishop toward the door.

Whatever was going on, it was obvious Kirsten suddenly wanted the man outta there.

"Bishop, wait!" Johanna shouted. "The money!" At the door, Dugan turned in time to see her jump up . . . and splash her martini down the front of her dress. "Oh darn!" she cried. "But wait a—"

"See you tomorrow, Bishop," Kirsten said, and closed the door behind them.

On the ride down the elevator, Dugan said he was sure Kirsten would explain later, but that just now—God knows why—she obviously had other things on her agenda. "You know how these women are, Bishop. Or, on the other hand, maybe you don't. I certainly don't. Not even with Kirsten, you know, because . . ."

He kept on talking until the bishop had joined his friend in the backseat of the cab. As it pulled away from the curb, Dugan leaned over to wave good-bye. That's when he saw that the driver was Cuffs Radovich.

When he got back upstairs, the two women had exchanged places, with Kirsten on the sofa now, and Johanna by the window. Kirsten must have been out to the kitchen while he was gone, because there was an open bottle of spring water on the coffee table in front of her.

He dropped into a chair near the front door. "Well," he said, "here we are."

"Yes," Kirsten said. "Can Dugan freshen your drink, Johanna?"

"How could you suggest such a thing?" Johanna was glaring at her.

"Well, you spilled—"

"I mean how could you possibly suggest that Bishop Keegan not try to find out whose money he has . . . and not return it? That's immoral, unconscionable." Johanna walked across to the sideboard and filled her glass again from the pitcher.

"Oh," Dugan said, "I thought you didn't want another—"

"He's never going to find out," Kirsten interrupted. "So why spin his wheels?"

"I know what you're up to," Johanna said.

"Oh?" That was all Kirsten said, and Dugan—clueless as to what anyone here was up to—resolved not to speak until spoken to.

"Yes," Johanna said. "You think you can talk Bishop Keegan into sharing that money with you."

"What?" He broke his resolution.

"If it's in his mother's trust," Kirsten said, "he should use it the way she would want it used."

"He should march straight to Liberty's Champions and find out whether the money came from them or not. I think it must have."

"And I think they won't say it's their money. First, it's not true. Second, if it were true, they'd have to admit they've been lying to the IRS—not to mention the explaining they'd have to do about why they wanted to buy the land, and what part they played in the deaths of Charles Banning and Walter Keegan, and why that man with a silencer on his gun—a professional killer—identified himself as their representative."

"That's a lie!" Johanna was indignant. "He said no such thing."

"Really? What about you, darling?" Kirsten said, turning to Dugan. "Did you hear him?"

"Whatever you say, dear."

Kirsten sipped her bottled water. "What I say is that Liberty's Champions aren't about to claim the money."

"Well, then . . ." Johanna lifted her glass and stared at it, then took a drink. "If it wasn't their money . . ." She'd calmed down, and seemed to be thinking hard. "Maybe some . . . businessman or something . . . gave them the money to buy the property for him. If it wasn't their money, they wouldn't be in trouble for not paying taxes on it."

"But why would they do that?" Kirsten seemed mildly interested in this theory.

"Well, maybe they were to get paid something to act as a . . . you know, a conduit or something."

"Uh-huh." Kirsten's interest was apparently waning. "So what? It's not their money, and they don't get it."

"But Bishop Keegan can ask them whose money it really is, and give it back."

"Do you actually think any of those Liberty's Champions people would admit they ever heard of the bishop—even if they have—and get themselves mixed up in this mess? You can forget that."

"But they have to. Otherwise the real owner won't get . . . his money back."

"Uh-huh." Kirsten smiled, then added, "Or *her* money."

"What?" Johanna choked a little, on the last swallow of her drink, then refilled her glass. "Why—"

"Or theirs, maybe. His and hers."

Dugan set down his empty coffee cup and, thinking he was starting to catch on, stood up. "I'm gonna go get a beer. That martini pitcher's almost empty, Johanna. Should I—"

"Stick around, darling." Kirsten reached down beside the sofa and came up with a bottle of Berghoff—along with an opener. "I think," she added, "Johanna has something to tell us."

SIXTY

don't understand," Johanna said. "I really *don't* have anything
to tell you."

Dugan opened his beer and sat back. This was Kirsten's
show, and he was content to watch it develop.

"You might start by explaining," Kirsten said, "why you said
the bishop should 'march straight to Liberty's Champions' a
minute ago. No one in this room had mentioned that name
until you did."

"I . . . one of you must have said it," Johanna shook her head.
"Anyway, I have nothing to say."

"That's unfortunate," Kirsten said. "For you, I mean. You
might avoid a long jail sentence—or worse. Several people have
died. One of them shot by you."

"But . . . but that was self-defense. You both saw it. The
police understand."

"But they haven't finished with us yet," Kirsten said. "And
did you tell them how you were listening in and heard the hit
man *not* say he was from Liberty's Champions? I don't think
so. In fact, I doubt you told them anything about your real part
in this."

"What in God's name are you talking about?"

"About how you and your husband want that land, and how you put up the earnest money."

"Why, you've come unhinged. Lost your sen—" Johanna put a fist to her mouth.

"Uh-huh," Kirsten said. "Not that common a phrase, is it, Dugan?"

"Not that common at all," he said, with no idea what she was talking about.

"We'll get back to that." Kirsten sipped her water. "You have a great head for business, Johanna, yet somehow couldn't tell me what business your husband was in. You came up with paper in South Africa. Nice try, except not many fortunes have been made in South African paper. But there are real riches there—and in Australia, too—buried in kimberlite, what Mark Brumstein says people call 'blue ground.' "

"Mark Brumstein, your landlord?" Dugan stared at her. "Blue ground?"

"Kimberlite. A mineral, I guess. Mark says it turns up in underground 'pipes,' whatever that means. What counts is that it's in kimberlite that you find diamonds. Not always, I guess, but often enough to arouse an investor's interest. Right, Johanna?"

"I'm sure I don't know." She seemed to be concentrating on her martini.

"For example, back in the seventies someone discovered a kimberlite pipe near a place called Lake Ellen, in Upper Michigan. Not that far north of the bishop's property, actually. A Canadian company paid something like twenty thousand dollars an acre for—"

"Twenty thousand an acre?" Dugan said. All he had were questions.

"And that's pre–nineteen eighty. Upfront money to the land owner, to lease the land for test drilling. Of course, in Lake Ellen they decided mining wouldn't be profitable. That's always been the case so far with diamond finds in Michigan and Wisconsin."

"Diamonds?" He couldn't believe it. "In Wisconsin?"

"Oh, yes," Kirsten said. "Mark says there's a kimberlite pipe—with diamonds, too—right up Interstate Ninety-four, between here and Milwaukee. Again, though, not in a quantity or quality worth mining."

"What does any of this have to do with me?" Johanna sounded bored.

"I think," Kirsten said, "that your husband found out about a kimberlite pipe on or near the bishop's mother's land, and subleased part of the property from whoever holds the lease. I'm still working on it, but I'll be able to document that."

"My husband's an avid outdoorsman," Johanna said. "If he or I subleased some property—and I'm not saying we did—it was so he could hunt and fish on it."

"Really?" Kirsten's voice rose. "Maybe the *story* was hunting and fishing, but I think what you did was drill. Unlike oil exploration, you don't even have to register with anyone in Wisconsin to look for diamonds." She leaned toward Johanna. "You did some exploration and . . . eureka! A diamond lode worth mining."

"*Eureka?*" Dugan said.

"Isn't that what they hollered at Sutter's Mill?" She turned back to Johanna. "But you didn't yell very loud, did you? When was it you learned the land you needed was in Mrs. Keegan's trust?"

"It's obvious you're making this whole thing up," Johanna said. "It's that militia group, Liberty's Champions, who wanted to buy the property. You can't—"

"That's what cinched it for me. 'Liberty's Champions,' you said. And not just today. Yesterday morning you wondered how many 'Liberty's Champions people' might show up with Banning. But I'd been careful not to tell you their name. Then

291

Banning started to say the name in the hallway last night, before you shot him. You made up that whole story."

"Of course," Dugan said. "Who'd want to buy a remote tract of woods and rocky soil? And keep the purchase secret? How about . . . there's this radical group that needs a secluded headquarters, a training ground?"

"Then," Kirsten said, "to broker the deal you'd need someone desperate enough to grab at any chance to make a good buck. You're quite an actress, Johanna, we've all noticed that. You made the calls to Banning yourself. Last night he was struck by your choice of words: 'He's lost his senses; he's come unhinged.' He recognized your voice, too. He would have dragged you into this." Kirsten stretched out a hand, palm up. "Look, we can go on, but . . ."

"This is absurd," Johanna said. "I've done nothing illegal."

"You'd really be better off facing it." Kirsten's voice had a new, almost motherly tone. "I have a man up there right now, looking at leases, checking out recent drilling operations. But I can't force you." She stood up. "You're free to go, and—"

"No, wait." Johanna seemed to be searching for words. "Look," she finally said, "I'll explain. But only because it will prove that I haven't commited any crime, and . . . and because I've invested money, and I need it back." She swirled her drink around. "My husband's not involved. But if he finds out, I'm ruined."

"If there's no need to tell him, we won't." Kirsten's voice was calm and soothing. "That's a promise."

Johanna sighed. "Gerard learned the diamond business in South Africa and made a fortune there, long before I met him. He made an even bigger fortune in Australia, and he's done explorations in the U.S., too, in Colorado and Utah. He knew about Lake Ellen, and a few years ago learned of a possible kimberlite pipe south of there. He gathered geological surveys and maps. Something more pressing came up, though, and he put the idea on hold, and then . . ." She stopped.

"And then you picked it up," Kirsten said.

"My husband's absurdly wealthy. That's his life, making money." An angry edge crept into her voice. "He hasn't a clue what I feel or—For years I've wanted a divorce, but there's a prenuptial agreement. I'd get nothing. I needed a way to set myself up. I managed to get access—temporary access—to some money, his money, and . . . I took it. He may never know, if I can put most of it back."

"So you subleased some land and arranged for test drilling?"

"I'd seen it done. It's not hard to keep the testing secret. You use out-of-state people and . . ." She paused. "Anyway the results were . . . surprisingly good."

"And you decided to buy the surrounding land."

"If I owned it I could lease out mining rights. You see? It's entirely legal."

"These days, exploration rights alone would lease for twenty or thirty thousand an acre, according to Mark," Kirsten said, "and maybe more."

"Jesus, three hundred fifty acres." Dugan swallowed and added up zeroes in his head. "That's . . . seven to ten million dollars."

"Minus expenses," Johanna said, "and not every acre could be leased. I learned early on that the bishop's mother owned the tract I'd most need. Obviously, I had to keep everything secret. I didn't trust Banning, so I hired actors to meet with him, give him the Liberty's Champions story. From then on I dealt with him myself, always on the phone, dropping bits of information that led him to the land I wanted, and finally to Mrs. Keegan's trust. But then . . . the bishop refused to sell."

"So you and Banning schemed to blackmail him, force him—"

"No! I'm telling you all this to prove I did nothing illegal. That's why I deserve my money back. Banning never even knew it was me. I didn't scheme with him. I simply . . . put pressure on him. I'd heard he was desperate for money. But I didn't know about his plan, not at—I mean, not how crazy he was."

"You almost said 'not at first.' But you found out," Kirsten said. "You could have stopped it."

"No." Johanna turned toward the window. "I *never* knew about all that."

Dugan was convinced she was lying, but kept quiet.

"Because if you did know, you were part of a conspiracy to commit extortion, blackmail, even the murders of—"

"Stop it!" Johanna's voice was shaking. "I had nothing to do with any murders."

"Ah, but you did," Kirsten said, her voice low and confident, not as kind as before. "You conspired with Banning to commit extortion—a felony. In carrying out that crime, at least three men were killed. Maybe a fourth, in Canada." Now it was clear she thought Johanna was lying, too. "The felony murder statute makes you as responsible for each killing as whoever physically did it."

Dugan thought she was exaggerating what she could prove, but stepped in anyway. "You could be facing a death sentence."

Johanna stood up, her face flushed. "Don't you threaten me! If I'm accused, the bishop is finished. I'll shout his sickening, degrading crime from the rooftops."

"A crime no one's mentioned until now," Kirsten said. "One he didn't commit."

"You've only his word for that. And I don't care whether he did it or not. That barmaid is dead and can't—" She stopped, but couldn't keep her hand from her mouth.

"No one's mentioned any barmaid, either," Kirsten said, "dead or alive. You knew the bishop agreed to meet her. No one else could have known that. Not Banning, not Walter. The bishop's phone isn't bugged. You were eavesdropping—probably in that conference room adjoining his office—when Dugan was there."

"No! I . . ." Johanna looked down, then seemed to change

her mind. "That is, yes. I did overhear, and I told Charles Banning some woman called and was meeting Bishop Keegan. I was afraid she'd interfere with the sale. But I had no idea he would kill her." She shook her head. "You don't believe me. But you can't prove anything. And if you try . . . the bishop's secret will be on the evening news that very same day. That much you better believe."

Dugan did.

And apparently Kirsten did, too. "So," she said, and Dugan marveled at how her tone changed again, now calm and businesslike, "let's make a deal. You—"

"I want my money," Johanna said. "The cashier's check, and the cash. All three hundred fifty thousand."

Kirsten ignored her. "The deal is: You keep quiet about the bishop; we keep quiet about you. If there's no deal, you talk about the bishop and he gets bad press; we talk about you and you get jail time . . . maybe a lethal injection."

"You're bluffing," Johanna said. "I need that money. All of it."

"No money. Just silence for silence. That's the deal."

"This is so unfair. You know my lawyers would tear your case apart. But you also know if I don't replace that money, my husband will find out. I'll be finished."

"Oh," Kirsten said, "poor baby. 'Finished.' Like the bishop?"

"I'll compromise," Johanna said. "The cashier's check that's already been deposited into the trust account, let the bishop keep that. I'll take just the cash."

"No way," Dugan said. "We already know what happened to—"

"No. She has a point, Dugan. Go get the bag with the money."

He did, although he didn't like the idea. He knew Kirsten couldn't have forgotten what he'd told her earlier about his phone call to the bank.

Johanna counted enough to satisfy herself that there was still a quarter million in hundred-dollar bills. She turned and headed for the door.

"Would you like a ride somewhere?" Kirsten asked. "That bag's rather heavy."

"I'll take a cab, damn you." She slammed the door behind her.

SIXTY-ONE

Dugan was disappointed. "I guess you let her have the money because you know you'd never make all that stick," he said, "not with Banning dead."

"And to keep her from ruining the bishop. She's scared, though. She has more to be scared about than you might think."

He didn't understand that, and let it go. "Did you really start suspecting she was involved just because she was unsure about her husband's business?"

"Well, it *did* seem odd. Then, when I was looking for mineral interests that might make that land valuable, I stumbled across the Lake Ellen kimberlite find and talked to Mark Brumstein. All along, I didn't like the way she was more interested in finding out what I knew than in helping. Finally, there was the fact of her knowing the name Liberty's Champions. Anyway, I told her about last night's meeting, thinking she'd show up if she was involved. I hoped somehow that might prove helpful."

"She should have snuck away when it all blew up, not let anyone see her."

"But she stayed, and *she* pushed me into the stairwell, not Banning. His hands are twice the size of hers. She thought I'd be locked out. She may have intended to kill Banning to keep her name out of it, even before he recognized her as his caller. I don't think it was the first . . ." She shook her head. "Maybe she did us all a favor. When the rest of the cops got there I spoke to Cuffs and in the confusion he managed to search Banning's body. He found that Canadian police report. Banning must have gone through Walter's pockets and lifted it."

"So . . . Banning has his hit man there to kill Walter, but comes in with his own hands in the air so we won't suspect him. Then Banning kills the hit man—unless he was already dead—and then . . ."

But Kirsten seemed to be thinking of something else. "If Johanna told Banning about the barmaid interfering," she said, "why didn't she tell him about you and me?"

"Just be happy about it. She didn't know he'd actually kill the girl."

"Maybe," she said, "but it's not consistent."

"She sure knew about the extortion and blackmail, though."

"Sad, isn't it? She knows the bishop well—even admires him, I think—and still, she'd have destroyed him."

"Ten million dollars is a lot of motivation."

"Ten million she didn't get. I just hope she's satisfied now, and—"

"Hell, she should be," he said. "She got all her money back. I told you earlier, I called the bank at eleven o'clock, about the cashier's check, and they said they voided it and returned the funds to the maker—which had to be Johanna, whatever the notation said. How could they just ignore a signed letter of direction?"

"For a millionaire's wife," Kirsten said, "maybe a customer, and a check for only a hundred thousand, they figure they'll sort things out later if they have to." Kirsten was back looking out the window. "Anyway, she doesn't know you're a co-trustee now and the bank told you what it did. She thinks she put one over on us."

"She did, dammit! Some compromise. She got the check back, and now the cash."

"Maybe not the cash. That's up to a higher power now."

"I don't think God's gonna get involved in—"

"Not *that* high a power. But I *did* tell Cuffs to drop the bishop at his friend's car in a hurry, and . . . I described that L.L. Bean bag to him." She stopped. "Oh, look!"

Dugan hurried to the window. "Yeah. Johanna found a cab right away."

"Yes."

As the cab pulled away, the driver stuck his arm out the window. It was a very large arm . . . and a very large hand that gave them a thumbs-up gesture as the cab drove down the street.

"Maybe we'll have to figure out pretty soon how to put all that cash to some use Mrs. Keegan would approve of," Kirsten said.

"Right." He pulled her close to his side and they watched the cab disappear around the corner. "But right now it's in the hands of a higher power."

SIXTY-TWO

Saturday morning Kirsten convinced Dugan he'd feel better if he went to the office, not pushing hard enough to make him suspicious.

When he was finally out the door she went to the phone. There was something she didn't want the others to know—not Dugan, not the bishop, not anyone. At least not anyone who'd lose any sleep over what she wasn't going to do. She called Cuffs.

He was there in half an hour. "You were right," he said.

"You're sure?"

"As sure as I am that you'd never prove it."

"What happened?"

"As soon as I had her in the cab I locked the doors and windows and started talking. From the backseat she couldn't override the locks. I told her I knew everything. I could prove it. Talked about trace chemicals and DNA and a shitload of other stuff I don't know shit about. She pulled the hysterical crap and I just kept talkin' pretty much nonstop all the way."

"All the way where?"

"Hell, the Moonglow Motel, the scene of the crime. Scared the crap outta her. I had the same goddamn room rented, for chrissake. Showed her the key. Said I'd show her a few things the evidence techs missed, but 'my people' found." He laughed. "Like I had some goddamn people."

"I hadn't thought of that."

"Yeah? Well, this was more fun than I've had in a long time, and I thought of everything. We didn't have to go inside, though," he said. "She did it."

"She confessed?"

"Hell, no. She's too tough and too smart for that. But she's scared and we made a deal. I got the cash and her promise to keep her trap shut about the bishop and his . . . his escapade. She got my promise not to turn over what I have to the cops."

"Which isn't much."

"Hell, they'd laugh their asses off. But she killed that woman. That was as plain as a turd on a white—Anyway, I saw it in her face. That's why she made the deal."

"When a person has reason to believe someone's committed a homicide," Kirsten said, "that person has a duty to notify the authorities."

"Right. So I go tell some brilliant assistant state's attorney that Johanna Gage—a millionaire's wife who volunteers every day for the goddamn Catholic Church—that Johanna Gage met a whore at a sleaze-bag motel, beat her about the head with a blunt instrument, and then strangled her."

"She wasn't a whore."

"But that's what they think she was. And they say what's my proof? And I say my proof is that the guy Johanna says did it, Charles Banning, couldn't have done it."

"They say that doesn't prove *she* did it, and ask how you know Banning didn't."

"And I say because I'd been following Walter Keegan at your request, and on the night before the murder he goes to Banning's apartment building. The next night, the night the girl's killed, Keegan's out of town and so are you. So I decide on my own to follow Banning. All he did was eat a Whopper at Burger King, buy some coke from a freak in Lincoln Park near the conservatory, and go home. Whether he sucked the shit up his nose that night or not I don't know. But he didn't go near Devon and Lincoln."

"Which doesn't prove Johanna did it."

"But she did, and I'm not goin' to nobody with nothin'."

"Me, too," she said. "Um . . . hold onto that two-fifty awhile, would you? Eventually, it has to go to some charity."

"Whatever." Cuffs stood up to leave. "I wonder . . . you think ol' Pete really got a blow job up there in Canada?"

"No, I don't."

"I don't, either," he said. "I don't understand why he didn't, though . . . and I sure as hell don't understand why I'm *glad* he didn't."

SIXTY-THREE

H er room's that way," he said, "at the end of the hall."

It was Wednesday, the bishop's day off, and Kirsten had arranged to meet him at the zoo. He'd seemed preoccupied, though not sad or worried, and he hadn't spoken much. They'd watched the lions for a while and then she'd given him the police report with the barmaid's statement. He read it, then tore it up and dropped the pieces in a waste container. When she reminded him that, despite what Walter had said, he might have made copies and they might somehow turn up, he'd seemed hardly interested. Then she'd driven him to the nursing home.

"May I come with you?" she asked. "I'd like to meet her."

"Certainly," he said, looking surprised. "I was hoping you would." Kirsten walked beside him, but he stopped after just a few steps and turned to her. "I want to tell you something," he said. "I . . . well, I resigned."

"Resigned? From what? I don't—"

"Not from being a bishop. You can't really resign from that, theologically speaking. And I'm staying a priest. But from carrying out the functions of a bishop, and all the rest of it— Catholic Charities, that national committee—I resigned. I always wanted to be just a priest. I never wanted to be a bishop. So . . . I quit."

"But you can't do that," she said, not even knowing why she was objecting. "I mean, aren't they counting on you? Haven't they, well, sort of *invested* a lot in you?"

"That's pretty much what the cardinal said when I told him. Our conversation didn't start out well at all. But I did my best to explain." He smiled, and it seemed a more relaxed, more comfortable smile than she was used to from him. "By the time we finished talking, he was starting to understand . . . at least a little."

"So what are you going to do, retire or something?"

"Oh, no. I'm going back to teaching," he said. "But much different from the seminary. There's this high school in the inner city, on the south side. Used to be a Catholic school. Now it's private and independent . . . but sort of unofficially Catholic. At least that's how I think of it. Anyway, it takes kids from the poorest neighborhoods, and it's like an island of sanity and hope for them in a crazy, hopeless environment. And . . ." He shrugged. "And that's where I'm going to teach. English."

"Wow!" That's all she could think of.

"I start in late August. Until then I'll just . . . go on sabbatical or something. Sort out my conflicting feelings about Walter being killed." Then suddenly he smiled again, almost a grin this time. "And maybe I'll take Bud Burgeson on vacation. And Kenny, too, to thank him for pushing through that sale of my mom's property on the spur of the moment, after he said it couldn't be done. I'll ask Larry Candle, too. Maybe a fishing trip. I own ten acres on a lake in Wisconsin, you know. Or there's this place I went to once, up in Canada."

She could tell he was enjoying his little joke, and she loved the animated look on his face. But still . . . "Are you sure you're not just worn out? Or maybe fantasizing about doing something heroic?"

"Interesting," he said, "because that's something else the cardinal said. You two must think alike."

"My God," she said, "I hope not."

"Anyway, the answer is simple." He shrugged and spread out his hands, palms up. "I don't know. I can't be certain how it's going to work out." He smiled again, and looked happy and embarrassed at the same time. "It's just something I want to do. So I'm doing it."

"Well, you know what? I think it's just great." And she did, too. And she also knew now where the first anonymous donation from the money Cuffs was holding would go. "And your mom?" she said. "You going to tell her?"

"I want to tell her about that. And about Walter, too, and . . ." He started down the hall again. "But she's pretty far gone. She doesn't understand much of what I say."

Kirsten followed after him, not sure now whether she should. "I'll stay out here," she said, when they reached the door to his mother's room. "I'd be intruding."

"No. I told you, I *want* you to meet her." He obviously meant it. "She . . . she could, you know, go . . . I mean die, at any time. Her heart. . . . Please, come in."

She followed him in. There was only one bed and beyond it a very old woman, tiny and shriveled, sat slumped in a chair by a huge window. The room was clean and plain, like a hospital room, but also bright and cheery. A faint odor of urine hung in the air, and somehow that didn't seem unpleasant or depressing at all. Maybe it was the glow of afternoon sunlight filling the space, but the room reminded her suddenly of a newborn infant's room—not a place where life was slipping away.

The bishop circled the end of the bed and stood looking down at the woman. "Mom?" he said softly. "Are you awake?"

She didn't move. Everything about her was pale—the thin, pink robe, her skin, the wisps of hair that barely covered her scalp. A wide strip of white flannel cloth was stretched across her chest, and Kirsten realized that it went around the back of the chair, to help hold her in an upright position.

"Mom? It's Peter. I brought you a visitor."

Kirsten thought she should say something, but didn't . . . couldn't. There was a chair against the wall near the foot of the bed, facing the bishop's mother. She sat down and folded her hands in her lap, tongue-tied, feeling very much like a little girl.

"Mom?" The bishop kept trying. "Mom? I've got things to tell you. Some of it's about . . . about Walter."

His mother moved then, very slowly, lifting her head. Her face was terribly gaunt, the face of a skull covered with skin as thin as tissue paper. She smiled. An unexpectedly pretty smile, but it faded almost at once, as though it were too much effort to hold onto. "Walter?" she said, in a soft, far-off voice. "Walter?"

"Yes, Mom, that's one thing."

His mother turned her head slightly and looked out the window, as though studying the fresh leaves on the trees in the yard outside. "Is it Christmas, then?"

"No, Mom, it's spring. See the grass? the trees? Not Christmas. Almost Easter. I'm your son. I'm Peter."

She turned and peered at him, as though from a long distance. "Peter," she said, and Kirsten saw something new in her eyes. "Peter? Is that you?"

"Yes, it is." She could tell he was excited. "It's me, Mom. And this woman is—"

"It's Good Friday, then."

"No, Mom, it's—"

"Good Friday. The day Jesus died. Tell me that part again. What Jesus said to that bad man on the cross."

The bishop sat on the edge of the bed and laid his hand gently on his mother's shoulder. "You mean the good thief." His voice was trembling. "Jesus told him, 'Amen, I say, this day thou shalt be with me in paradise.'"

"Ah," she said. "So . . . maybe Walter . . ."

"Walter's dead, Mom." He was leaning close to his mother's ear. "And I was there and . . . and Walter died to save my life. It was just like Jesus said. He got turned around, right there at the end. Walter made it, Mom."

The old woman stared at him, eyes wide. She opened her mouth as though to say something, but seemed too weak to go ahead with it. She smiled again—that same lovely smile—until that faded away and her head fell forward and her body sagged against the flannel restraint that was all that held her up now in the chair.

And her lovely smile was gone for good.

Tears flooded Kirsten's eyes, and they stung a little as she tried to wipe them away. But they just kept coming, so she let them flow. She wasn't at all sure Walter had *made it* somewhere, really didn't know what that meant anymore. What she did know, though, was that the bishop had made it—or was well on his way, at least.

She hadn't even seen him get up, but he was standing now, holding his hands palms down in the air above his mother's head. "May almighty God bless you," he said, his voice clear and firm, his right hand tracing a cross in the air over her, "the Father, the Son, and the Holy Spirit . . ." He lowered his hands and clasped them on the top of her head, then leaned and rested his cheek on his hands.

Standing now and still crying, Kirsten felt embarrassed, out of place, and very, very grateful to be right where she was.

". . . forever and ever," Peter Keegan whispered. "Amen."